AN *Aster Bay* NOVEL

# FIRST COMES *Marriage*

## CARA DION

Print ISBN: 979-8-9882826-8-6
Ebook ISBN:979-8-9882826-7-9
Imprint: Independently published

First edition

Cover designed by Stephanie Anderson at Alt 19 Creative.

# Also by Cara Dion

### Love Song Series
*Irreplaceable*

*Indiscreet*

*Undeniable*


### Aster Bay Series
*Whisking It All*

*Just For Show*

*First Comes Marriage*


**Visit my website to learn more and download free bonus content:**

# Content Warning

This books contains discussions of
polycystic ovarian syndrome (PCOS) and (in)fertility.

*For Nana*

# Chapter One

Sebastian Graham was sitting in the dunk tank at the center of the St. Anthony's Bazaar, sweating his ass off in a Darth Vader costume, when the woman he hated most reappeared in his life.

And he had plenty of reasons to hate Sabrina Page.

First: the last time he'd seen her, ten years ago, she had destroyed his wedding. He wasn't sure how exactly she had convinced her sister to leave him at the altar, not that *how* really mattered when the fact remained that he'd stood at the front of that church waiting for a bride that would never come while everyone he cared about watched.

Second: no sooner had she ensured his public humiliation than she had disappeared, fucking off to Morocco or Paris or who-the-fuck-cares-where and leaving him to clean up the mess she and her sister had made.

Third: despite the rest of the Page family having the good graces to avoid him at all costs, Sabrina's great aunt Lucy remained in Aster Bay, clucking her tongue and patting his shoulder every time they crossed paths in the grocery store as though he were some kind of wounded animal. As if her niece deciding she could, in fact, live quite happily without him hadn't been mortifying enough.

He had more than enough reasons to hate Sabrina, but the icing on the uneaten wedding cake was that before she'd dropped a grenade in the middle of his carefully laid plans for his picture-perfect future, she'd made him believe they were friends.

So when he caught sight of Sabrina's auburn hair falling in loose waves around a face that he knew would be dusted with freckles, Baz knew he must be mistaken. The slightly too-loud, too-brash laugh floating on the summer breeze from the fried dough stand and smacking him in the face as he sat in the dunk tank couldn't be hers. There was no way Sabrina Page had returned to Aster Bay. She was in Barcelona or Athens or Tibet, one of the countless places she'd always talked about visiting while they'd stood side by side stocking shelves at the food pantry, building a friendship that had clearly meant more to him than it ever did to her. She was *not* standing in the middle of St. Anthony's Bazaar in a pair of pressed pants and a silk blouse, of all things. Not in *his town*. When the Page sisters discarded him, they may have taken his dignity, but he got to keep his town.

"Hey, stormtrooper! Take this!" a kid yelled as he hurled a tennis ball at the target.

The ball made contact with a loud crack and the seat beneath Baz fell away, dropping him into the water, helmet and all, but not before he heard Gavin groan, "Darth Vader was never a stormtrooper."

Gavin's lecture on the history of his favorite villain disappeared as Baz slipped beneath the water. He blew all the air out of his lungs and let himself sink to the bottom of the (admittedly shallow) tank. How long could he stay down there? Long enough for Sabrina to disappear again? Long enough for the rage and shame that burned in his chest to melt back into the disdain he'd cultivated in its place?

He pushed back to the surface, yanking off the helmet in the process and wiping water out of his eyes as he pulled himself back onto the bench. He found her again in an instant, taking a giant bite of her fried dough and laughing as she licked the powdered sugar off her lips. His eyes narrowed, as though her enjoyment was a personal affront.

Before he could put his helmet back in place, another ball hit the target, plunging him back beneath the water.

"Son of a bitch!" he cursed, sputtering, when he resurfaced, the helmet bobbing in the tank beside him.

"He swore!" the tennis-ball-thrower shouted, his arm outstretched, finger pointing at Baz.

Baz tried to pull himself back up onto the bench, but his hands tangled in the wet fabric of his cape and he slid off again. "Motherfu—" He disappeared beneath the water before he could finish the word, which was honestly for the best considering the size of the crowd gathering to watch Darth Vader be defeated by a ten-year-old with a tennis ball.

"Sebastian Graham, get back up on that bench!" Mrs. Greene's shout cut through the hum of carnival rides and children begging for cotton candy as she marched across the field-turned-fairgrounds behind St. Anthony's. She tapped the tank with the edge of her clipboard. "We have money to raise, young man."

Baz wasn't listening to her lecture, however. At the sound of his name shouted across the field, Sabrina had frozen, her shoulders stiff. He watched as she turned, searching, her auburn hair lifting on the breeze and all the color draining from her face.

She'd grown up in the ten years since he'd seen her last, her cheekbones somehow higher, her hips wider. A bright burst of awareness hummed through him as he took in the dip of her waist, the wisps of hair fluttering around her face.

Finally, she located him, her green eyes widening as they took in the sodden costume, his hair still dripping into his eyes. He tucked the helmet beneath his arm as he stood in the dunk tank, water waist high and sloshing against the enclosure walls, and refused to be the first to look away.

Their gazes locked and he swore he could hear her gasp even at this distance. He clenched his jaw and straightened his shoulders defiantly. This was his town, goddamn it, and he was not going to let *Sabrina Page* of all people rattle him, even if the awkward twenty-year-old he'd known had been replaced by a knockout of a woman in expensively tailored clothes.

"Are you listening to me?" Mrs. Greene demanded, practically stomping her foot.

"What's going on?" Ethan asked, appearing beside Mrs. Greene.

"I got it," Gavin said, stepping up to the edge of the tank and reaching for the helmet. "It's my turn in the tank anyway." He looked sadly at the helmet and handed it to Ethan. "No point in wearing the costume anymore, I guess."

"Don't worry. I'll still dunk you," Ethan said.

By the time Baz hauled himself out of the tank, Sabrina was gone.

# Chapter Two

"Aunt Lucy!" Sabrina shouted, the screen door slamming behind her. "I'm home!"

Her great aunt's house was creaky and badly in need of updating, but the sunshine streaming through the oversized windows danced on the dust in the air, and the faint smell of potpourri permanently emanated from the curtains and cushions in the living room.

It felt more like home than any place she'd lived, including her parents' Brookline estate. Even the little house she and her ex-husband had shared in Kennebunkport for the last four years hadn't felt like home. Not like Great Aunt Lucy's house did. Not like Aster Bay.

Sabrina stepped out of her tasteful flats and slid them into position on the mat by the front door like her mother had taught her. "Aunt Lucy!" She plucked a thumbprint cookie off the plate on the counter, dipping her finger into the raspberry jam in the center and sucking the sugary gel from her fingertip.

At the edge of the kitchen, the curled cord of the wall-mounted telephone disappeared around the corner into the sunroom. Grabbing a second cookie and grinning to herself, Sabrina followed the cord into the airy room where her father's aunt preferred to take her afternoon tea. There, on the small loveseat facing the picture window overlooking her garden, sat Aunt Lucy, the banana yellow phone receiver pressed to her ear.

"Oh, Ruthie, she just got home," Aunt Lucy said into the phone. Then, tilting the mouthpiece away from her lipsticked smile, she said to Sabrina, "Come in, dear. Ruth Greene is telling me about the Bazaar."

Sabrina flopped into the floral-patterned armchair at the side of the room as her aunt "uh-huh"ed and "mm-hmm"ed her way through the next few minutes of her phone call. Aunt Lucy's eyes flitted towards Sabrina, her brow wrinkling. "Yes, very interesting."

Sabrina mouthed "What?" but her aunt ignored her, choosing to instead run her eyes appraisingly over Sabrina's outfit.

She shifted uneasily in the seat, popping a cookie into her mouth to have something to do as she felt her aunt taking silent inventory of her appearance. The tailored khakis and sage green silk blouse were exactly the kind of outfit her mother would have approved of, but she wasn't supposed to worry about that kind of thing. She and her therapist had agreed that, at age thirty-one, it was high time she stopped concerning herself with what her mother might think.

So why had Sabrina hesitated when faced with the option to wear jeans and the comfortable crochet crop top she'd originally pulled from her closet that morning? Why had she instead ironed her trousers and fussed over how many delicate gold chains to string around her neck before going to a church bazaar?

*Because you can still hear her voice in your head, even if you know you shouldn't care.*

Sabrina slouched a little in the armchair, because she knew her mother would have hated it if she'd been there to see. Which, of course, she wasn't. Sabrina had chosen to move in with her great aunt after her divorce precisely to avoid the kind of running commentary on her life choices that would have dogged her steps in her parents' home.

"I certainly shall," Aunt Lucy said into the phone. "And tell Norm it's settled. I'm sure Sabrina will be more than happy to help. Thank you, Ruthie."

Sabrina waited while her aunt returned to the kitchen to hang up the phone, reappearing in the sunroom with two glasses of iced tea. "What's settled?"

Aunt Lucy pursed her lips in that way she did when she was keeping a secret. It was the same look she'd give Sabrina when, as a child, Sabrina asked where her parents had hidden the Christmas presents. But Aunt Lucy could never keep a secret for long. Sabrina just had to be patient.

Aunt Lucy eyed her over the top of her iced tea as she took a long sip before firmly changing the topic. "Apparently there was quite a stir at the Bazaar. You didn't happen to notice a commotion at the dunk tank, did you, dear?"

Sabrina's stomach clenched, reminding her of the knots that had formed there that afternoon and refused to budge since. "No, I don't think so," she lied.

"Hmm. You might be the only one."

"Did something happen?"

The image of Sebastian Graham, dripping wet and staring daggers at her across the fairgrounds, came to her unbidden. He'd always been attractive in that tall, dark, and broody way, but she was surprised to learn the simmering anger in his gaze had a rather inconvenient affect on her ability to form complete thoughts. Her therapist would have plenty to say about that, she was sure. Sabrina forced herself to focus on her last cookie, dragging her finger through the jam as though baked goods could make her forget the look in his eyes.

"Well, you see, for several years we've had a mystery man in the dunk tank. In costume. And today, he was unmasked." Sabrina hummed in acknowledgment but kept her eyes on her cookie. "You'll never guess who it was."

"I don't know many people in town anymore, Aunt Lucy."

"You know him."

Sabrina shot her aunt a warning glance. "No, I really don't anymore."

Aunt Lucy sighed. "Once upon a time you used to think he was a very nice man. We could hardly get you to stop talking about him. Why, if he hadn't been engaged to Holly, I almost would have believed that you—"

"Yes, Auntie, we all know how much you like Sebastian." Best to put an end to that line of conversation. No good could come from revisiting what Sabrina may or may not have felt about her sister's former fiancé.

Her aunt sniffed the air and resettled in her seat. "He'll make *someone* a fine husband one day."

Heat crept up Sabrina's neck. She knew everyone blamed her for turning her sister into a runaway bride, and she'd never be able to convince them it hadn't been her fault. Holly was the perfect daughter, the picture of Ivy-league propriety, the beautiful one, the successful one, the sensible one. Everything Sabrina wasn't. No one wanted to know that Holly had been having an affair with a partner in her law firm. They would much rather believe that Sabrina was to blame for the embarrassment of Holly leaving her fiancé at the altar.

And for ten years she'd let them. It had seemed like a small price to pay for Sebastian's happiness. Even if it meant he hated her.

But that was before he had looked right through her, as though he could erase her from existence with a glare.

That was before Sabrina had lost everything in a painful divorce and been forced to move into the spare bedroom at her great aunt's house in a town far too small for her to have any hope of avoiding Sebastian Graham.

There had been a time when Sabrina had counted down the hours until she could see him again. When she would have done anything to make him happy, even confront her sister on their wedding day.

There was a time when she thought he would have done the same for her.

It seemed like a lifetime ago.

Aunt Lucy sighed. "Well, never mind. Let's enjoy our night together before you jet off."

Sabrina narrowed her eyes. "I just got here a few days ago."

"Yes, well, when one is trying to start over, it's best to dive right into the starting," Aunt Lucy declared, as if she hadn't spouted some kind of fortune cookie nonsense.

"I have started. Being here is the start." An uncomfortable thought turned her stomach and she leaned closer to her aunt. "I thought when you offered me the guest room that you understood I'd be staying. Indefinitely. It's going to take a little while before the studio can open and then probably even longer until it's turning enough of a profit for me to get a place of my own. I guess if I wait to buy health insurance, I could probably move out sooner, but—"

"Don't you worry about that, dear heart. You stay as long as you like," Aunt Lucy said with an exaggerated flutter of her hands.

Sabrina smiled uneasily. "Thanks, Auntie. Now if I could just get my business permits—"

"Oh, did I not tell you?" Aunt Lucy's eyes went wide in a poor approximation of an innocent expression.

"Tell me what?"

"Ruthie Greene and I have arranged a way for you to get into the good graces of the Merchants' Association and speed up that pesky permitting. Think of it as a sort of extended play date."

"Auntie, I'm thirty-one years old. You can't arrange a play date for a woman in her thirties."

"I can and I did," she said smugly. "There's a charming young woman who owns a lingerie shop in town, helped me figure out my correct bra size—did you know most women are wearing the wrong bra size? You see—oh, how did she explain it—it's something about bands that are too large and cups that are too small. Or was it the other way around?"

"You want me to have a play date with the woman who sells you bras?"

"Natalia. You'll love her. But no, dear, that's not who I've arranged this meeting with."

"I thought it was a play date."

"Play date, meeting, they're all the same. Anyway, last week when I was in Natalia's shop getting fitted for a new bra, she mentioned that the Merchants' Association was having a doozy of a time finding someone to represent the town at some sort of convention. To help with the tourism, you see. Someone to take notes at all the sessions and share what they've learned when they return. And I thought to myself, who do I know who has quite a head for these sorts of things? Who might, oh, I don't know, have a somewhat risqué pottery studio they're hoping to open sooner rather than later, who would benefit from making herself indispensable to that very same Association that needs to approve her plan before she can open?"

For all she pretended to be an unassuming old woman, Great Aunt Lucy could plot with the best of them. "Where is this convention?"

Aunt Lucy fluttered about as she gathered up their iced tea glasses. "The Association takes care of everything—your travel and hotel and food. And someone else will be joining you. A nice young man from town, if I'm not mistaken."

Sabrina's stomach dropped. "Who?"

"I'm not entirely sure. Natalia was a bit fuzzy on that detail, but I'm sure she said it was one of the young men who plays trivia with Ruthie and her friends every week, and Ruthie confirmed that they are all fine, upstanding gentlemen."

"Auntie, I thought we talked about this. I don't care how upstanding he is, I'm not looking to get involved with anyone."

"Yes, of course, dear heart. All I'm suggesting is that whoever is joining you, the two of you will have a wonderful time in Las Vegas. And if you happen to have a glass of wine together at the end of a long day, and he happens to be single and attractive—" Sabrina arched an eyebrow at her aunt. "Now don't give me that look. Ruthie tells me the Association is so grateful for your willingness to step in—everyone else has a family or a shop they need to tend, you see—that you'll have an answer about your studio by the time you return."

Sabrina sighed. "What a fortunate coincidence you just happened to hear that they needed someone to go to this mysterious convention."

It wouldn't be the worst thing to spend a few days doing a good deed for the town she intended to call home. If it fast-tracked her approval to open Get Clayed, it would be worth it. And it would be nice to get to know another business owner in town, even if this whole thing reeked of a set up. The last thing she needed in her new post-divorce life was a 'nice young man.' She'd already had her rebound fling, thank you very much, and now she was ready to settle into spinsterhood.

"Make sure you pack something sparkly. Men like a little sparkle."

"Auntie, I'm doing a favor for the Association, not looking for men."

"Who says you can't do both?" Aunt Lucy laughed. "You know, Aster Bay has quite a few eligible bachelors—and only one of them used to be engaged to your sister."

The knocking on the door resumed, but Baz turned up the volume on his stereo, the music filling his apartment and bouncing off the steel and concrete finishes. He took another sip of his Scotch and slumped down in his chair, the glass dangling from his fingers as he closed his eyes and tried to sink into the sea of sound.

Maybe if he stayed this way long enough, he'd drown in it, inhale enough of it that he'd no longer see Sabrina when he closed his eyes, the shock and hurt on her face, as though she had anything to be hurt about. She was the one who'd betrayed him, goddamn it. Maybe if he had another Scotch, he'd stop thinking about the way her hair fluttered about her face and the full curve of her hips in pants that looked too expensive to wear while eating fried food sold from a roadside cart.

Maybe he could forget she existed altogether.

The sound of a key turning in the deadbolt on his front door broke through the music, but Baz ignored it. Ignored, too, the muttered curses and clomping of heavy shoes moving across his apartment. He took another sip of his Scotch, never opening his eyes, as someone turned off the music.

"So much for not caring," Ethan muttered at his side.

"Fuck you."

Gavin sighed. "I told you we should have come earlier."

"I'll make coffee," Jamie announced from the open concept kitchen.

Baz slowly opened his eyes, keeping his gaze locked on the rolling waves of the bay through the wall of windows at one end of his apartment. He lifted his glass to his lips again, but Ethan snatched it from his hands. "I think you've had enough for one night."

"I'm pissed off, not drunk," Baz grumbled.

"We brought food," Jamie said over the sound of Baz's microwave whirring to life. "Pizza."

"To soak up the booze," Ethan said with a pointed look.

"I'm fine. You can go."

"Doubtful. Besides, we need to settle this before the Merchants' Association meeting tomorrow night." Gavin held up a worn Scrabble box in one hand and a tin of Uno cards in the other. "What'll it be?"

"Pain in my ass."

"We love you too." Jamie thrust a mug of coffee at him.

He accepted the mug and went to the wall of glass overlooking the bay as Gavin and Jamie set up the evening's board game at his dining room table. Baz rested his forehead against the glass, letting the coolness seep into his skin. Ethan came up beside him, his hands dug into his pants pockets.

"You wouldn't be day drinking because of a certain redhead who happens to be back in town, now, would you?" Ethan asked.

If Ethan was surprised that Sabrina's reappearance in town had rattled Baz, he didn't show it, and Baz wasn't sure if he was grateful or frustrated. He deserved to have someone call him out for the hypocrite he was, for tying himself up in knots after a fleeting glimpse of the woman he claimed to hate. Someone should point out that he hadn't had a single feeling about a woman in a decade, and it was fucking ridiculous for Sabrina, of all people, to be the first to get under his skin. But he should have known Ethan wouldn't be that person.

"I heard she's staying with Mrs. Page," Ethan offered.

Baz took a sip of the coffee, wincing as it burned his tongue. He glanced at Ethan, clocking the thoughtful narrowing of his eyes. "Just fucking say it."

"Is all this, the Scotch and the music, because you're upset she's back, or because you're upset you care?"

Baz ignored the question, which was its own kind of admission.

"She submitted an application to the Merchants' Association for some kind of pottery studio. Seems like she might be planning to stick around for a while," Ethan continued.

Baz snorted. "A pottery studio? Guess she decided not to get that MBA after all."

"Maybe it's time the two of you actually talked about what

happened. You used to be friends."

Again, he ignored Ethan. He didn't need to talk to Sabrina to know what had happened. He had never been good enough to marry Holly Page. Everyone knew it. It had been stupid of him to have ever thought Sabrina felt differently.

"Are we playing or what?" Gavin called.

Baz took another sip of his coffee and turned to face his friends. "You ready for me to kick your ass?"

Ethan laughed. "Big talk from the guy who's slurring his speech."

"Even if I was drunk, which I'm not, I'm better at this game than you'll ever be." Baz took a seat across from Gavin at the dining room table.

"Prove it."

Jamie slid a plate of pizza next to Baz's elbow. "Standard rules—no proper nouns, and no words that aren't in the dictionary." He tapped a weathered paperback copy of the Miriam Webster dictionary that Baz kept in the game box. "No Dothraki, Quenya, Klingon, or any other made-up languages."

"All languages are made up," Gavin grumbled.

"Point of order—" Ethan began.

"Yes, the Portuguese names of foods count, but only if there isn't really an English equivalent," Jamie said. Ethan leaned back in his chair, mollified. "Mnemonic device acronyms are allowed but only if you have the entire acronym. Loser has to go to this convention next week. No rematches unless there's a tie for last place. Did I forget anything?"

"Nope. Let's play," Gavin said.

"Aren't you playing?" Baz asked, noting the lack of Scrabble tiles in front of Jamie.

"Tessa's seven months pregnant. No way am I traveling anywhere. This is between the three of you."

"And yet, you're the one who promised Norm one of us would go," Baz said with a shake of his head. "Isn't that convenient?"

"That's my grandbaby about to be born. I think I should be off the list too," Ethan said.

"Nice try." Gavin shuffled the tiles on his rack. "You go first."

Baz stared at his tiles, the letters blurring and shifting in front of him. He blinked but it was no use. Maybe he was a little drunk after all. And now he was going to lose this game.

Of course, losing might not be that bad. Then he'd be the one flying off to the small-town tourism conference in Vegas, putting a whole country between himself and Sabrina. It would only be a temporary solution, but maybe it would be long enough for him to figure out how to be civil to her when they inevitably ran into each other in the cheese aisle at the grocery store. Long enough to remember that he wasn't supposed to be attracted to someone he hated.

"Didn't Norm say something about sending two delegates?" Gavin asked. "Two of us have to go to this thing?"

Jamie shook his head. "Mrs. Greene said she's filled the second spot already."

"Then one of us has to spend a few days in Vegas with our former elementary school teacher. Nothing weird about that at all. You're up, Baz." Ethan leaned back in his chair with a smug smile.

Ethan and Gavin had already played their opening words, each one six letters and worth more points than Baz could calculate after drinking four fingers of Scotch. Squinting at the board, he lay down two tiles.

"That's the best you can do?" Ethan laughed. "Do you *want* to go to this conference?"

Baz glared at him.

"If you're only going to play swear words, you're going to have to get more creative than that," Gavin said, inclining his head towards Baz's move.

"Shit isn't a swear. They don't even bleep it on TV," Jamie said.

"Huh. I guess you're right." Gavin lay out his own tiles.

"I thought we said no made-up words." Baz pointed at Gavin's mess of consonants. "How the hell do you even say that?"

"Every Good Boy Deserves Fudge," Gavin said. "Mnemonic device. Didn't you take piano lessons with Mrs. Blumenthal when you were a kid?"

"I thought it was Every Good Boy Does Fine," Ethan said.

Gavin shrugged. "Either way."

It didn't take long for his friends to completely destroy him, putting more than a hundred points between their scores and his.

Jamie clapped him on the shoulder as he stood from the table. "I'll let Norm know to put the plane ticket in your name."

Playing Scrabble when he was the only one who'd been drinking might not have been his best idea, but as much as he hated losing, he was starting to think that going to this conference might be exactly what he needed to get his head on straight. A few nights in the city of sin on the town's dime, an anonymous out-of-town hookup or two, and by the time he returned to Aster Bay he'd be prepared to face his ex-fiancée's little sister.

# Chapter Three

Sabrina shoved her overstuffed carry-on under the seat in front of her with a grunt. It shifted a fraction of an inch, barely fitting in the meager space. She sighed and sank down into her window seat overlooking the wing of the airplane. Closing her eyes, she focused on her breathing. In for five, out for five, in for five, out for five, just the way she'd practiced.

*You are not going to die today. You are safe in this giant metal projectile that defies the laws of physics. You will not plummet from the sky in a fiery blaze and crash in a flyover state. Not today.*

It wasn't exactly the type of mantra her therapist had recommended but, after everything that happened with her now ex-husband, Sabrina had learned that acknowledging the doomsday scenarios playing in her head was more helpful than pretending they didn't exist.

She stabbed at the button overhead to turn on the fan above her seat, but all it did was spit out a burst of hot air. As if she wasn't already sweating to death. Thank God she had the foresight to block out her mother's voice this morning—*Respectable people do not wear sweatpants on an airplane, Sabrina.* Flying might have been Sabrina's own personal version of hell, but at least she was wearing an elastic waistband and a wire-free bra. Could be worse.

"Fucking hell."

*It just got worse.*

Sabrina forgot to breathe. She'd know that gruff voice anywhere. The gravel of it scraped across her skin, and she grew lightheaded as his mere presence sucked all the oxygen out of the tiny space.

*You are* not *going to die today.*

Opening her eyes, she met the hard stare of Sebastian Graham. He stood in the aisle beside her row, an immovable tower of censure in a three-piece suit. The sharp slash of his eyebrows and slight flare of his nostrils would be comical on any other man, but only made Sebastian more handsome. How was he so beautiful when he was this angry? The silent wrath rolling off him in waves bent the air around him, like the heat rising on the tarmac below.

"What are you doing here?" she asked.

He arched an eyebrow at her as though the question offended him.

"I mean, you're going to Vegas. Obviously. But why?" she stammered.

He shook his head and shoved his carry-on into the overhead compartment with an alarming ease. Swearing under his breath, he unbuttoned his suit jacket and dropped into the seat next to her. She pressed herself against the wall of the cabin, as if that half an inch of space could give her enough room to breathe. As if his thigh wasn't dangerously close to pressing against hers. Why did they even make planes with only two seats together? What happened to three seats in a row?

*You are not going to die today. Not from this hunk of metal falling out of the sky and not from Sebastian Graham's death glare.*

Out of the corner of her eye, Sabrina watched as he settled into his seat, put in his earbuds, and rested his head back, his eyes falling closed, without ever answering her question. Clearly, he had no intention of talking to her, even if they were trapped with each other for the next seven hours. What were the odds?

But then she remembered—Aunt Lucy had said the other person going to this convention on behalf of Aster Bay was a "young man" who played bar trivia every week. Sabrina winced as she remembered the hours of Trivial Pursuit she and Sebastian had played in the food pantry break room between stocking shelves with canned soup and packing care packages of mini toiletries.

She placed her hand on his forearm to get his attention. His icy blue eyes flew open and stared at the offending point of contact. She motioned to his ears. With a harsh exhale through his nose, he removed the earbud closest to her and watched her expectantly, but he still didn't say a word.

"Are you—" She stopped herself, swallowing to bring moisture back to her mouth, and tried again, pulling her hand back into her own lap. "You're the other rep from the Merchants' Association."

His eyes flared slightly in surprise before narrowing at her. "The *other*?"

"Aunt Lucy volunteered me." When he didn't say anything, she continued, words tumbling over themselves. "I moved back. In. With her. I want to open a pottery studio, like the one I had in Maine. Kennebunkport. That's where I've been, the last few years at least. Not that you asked. But I was. And I had a studio there. And a—" She stopped herself. *No need to dump all your baggage at his feet.* "But now I'm here and I want another one. Studio, that is. And the Merchants' Association hasn't approved my application yet for a permit to open. Apparently, pottery's controversial, which is really saying something, if you think about it, in a town that already has a lingerie store, a boudoir studio, and a sex toy store."

Her face heated at the mention of the sex toy store, filthy fantasies that had kept her company since she'd spotted him at the Bazaar flashing behind her eyes: Sebastian pressing a toy between her legs, the way he'd punish her for the last ten years with an endless string of orgasms.

*You will not think about orgasms while you're sitting next to him in this death trap.*

"Not that there's anything wrong with a sex toy store. I mean, it really is progressive of the town to welcome a sex shop in the heart of downtown. And quality toys can be hard to find, you know? I mean, maybe you don't know. I mean, *I know*."

A muscle in his jaw jumped, drawing her attention, and she was momentarily fascinated by the movement of the tiny muscles keeping his jaw tightly clenched.

"What was I talking about? Oh! My pottery studio. Aunt Lucy—you remember Aunt Lucy—she told the Merchants' Association that I'd go to this conference because she thought it would put me in their good graces to get my application approved and no one else wanted to go. Well, no one else except you. Apparently."

"Apparently."

She opened her mouth to say something else when the flight attendant at the front of the plane started her speech about seatbelts and how to use the oxygen masks if they should drop from the ceiling of the plane. Sebastian turned his attention to the flight attendant, his laser focus on the safety monologue making it clear that he was done listening to her babble. Sabrina slunk down in her seat, trying to absorb the information, but it all sounded like white noise. And the less she heard, the more panic clawed at her throat. How would she inflate the oxygen mask if she hadn't heard the directions? Was she supposed to pull down and then put it on, or put it on and then pull down? And what was that about the seat cushion?

*You are not going to die today. You are not going to die today. You are not going to die today.*

*Unless there's a sudden loss of cabin pressure and you can't figure out how to put the oxygen mask on. Or the plane crash lands in water and you drown before you figure out how to use the flotation device.*

*Are we even going to fly over water? A flotation device won't help me if we crash in a field.*

*Which is more likely to cause fatalities—going down nose first into a Great Lake or a corn field?*

*Holy shit, what if I die today?*

"Sabrina!"

Sebastian's harsh bark pulled her attention, and she jerked her head towards him, but she didn't see him. Not really.

*You are not going to die today. You are not going to die today.*

"Jesus Christ," he muttered. He took her hand and pressed it to his chest. "Breathe," he ordered, and then began counting, a slow chanting of "one two three four five" over and over.

As her breathing slowed and air rushed into her lungs, embarrassment crept in. It had been months since she'd had a panic attack. Maybe she should have listened to her therapist about the inane, happy mantras instead of ones that included words like "death trap" and "fiery blaze."

"Everyone alright over here?" the cheery voice of the flight attendant asked from the aisle.

Baz kept his eyes locked on Sabrina's, waiting for her to answer.

"Y-yes," she stammered. "I'm fine."

The flight attendant's plastic smile flickered towards Sebastian, looking for confirmation.

"Fine," he grunted.

"Alright," the flight attendant said with a smile. "Then please fasten your seatbelt, ma'am. We'll be taking off in a few moments."

She reluctantly pulled her hand away from the heat of Sebastian's chest. Her fingers were clumsy as they fumbled with the belt buckle.

"Christ's sake," he muttered, reaching over and buckling her seatbelt with a metallic clang.

"Thank you."

The plane jolted as it started down the tarmac and, before she realized what she was doing, she reached over the arm rest and grasped his hand in hers, clinging to him.

*I can't die today. I can't die when Sebastian thinks I ruined his life.*

He stared at their interlocked hands and she knew she should release him, but she couldn't.

"You are not going to die today," he said in a low, deep voice.

"What?"

"You said, 'I can't die today.'"

Her heart sank into her stomach. She'd said that out loud?

"You're right. You are not dying today. You said it yourself. You can't die while I think you ruined my life."

Oh fuck. Stupid mantras.

With his free hand, he replaced his earbuds, then closed his eyes and leaned back as if he'd go to sleep. "And you did ruin my life. So obviously you cannot die today."

"Check again." Baz gritted his teeth and used every ounce of his self-control not to reach across the concierge desk and throttle the poor sap who had the misfortune of checking him into the hotel.

The baby-faced twenty-something wiped a bead of sweat away with the back of his forearm before typing furiously, each clack of the keys twisting his face into a deeper grimace. "I'm sorry, sir. Both of your names are in the system but there's only one room. Whoever booked your reservation—"

"Fuck!" Baz slammed his fist down on the desk, causing the

kid to jump.

He spun away, raking his fingers through his hair. It wasn't this kid's fault that Norm was a cheap asshole. He pulled his phone from his pocket and fired off a text to the President of the Merchants' Association, staring at the screen in stunned silence as the status changed from 'delivered' to 'read' and still no reply came.

*The bastard left me on read.*

"Are there any other available rooms?" Sabrina asked the desk agent with a conciliatory smile.

"Yes, ma'am. I could put you in a junior suite for six hundred dollard per night."

"Per night?" Sabrina squeaked. "That's—"

"Too fucking expensive," Baz grunted.

The kid winced. "There are several conferences in the hotel at the moment, sir. The only rooms I have left are suites. But the room reserved for you both does have a pull-out couch. You could—"

"That will be fine." Sabrina shot a wary glance towards Baz.

*Stop being an asshole. You let her sleep on your shoulder on the plane, but you can't share a room with her in the hotel? Fucking hypocrite.*

With any luck he'd meet someone in the hotel bar and need never find out exactly what kind of hell came folded up in a hotel pull-out couch.

He scrubbed his hand over his face, then thrust it out towards the desk agent. "Keys."

Across the lobby, the elevator doors slid open with a ding and Baz strode across the ostentatious space, determined to put some distance between himself and Sabrina, even if only for a moment. But once he was inside the elevator, pressing his palm to the door to keep it open and watching her struggle to drag her luggage after him, he realized his mistake. Now there was nothing to do but watch her, and if he'd thought she was a menace in her fancy silk blouse at the Bazaar, it was nothing compared to Sabrina Page in loungewear. He cleared his throat and looked away, determined not to focus on the way her chest moved each time she tugged on her bag.

*You hate her. Stop looking at her tits.*

No sooner had Sabrina joined him in the elevator, than a laughing, drunk couple pushed their way inside as well. They ricocheted off the gilt mirror-like walls of the elevator in their hurry to paw at each other, hardly coming up for air long enough for the man to slam his hand against the button for the twentieth floor. The woman giggled as her partner buried his head in her neck, his hands everywhere. It was like they consumed every bit of air in the elevator, taunting Baz and Sabrina, daring them to watch their ridiculous public display of affection.

Baz inadvertently caught Sabrina's eye, a blush rising rapidly in her cheeks, and looked away quickly. He didn't want to know what that blush was about—if she was embarrassed or scandalized or, even worse, turned on. He just wanted to get to their room and forget this day had ever happened.

Their room was on the seventeenth floor and overlooked the strip, the obnoxious neon flashing lights below bleeding in through the thin curtains. After the company in the elevator, their room felt enormous. Baz dropped his bag on the pull-out couch in the corner as Sabrina closed the door behind them.

"Sorry about this," she said over the sound of her bag dragging across the carpet.

Baz rolled his eyes and snatched her bag from her grasp, lifting it easily and placing it on the luggage rack in the corner. "Did you make the reservation?"

"No."

"Then don't fucking apologize for things you didn't do."

She chuckled under her breath as she unzipped her bag, digging out a toiletry kit. "Some things never change." He narrowed his eyes at her, but that only served to make her laugh more.

"You always did have to be the grumpiest guy in the room."

"Do not," he muttered.

She pressed her lips together to suppress her laughter, but her eyes sparkled as if to say, *told you so.*

"I need a drink." He stalked across the room to the mini bar, not caring that a single glass of Scotch was about to cost him the same as a steak dinner back home.

Before he could untwist the cap, Sabrina said, "Why don't we go down to one of the bars? I wouldn't say no to a margarita after that flight."

This Sabrina, the one who smiled charmingly at desk agents and made fun of his attitude, was more familiar than the woman who'd gripped his hand on the plane like he was the only thing between her and certain doom. He'd never known Sabrina to be afraid of flying. All those vacations she'd talked about wanting to take, the trips to Egypt and Peru she'd planned in between unloading boxes of cereal at the food pantry, they all required lengthy flights. But this woman—both the version that panicked on the tarmac and the one who confidently spoke to customer service employees—was different from the girl he'd known all those years ago.

Different and yet unsettlingly familiar.

Baz frowned at the bottle in his hand before putting it back in the mini bar. The sight of her answering smile hit him squarely in the chest, knocking the wind out of him. There had been a time when she'd smiled at him constantly, when he'd gone out of his way to make her smile, when he'd known a thousand ways to paint that particular expression on her face. But it had been a decade since he'd last felt its warmth directed at him. A decade since he'd cared.

*Liar.*

"Give me five minutes to freshen up," she said as she disappeared into the bathroom.

*Freshen up* was apparently secret girl code for change out of her cotton loungewear and pour herself into a little black dress that showed off her legs and cleavage in a display designed to drive men out of their minds. A gold chain around her neck disappeared down the front of her dress and he found himself wondering what was on the end of that chain.

*Don't look at her tits.*

But when had she gotten curves like that, the kind that begged for his hands? When had Sabrina Page, the quirky kid at the food pantry and his almost sister-in-law, turned into this knockout with tits that defied gravity and legs he wanted to feel wrapped around his waist? If she were any other woman, he would have already made filthy promises to her, every one of which he would make good on. If she were any other woman—

"Ready?" she asked, smoothing her hands over her thighs to straighten the dress.

Baz could think of a thousand things he was ready for in that moment, none of which involved leaving that hotel room and all of which ended with her lipstick smeared all over his cock.

*Fuck. Stop.*

*Sabrina Page is the last person you can think about that way.*

"Sebastian?" she asked, her brow wrinkling.

Jesus Christ, why did he like the way she said his name so much? If anyone else insisted on calling him by his given name he'd bite their head off. But he liked the sound of the consonants on her lips.

"Let's go," he grunted, buttoning his suit jacket and striding out of the room.

The bar in the hotel lobby was crowded, but they found a small booth in the corner and ordered their drinks. Sabrina practically clapped when her margarita arrived. She took a slow sip, her tongue darting out to lick salt off the rim. That flash of pink was how Baz knew he was in hell. Their plane had fallen from the sky after all and he was in his own personal hell watching Sabrina Page's tongue flick in and out of her mouth. He threw back half his drink in one sip.

*What is wrong with you? You hate this woman.*

Didn't he?

"Nice suit," she said.

He grunted, because what the fuck was that supposed to mean? "Nice dress."

"I don't remember you wearing suits." When he didn't answer, she leaned forward, a grin tugging at her lips. "Do you even own jeans anymore, or is it all suits and Darth Vader costumes now?"

"Do you always dress like your mother?" he shot back. She flinched slightly at his words and he turned away. *You are such an asshole.* "Your mom wouldn't have worn spandex on a plane," he conceded.

She chuckled. "No, she definitely would not.

They sat in silence for another few minutes, Baz trying not to think about why he cared what she thought of his wardrobe and Sabrina seemingly focused on her drink.

"The way I see it, we have two options." Sabrina twisted the stem of her margarita glass between two fingers, leaving a widening circle of condensation on the table. "We can spend the next few days walking on eggshells, with you grunting and scowling and me babbling like an anxious lunatic, or we can actually talk about what happened."

"When you broke up my wedding," he said.

She huffed out a breath. "It's not that simple."

"You told your sister not to marry me."

Her face went pale and she swallowed, rolling those distracting bright red lips over each other. "I did."

"Seems simple to me."

Sabrina took a long sip from her margarita, that fucking

tongue gliding over her lips to catch the last bits of salt and tequila. She threw a nervous glance his way and he almost felt bad for being such a jerk.

Almost.

He let himself sink down in the booth and drank his Scotch, his thighs spreading as he adopted a posture far more casual than he felt. Let her think it no longer bothered him, that her betrayal on what should have been the happiest day of his life didn't still sting. That he hadn't spent ten fucking years wondering what he had done wrong.

Except he didn't have to wonder. He'd been born into a middle-class family in a middle-class town where he worked a middle-class job. He went to college on loans that would take him too long to pay off and he scraped and clawed and worked for every damn thing he had. He didn't belong on the golf course at the country club and he sure as fuck didn't fit in with the Pages, with their generational wealth and all the moral high ground they thought came with it.

He hadn't been good enough. That was his crime.

He just hadn't thought Sabrina had felt that way.

So damn-fucking-right he wore suits now. He wasn't the loser her family had thought he was anymore. He'd made something of himself, and if he wanted to broadcast that to the entire goddamn world through a wardrobe full of tailored business wear, he would.

Sabrina's eyes raked over him, something like interest sparking in their depths as they lingered on the pull of his suit jacket over his biceps and the flat planes of his stomach. He bit back a smirk.

*Good.* He wanted her to want him, the guy who hadn't been good enough to marry her sister. Wanted her to sit there in that fucking tease of a dress and squirm thinking about all the things he could do to make her scream his name.

If he didn't hate her, that is.

"You're different," she said, sadness pulling at the corners of her mouth.

"It's been ten years."

"No, it's not that. You didn't use to be this...cold."

He grunted, draining his drink.

"The morning of your wedding—"

"We're not talking about this."

"Sebastian, you deserve to know. That morning—"

"I'm not fucking talking about this," he growled. "It won't change anything."

"It might."

"What would it change?"

"Maybe you wouldn't hate me."

"I don't hate you, Sabrina." He dug a handful of bills out of his wallet and tossed them on the table as he got to his feet, buttoning his suit jacket. "I don't feel anything for you at all."

# Chapter Four

*Then*

"I never would've believed you'd be the next of us to tie the knot," Ethan said, shaking his head as he refilled Baz's tumbler of Scotch from the bar cart in the corner of the groomsmen's suite at The Barclay.

Baz waved him away. "Get out of here with that. Don't want to be drunk when I walk down the aisle."

Ethan shrugged and took a sip from the glass himself before setting it down.

"You nervous?" Gavin asked.

"Not really."

"The reality hasn't sunk in yet, that's all," Jamie teased.

Baz supposed he should be nervous. Two hundred of his closest friends and family had gathered to watch him get married. Who was he kidding? There were about twenty people there for him and the rest were Holly's guests.

"I was nervous as h-e-double-hockey-sticks on my wedding day," Gavin said.

Brodie, Gavin's thirteen-year-old son, looked up from his handheld video game. "I'm a teenager now, old man. You can say 'hell' around me."

"Is it bad that I'm not nervous?" Baz asked, turning to his friends, genuine concern sinking into his gut.

"Don't overthink it," Ethan said.

Baz turned back to the mirror and straightened his bow tie. In less than an hour, he was getting married.

He stared at the man in the mirror and hardly recognized him. And it wasn't about the clean-shaven jawline—because Holly complained of beard burn if he didn't shave for even a day—and slicked back hair—because Holly said it made him look more sophisticated. He wasn't this guy. the guy who jumped into things headfirst, who let his emotions determine his next move, who was willing to give up his entire life in Aster Bay—his friends, his fledgling accounting business—to follow a woman to Brookline.

He had only met Holly six months ago when she'd arrived in town to spend the summer with her sister and great aunt. She'd shown up at the food pantry where Baz and Sabrina volunteered together and turned his entire life upside down. He'd never thought he'd be that guy, yet here he was, preparing to marry a woman who, until last week, he hadn't known hated board games.

But he wanted to be the guy she thought he was, or thought he could be—a guy worthy of Holly Page, country club princess and rising star lawyer at one of Boston's top law firms. Still, in his rented tuxedo in this too-expensive suite in the fanciest hotel in his hometown, he felt like an imposter.

"Uncle Baz, are you gonna throw up?" Brodie eyed him warily from his perch on the ottoman.

"I need some air." He pushed past his friends towards the door to the suite.

"We'll come with you," Gavin offered.

Baz shook his head. "Give me a minute."

He was stomping down the hallway towards the bridal suite before he even recognized where he was headed. As he approached the room, his footsteps slowed and he tried to steady his breathing. He needed to see Holly, to touch her, to look into her eyes and remember how much he loved her, and then it wouldn't matter that her family's bank account had more figures in it than his family would see in a lifetime, that she was so far out of his league it was laughable. None of it would matter, because she had chosen him, because he had asked her to be his wife and she'd said yes.

"I won't let you do this." Sabrina's tight voice drifted into the hallway through a crack in the bridal suite door.

Baz paused, leaning against the wall. He didn't want to interrupt whatever sibling drama was unfolding behind that door. He knew Holly and Sabrina didn't always see eye to eye, and his friendship with Sabrina had already caused more than a few arguments with Holly when Baz had made the mistake of trying to help Holly see her sister's side of things. Sabrina was his friend, but Holly was about to be his wife. The last thing he wanted to do was put himself between them.

"I don't think you really get a say here," came Holly's laughing reply. "You're making a big deal out of nothing. Everybody does it."

"Not you. Not Sebastian."

Baz's heart stopped at the mention of his name, at the vehemence in Sabrina's tone.

"Are you jealous? Is that what this is about?" Holly asked. "You picked a hell of a time to tell me you're in love with my fiancé."

"I'm n—it's not about that and you know it."

"What I know, little sister, is that you are out of line."

"You can't marry him."

Baz sucked in a breath, anger and confusion souring in his gut as he leaned against the wall.

"Why not? Why shouldn't I have some fun?"

"Fun? You know this will never work. He doesn't deserve—"

"I've had about enough of hearing what you think my fiancé deserves."

What the hell was happening? He and Sabrina were friends—weren't they? Since when did she think he wasn't good enough for her sister? That he didn't deserve her?

"I'll never forgive you for this," Sabrina said, her voice tearful.

But Baz had heard enough. He turned and walked away, the voices of the arguing sisters receding into the background of the static slowly filling his brain.

It would be fine. He and Holly would get married and Sabrina would see how much he would do to deserve Holly, how hard he would work to make her happy. He'd prove it to everyone. And if Sabrina couldn't be happy for him, if she really believed that her sister shouldn't marry him, then maybe they were never really friends to begin with.

"Don't forget to breathe," Gavin whispered at Baz's back.

Baz glanced over his shoulder at his friends lined up in their matching tuxes at the front of St. Anthony's, and gave a small nod. He hated standing there, at the front of the church he'd been attending his whole life, with all those people looking at him. He felt certain they could all tell that he didn't belong in this life, in the tuxedo with the too-tight shoes surrounded by flower arrangements that cost more than he made in a year, preparing to marry a woman who should have never even known his name. If Sabrina could see that they didn't fit, surely everyone else in this cavernous church could too.

The music changed and the first of the bridesmaids appeared at the back of the church in a long, pale pink dress—one of Holly's college roommates. The one who married the doctor. She was followed by Holly's cousin, the one who competed in dressage tournaments, not that Baz had even known what dressage was when they'd been introduced. Another college roommate—the one who clerked for the Senator. And then Sabrina appeared at the back of the church. Her face was red, eyes puffy, and she kept her gaze focused on the ground in front of her as she walked.

She couldn't even look at him. Did she hate him that much? After all this time, months of volunteering together, laughing together, and it was all, what, a fucking game to her? It didn't make sense. And he hated that he was even trying to puzzle it out on what should have been the happiest day of his life. He was marrying Holly Page. He was going to have the picture-perfect future that no one believed he could have.

*Fuck Sabrina.*

Sabrina took her place at the front of the line of bridesmaids, directly opposite from Baz, her eyes locked on his shoes.

The music changed and the crowd turned as one to face the back of the church. But not Baz. He couldn't stop staring at Sabrina, daring her to look at him, so it took him a beat longer than everyone else to notice that something was wrong.

Holly should have entered the church already. The song had gone on too long, the organist glancing around as he continued playing, uneasy murmuring rippling through the crowd. Baz turned his head to look over his shoulder at Gavin, who clapped him on the back. "Probably just fixing her veil," Gavin said.

Baz nodded and turned back towards the church, towards the empty doorway where his fiancée should have appeared by now. At the front of the church, his mother sent a concerned look his way, but Baz shook his head roughly. Everything was *fine.*

As the organist started the song over and the crowd began shuffling in their seats, the murmurs growing louder, something sickly and cold turned in Baz's gut, gathering size and weight with each moment that passed. In his jacket pocket, his cell phone vibrated and he whipped around, turning his back to the assembled congregation as he pulled out his phone.

Gavin, Ethan, and Jamie huddled around Baz as he stared at the screen in disbelief.

**Holly:** I can't do this. Sabrina was right.
**Holly:** It's over.

"What is it?" Ethan asked.

Baz shoved the phone towards him, each inch of his body growing hot with awareness of the hundreds of eyes watching his every move, waiting for him to come to grips with what they had already realized.

"What do you want to do?" Jamie asked, handing Baz back his phone.

"I—I don't know."

"Baz, let's get out of here," Gavin said.

"I'll handle the guests," Ethan offered.

Baz nodded numbly. Gavin and Jamie flanked him, moving as one to escort him out of the church, as though they could somehow lessen the embarrassment of literally being left at the altar.

"What's going on?" Baz froze at the sound of Sabrina's voice behind him. He spun around, meeting her eyes for the first time all day, and clenched his jaw to keep from shouting. "Is everything alright?"

"You got what you wanted," he snarled.

"What do you—" Her face went white, her lip quivered, and fuck her. She didn't get to cry. Not when he was the one who'd been humiliated. Not when she was the one who'd caused it all in the first place. "Oh, I didn't—This isn't what I wanted."

Baz scoffed and scraped his hand over his jaw, aware of all the people staring at them now—the cousin who competed in fancy horse competitions and the great aunt who baked the best thumbprint cookies in Aster Bay, Ethan's parents who'd been the first to take a chance on Baz's new accounting firm, his own mother. They were all witness to his humiliation. There wouldn't be a place in Aster Bay he could go after this where people wouldn't know that Sebastian Graham had been publicly rejected, weighed and measured and found lacking.

And it was her fault.

Baz leaned close to Sabrina, his lungs burning with the rage he refused to let loose in a church, and dropped his voice dangerously low. "Get the fuck out of my town."

# Chapter Five



*Now*

Sabrina stifled another yawn behind her hand as she scribbled notes from the slideshow on the screen at the front of the packed conference room. She wasn't sure if she was struggling to pay attention to the session on dynamic pricing because math had never been her strong suit, or if it had more to do with the lack of sleep.

She'd gone back to their room after Sebastian left the bar and waited for him to return, flipping through endless cable channels until well after midnight. By the time she finally gave up and went to bed, he still hadn't returned. But when she woke the next morning, his suitcase had been moved and there was evidence that he'd slept on the couch in the corner without ever bothering to pull it out.

She hadn't seen him at all yesterday, falling asleep before he returned to the room. But again, this morning, it was clear he'd slipped in and out of their room undetected, the balled-up blanket in the corner of the couch and the smell of his body wash in the bathroom the only clues that he'd been back to the room at all.

She shouldn't care that he was avoiding her—they'd avoided

each other for the last ten years, hadn't they? But she also couldn't deny that his words stung. Somehow his apathy was even worse than his anger. And some part of her, however tiny and irrational, had thought that maybe being on this trip together was a sign. Maybe they could finally hash out what had happened all those years ago and move past it.

But tomorrow they'd fly back to Rhode Island, and they were no closer to reconciling than when they'd arrived.

Around her, conference attendees burst into applause, the lanyards around their necks swinging back and forth as they got to their feet. *Shit. Now you've missed what he was saying about identifying peak demand times.*

Sabrina reluctantly gathered her things. She'd have to hope it was in the slides the presenter had promised to upload to the conference website, or that it overlapped enough with what she'd learned in her undergraduate business administration program that she could wing it. Attending this conference might not get her back into Sebastian's good graces, but if she learned enough to share with the Aster Bay Merchants' Association, she might manage to get her pottery studio approved.

She moved with the crowd towards the last session of the conference—a keynote address on leveraging the unique character of your small town to increase tourism. As she approached the auditorium, she spotted Sebastian outside the doors. His suit jacket was slung over his arm, shirtsleeves rolled up to reveal tanned and toned forearms, as he spoke with a short, balding man in lime green suspenders. She was transfixed by the ease with which he moved, by the familiarity of it, and yet the awareness that all that ease turned hard and cold when he was around her.

For a moment he looked like the man she used to know, a man who would catch the spiders in the stock room in a paper cup and safely bring them outside, all the while teasing her for being afraid of such a small bug.

God, she missed that man.

Her cell phone buzzed to life in her hand, shaking her from her reverie. Her mother's name flashed across the screen, and she backed away from the auditorium, ducking into an alcove off the main hallway as she answered the call.

"Can you please explain to me why I had to hear from Aunt Lucy that my youngest daughter has moved to Aster Bay?" her mother asked from the other end of the line.

"Hi, Mom." Sabrina slumped against the wall of the alcove, setting down her notebook and bag of conference swag on the little side table.

"Answer the question, Sabrina."

"I was going to tell you once I was settled." It might have been true. At least, she hadn't decided *not* to tell her parents she was in Aster Bay.

Her mother huffed. "When have you ever been *settled*?" Sabrina closed her eyes against the jab as her mother barreled ahead. "If I hadn't called Aunt Lucy to invite her to the Labor Day Party, I never would have known you'd finally decided to move on with your life, though why you chose to go live with an elderly woman instead of coming home to your parents, I'll never understand."

*You will not dump thirty years of resentment on your mother over the phone. You will not spontaneously combust from holding it in for one more day.*

"I like Aster Bay, Mom. I always have."

"You liked sneaking off to take your art classes when you were supposed to be looking for graduate programs," her mother snapped

Would she ever live down the sin of embarrassing her parents by not following the prescriptive path they'd set out for her? For preferring working with her hands to sitting behind a desk all day?

"At least now you can put that whole unpleasant chapter in

Maine behind you. It will be good to have the whole family together again for the long weekend," her mother said.

Sabrina's eyes flew open. "Aunt Lucy said she'd go to the party?"

"No, of course not. She's *elderly*, Sabrina. She has no interest in traveling for a party." Her stomach sank. That meant— "We're going with a patriotic theme this year. Make sure you wear something suitable. Preferably something blue or white. Red would be terrible with your coloring."

"Mom, I wasn't planning on going back to Brookline for the long weekend. You know, Aster Bay has a whole celebration of its own that I thought I might stay for this year."

Her mother laughed. "Of course, you're coming home. You know this is the largest social event of the year for our family. How would it look if one of my daughters didn't attend?"

"How would it look to *who*?"

"To everyone! Don't be obtuse, Sabrina. It's not flattering."

*You will not hang up on your mother. You will not daydream about ways to sabotage her precious party.*

"Oh! I almost forgot," her mother said. But Sabrina knew better. Maryann Page never forgot anything. "We'll have a special toast to celebrate Holly making partner. I expect you'll want to prepare a few remarks to contribute. And do *try* to find a suitable date to accompany you. You know how I hate odd numbers at a party."

"Or I could not go."

"You'll come, Sabrina, and you will play nice. You and Holly used to be close before that unpleasantness with the Graham boy."

"You mean before she blamed me for ruining her wedding? That unpleasantness?"

"Yes, yes, I'm aware of your version of events," her mother said as though the truth were exhausting, as though Sabrina's statements were merely one interpretation rather than the truth.

It had been ten years and still her mother couldn't fathom that her perfect eldest daughter might have done anything wrong, that maybe Sabrina wasn't a jealous monster hellbent on destroying her sister's happiness. Ten years and nothing had changed.

*You will not let her lack of faith in you hurt you anymore. You will not give her the power to affect how you feel about yourself. You will not question what you know to be true because of your mother's inability to acknowledge it.*

"I'll forward the details and we'll see you next weekend. And do remember to do something with your hair."

The line went dead and Sabrina shoved the phone into her purse.

*You will not cry in a hotel hallway because your mother is exactly the person she has always been. You will not cry over things you cannot control. You will not cry.*

No, she wouldn't cry. But she also wasn't sure she could sit in an auditorium and pretend she wasn't barely holding it together, that her mother's casual dismissal—of the heartache she'd endured over the last few years, of her desires, of her integrity—hadn't left her raw, like the stinging pain of an old wound reopened. And if she did somehow manage to pull it together long enough to sit through the keynote, to take halfhearted notes she'd struggle to decode later, she knew all it would take is one look from Sebastian for her to crumble.

Crying wouldn't help.

But tequila might.

She'd worn a pencil skirt.

How was Baz supposed to focus on partnership opportunities with tour bus companies when Sabrina was wearing a fucking pencil skirt?

Despite his best efforts to avoid Sabrina, he kept running into her. And each time he passed her in the crowded hallway or narrowly avoided joining the same break-out session that she'd chosen, his frustration increased.

Frustration that she was here at all, that she was headed back to Aster Bay when this was all over, that she existed on the same plane of existence as him.

Frustration that in the years since they'd last seen each other, she'd somehow gone from being a cute kid barely old enough to drink to being this knockout of a woman in red lipstick and flirty little dresses and goddamn pencil skirts.

But most of all, frustration at himself for even noticing the lipstick and the skirts, for wanting to wrap his fist in that cascade of auburn hair and tug until she gasped, for wanting anything to do with her at all.

Baz had spent the decade since his failed attempt at marriage making sure he would never be in a vulnerable position with a woman again. Sure, he flirted and he fucked but he didn't *feel* anything.

It wasn't fair that Sabrina could make his blood hum with just a bat of her eyelashes and a flash of toned calf muscle—and he couldn't even begin to think about the strange sensations she'd inspired when she gripped his hand and slept on his shoulder on the plane the day before, the strange mix of calm and protectiveness that had rapidly usurped his usual state of annoyance. What the fuck was he supposed to do with that?

When the audience around him burst into applause, he realized he had hardly heard a word of the keynote—he'd been too busy hating himself for wondering what Sabrina Page wore under her skirt. There was no way he could go back to their shared hotel room and risk being cooped up with her in that confined space for hours on end. It had been hard enough to sleep on the couch for the last two nights, to slip in and out of the room without having to converse with her, to force himself to fall asleep in a room that smelled like her. He wasn't sure he could do it for another night.

Which only left two options: he could get absolutely shit faced and pass out for the rest of the night, or he could find a willing woman who was interested in helping him work out some of this…whatever this was. Either way, the initial destination was the same.

He heard Sabrina before he saw her.

Hardly two steps into the hotel bar and Sabrina's laugh slammed into his chest like a battering ram. He scanned the room, skipping over the table of women wearing tiaras adorned with penises surrounding a very drunk looking bride-to-be, until his eyes landed on Sabrina. She sat at the polished mahogany bar, one black patent leather pump dangling from her toes and her conference materials in a stack forgotten at her feet by her open purse. She smiled at the bartender when he slid a fresh margarita in front of her, the expression not quite meeting her eyes despite the flirtatious way she ran her finger over the bartender's hand.

Baz stalked across the room before he even registered that he was moving. As he drew closer, Sabrina stiffened where she sat, her shoulders straightening and her head swiveling, as though she could sense him approaching. Their eyes locked and her mouth fell open in a surprised little 'o' before stretching into a wide smile, white teeth flashing against red lips.

"Sebastian!" She threw her arms out to the side, wobbling on her stool. Then, to the bartender, "This is Sebastian. He hates me."

"Jesus Christ," Baz grumbled as he slid onto the stool beside her, nudging her purse further under the lip of the bar and out of sight of any would-be thieves. "I don't hate you."

Sabrina took a long sip of her drink, popping off the rim of the glass with a smacking of her lips. "Yes, you do. You hate me."

"I don't hate you," he repeated, louder this time.

Her eyes sparkled. "Oh, that's right. What was it you said?" She drew her brows down and scrunched up her lips in an adorable pout before lowering her voice in a ridiculous impression of him. "I don't feel anything for you at all."

"That's not what I sound like."

"Mmhmm. Yup. Yuppers. It definitely is." She drew her finger through the salt on the rim of her glass and popped the fingertip into her mouth, sucking it clean.

Baz closed his eyes against the sight, willing the filthy, inappropriate thoughts flooding his brain to leave him the fuck alone. "You're drunk."

"I am?" She gasped in mock surprise and pressed her hand to her chest.

*Don't look at her chest.*

He ground his back teeth together.

She poked him in the arm, her whole body swaying with the movement. "Have a drink with me."

"No."

"You're no fun. But my friend here—" She pointed at the bartender. "He's fun. What was your name? Billy? Willy?"

The bartender chuckled and held out a hand to Baz. "Philip. What can I get you?"

"Mr. Grumpy Pants isn't drinking." She batted the bartender's hand away before Baz could shake it. "Told you he hates me."

Baz scraped his hand over his face and fought for patience. The last thing he wanted to do was have a drink with Sabrina but he couldn't very well leave her like this. Aunt Lucy and the Granny Squad would string him up by his balls if anything happened to her while they were away.

"Scotch, neat. And keep 'em coming."

Sabrina leveled the bartender with a serious look. "He's

got catching up to do." She drained the last of her margarita and slid the empty glass across the bar towards the bartender. "Keep 'em coming for me too."

"How many have you had?" Baz asked her as Philip rimmed a fresh glass with salt.

Sabrina shrugged and plucked a pretzel stick from the bowl on the table. "More than one, less than five." She shot him a mischievous grin as she slipped the pretzel between her lips, sucking on the end of it like it was a lollipop.

Baz forced his eyes away from her to accept his drink from the bartender. "Do you usually get drunk in the middle of the afternoon?"

"Pssh, it's practically dinner time, which means it's practically nighttime."

"You're chugging tequila like a college freshman on spring break." He slid her glass away from her.

"You don't know what I was like as a college freshman," she scoffed. "You didn't meet me until I was a *senior*, Grumpy Pants McGee." He arched an eyebrow at her and she waved her hand in the general direction of his lower half. "Those are grumpy pants."

"They're regular pants."

"Nope. They are the grumpiest pants that ever grumped." She sighed heavily, the force of it pushing out her lower lip into a pout that would have been adorable on someone he didn't thoroughly despise. "You used to be *fun*. Remember fun? Like when we used to dance to Wham! in the back room of the food pantry?"

He fought back a smile at the memory. "I didn't dance."

"You did. You absolutely did. Moved your hips and everything." She'd pulled her drink back towards herself and took another sip. "Remember that time you tried to dip the mop and you knocked over the bucket?" She snorted with laughter.

"At least I didn't knock over a whole shelf of pasta."

She gasped. "Because there was a spider!"

"I remember."

He scraped his hand over his jaw, tamping down the urge to laugh with her. He had no interest in taking a walk down memory lane. "What are you even doing here?"

"Same thing as you, Mr. Grumpasaurus Rex." She threw her arms out to indicate their surroundings, wobbling precariously again. He gripped the bottom of the stool to steady her.

"Not *here*. In Aster Bay. Why the hell did you come back?"

She bit off the end of the pretzel and chewed it thoughtfully, the corners of her lips turning down as her eyes grew misty.

"Sabrina."

She waved him away with what was left of the pretzel. "It's fine. I'm fine." She took an overlarge sip of her margarita.

"Did something happen?"

She got a far off look in her eye and, for a moment, he thought she wasn't going to answer him. He sipped his Scotch and waited.

Finally, she turned back to him. "My parents never wanted a second daughter. Did I ever tell you that? Probably not. Even when we were friends, we weren't *those kind* of friends." He arched an eyebrow in question. "You know, the tell-each-other-about-our-childhood-trauma kind of friends. That wasn't us. Anyway. My mom was convinced I was going to be a boy, but really, I think she just wanted me to be. Gregory. That's what they were going to name me. What did she need another girl for? She already had Holly." She blinked, looking away from him and taking another sip of her margarita.

Something tightened in his chest at the sadness in her face and he found himself throwing back the rest of his Scotch to keep himself from trying to comfort her. Baz didn't comfort women in bars—that was more of Gavin's domain. And she still hadn't answered his initial question.

"Holly was right, you know," Sabrina said with a sad kind of half smile. "The day you were supposed to marry her, she said I was jealous. I was. I was so jealous. But that's not why I asked her not to marry you."

He clenched his jaw, his shoulders stiffening. "Sabrina, stop."

"I didn't want to be your sister-in-law, but I would have been. No one believes me. Everyone still thinks I ruined your wedding to be spiteful. Even you think that. How could you think that, Sebastian? We might not have been trauma-sharing friends, but we *were* friends."

Baz accepted a new Scotch from the bartender as guilt twisted in his stomach. They had been friends and she'd betrayed him—at least, that's what he thought had happened, what Holly led him to believe had happened. But here, now, Sabrina seemed so sad, like he'd been the one to betray her.

"I wouldn't have believed me either," she said with a sigh. "Sometimes, when Holly tells it her way, I wonder if I made it all up. She's very convincing. That's why she's the lawyer and I'm the fuck up."

"You're not a fuck up."

"I am. Everyone thinks it. My mom and Holly and you—"

"I do not think you're a fuck up," he growled. He turned on his stool to face her more completely, his knees brushing against hers.

"But you still hate me."

"I don't—"

She closed her eyes. "Don't say you don't feel anything. That's so much worse."

He sipped his Scotch, the pain in her voice rendering him temporarily speechless.

"I wanted to tell you the truth," she continued, oblivious to the guilt gnawing at his bones. "But you didn't want to hear it. Not from me. No one wanted to hear it from me."

"Tell me now." Her eyes flew open, meeting his with a confused wrinkle of her brow. "I want to hear it now."

She opened and closed her mouth as though she didn't know how to begin, then blinked and turned back to the bar, downing her margarita.

"That morning, I went to Holly's hotel suite early. I wanted to surprise her with a wedding day mimosa, just us two, before everyone else got there." She glanced at him, as if to confirm that he was listening. He inclined his head in encouragement, and she wet her lips before continuing. "I had a key. Took it the night before because I wanted to surprise her. She didn't answer when I knocked so I let myself in. Mimosas in bed to start her wedding day." Sabrina's face fell, lost in her memory. "She was with another man."

All the air rushed from Baz's lungs like he'd been punched in the gut.

She glanced at him, barely seeing him, and he drained the rest of his Scotch, setting it down on the bar and tapping next to the empty glass to get the bartender's attention. They both watched as the amber liquid rushed into the glass, waiting until the bartender had moved along again before Baz chanced a glance at her.

"Who was he?"

"Harry something-or-other. He was a partner in her law firm."

Baz had expected the name to set off a storm inside his chest, to reignite the smoldering remains of his hatred for his ex-fiancée, but instead of a glowing ball of anger burning through his skin, he felt empty.

"He was married to his first wife back then. I don't remember her name," Sabrina continued. "I waited in the hallway outside her room until he left. He still had her lipstick…" She trailed her fingers over the column of her throat. "She denied it. But I know what I saw. What I heard. I told her if she didn't tell you the truth, I would."

"And instead she left."

"I didn't know she was going to do that. I didn't think she'd… I didn't think."

Baz closed his eyes, remembering the vehemence with which Sabrina had vowed she wouldn't let her sister marry him, the immediate hurt that had flooded through him that someone he had considered his friend would want to snatch his happiness from him. He'd been blinded by the vision in his head of the white picket fence and two-point-five kids with Holly's smile and his eyes. By his desperation to believe that she had loved him, that he could marry the perfect girl from the perfect family and somehow that would make his life perfect.

"I'm so sorry," Sabrina said, her voice tight.

He threw back the rest of his Scotch. Whether his head spun from the alcohol or from the realization that everything he thought he knew about what happened that day was wrong, he wasn't sure. Not that it really mattered.

"Don't be. You saved me from an expensive divorce."

"I should have found you. After. Made sure you were alright. You were my friend and I—"

"I wouldn't have listened," he said. "I wanted to believe it was your fault."

"Why?" That single syllable tugged at his heart.

"Because it was easier that way."

She deflated in front him as the full force of his words settled over her. He'd been ready to believe the worst of her because doing so meant he didn't have to acknowledge his own disastrous choices. If Sabrina was the reason his wedding fell apart, then he didn't have to face the fact that he shouldn't have been getting married in the first place. He'd thought he was in love, but he hadn't known Holly at all.

"I'm sorry, wildflower," he said, the old nickname falling from his lips too easily.

Her eyes softened, her red-stained lips pressing together to hide the way they quivered. "I forgive you."

"You shouldn't."

"But I do. Friends?" she asked, holding out a hand to him.

He huffed out a breath, something loosening inside his chest. "Friends."

He squeezed her hand lightly, the feel of her skin on his remaining even after he'd released her. She stared at the hand he'd been holding, flexing it as though she felt it too.

"Thank you for believing me," she said softly. "If anyone was going to, I'm glad it was you."

"How is it possible that your parents don't know the truth?"

She sighed. "Maybe they also thought it was easier to believe it was my fault. You know, when I started volunteering at the food pantry that summer, my mom tried to convince me it was a waste of time. She thought I was doing it to avoid finishing my grad school applications."

"Which you kind of were."

"But as soon as I introduced you to Holly, suddenly Mom was happy I'd been working there. At least until the wedding. Then she was right back to accusing me of embarrassing the family."

"Holly never told them what happened?"

Sabrina sputtered an incredulous laugh. "Holly have an uncomfortable conversation? Holly admit she messed up? You should know better than anyone that my sister doesn't do either of those things."

The memory of receiving that text message on his wedding day washed over him, shame and anger sinking in his stomach. It was bad enough to be left at the altar, but to have your wedding called off over text message? It was unforgiveable.

Beside him, Sabrina had begun spinning her margarita glass again, leaving patterns of condensation on the bar top, her lips turned down and brow furrowed. He gripped her knee and turned her towards him, using his own leg to stop her momentum when she was positioned between his thighs. "What happened today?"

"Nothing out of the ordinary. Mom wanted to remind me how successful and *appropriate* my sister is. Not like me. I'm the family fuck up."

A low noise rumbled in Baz's chest. "Will you stop saying that?"

"Just once I wish Holly felt like the fuck up, ya know? Just once I wish she was jealous of me."

Baz studied her eyes, a deep green that reminded him of a forest, of getting lost in the twists and turns of trees and overgrowth, of inhaling the sweet summer scent of moss and damp earth, of wildflowers. How did she always smell like wildflowers?

Her eyes dropped to his mouth, and he felt the ghost of her gaze as it traced his lips. At the back of his mind, an idea pushed through the cloud of alcohol, the twining branches of guilt and anger and a strange sort of relief.

Without taking his eyes from her, he lifted a hand to hail the bartender. "Another round." She raised her eyes to his and he lowered his voice, for only her to hear. "Then let's make her jealous."

# Chapter Six

"That's definitely the one." Sabrina stabbed her finger at the photo on Sebastian's phone.

It had taken several tries before they had managed to snap the selfie of the two of them without his thumb in the frame, or one of them making a weird face. But the final image, of Sabrina sitting on his lap at the bar, his hand curled around her waist and tugging her back against his chest, was perfect. Holly was going to lose her mind.

Sabrina wiggled happily in his lap. Beneath her, Sebastian's cock stirred, and a strange new giddiness bubbled up behind Sabrina's lips.

"Send it to me and I'll post it," she said.

"You're sure she'll see it?" He handed her his phone to type in her number and send off the image.

"Oh yeah." She pulled her own phone out, her fingers flying over the screen. "Holly is an Instagram addict. There." She turned the phone to show him her handiwork. Above a photo of a hunk of clay on a pottery wheel, their selfie was posted with the caption "Second time's a charm #Reunited."

"Now what?" he asked.

"Now we wait."

She slid off his lap and moved back to her own bar stool.

Instantly she missed the pressure of his hand on her waist, the impressive bulge in his pants growing larger beneath her.

Heat crawled up her neck as she looked away. "I hate waiting."

He barked out a laugh that surprised them both, her mouth quirking up into a delighted grin.

"What if we take one more? Just to be sure she'll see it?" she asked.

Before he could respond, she was back in his lap, her ass pressed against his groin as she leaned back into his chest. He banded his arm around her waist, holding her against him as he thickened beneath her. She wiggled her hips experimentally and his hand tightened on her waist.

"Hold still," he grunted.

She turned to see him better, her head resting on his shoulder. A deep crevice had formed between his brows, his pupils blown large until they were ringed by the thinnest band of blue.

"I have an idea," she said.

He raised his phone, camera at the ready, the shutter snapping as she pressed her lips to the place where his pulse thrummed against his throat. He sucked in a sharp breath as her mouth brushed his skin and something deep and hungry thrilled within her.

Sebastian had always been handsome—actually, handsome was too mundane of a word. He was beautiful. Ice blue eyes and sharp cheekbones, all angles and muscle, a predatory grace to his movements despite his grunts and silence. And just then, with her face tucked against his throat and the scent of him surrounding her—something spicy and luxurious, like cardamom and old books—he had never been more beautiful.

"Did you get it?" she asked, her lips still grazing his throat.

"One more. To be sure," he rumbled.

She smiled and kissed him again, this time closer to his Adam's apple, tilting her face up towards the sharp line of his jaw, and listened for the click of the camera. When she pulled away, his eyes were closed, that crevice between his brows even more pronounced. She ran her thumb over it, smoothing out the skin.

He opened his eyes slowly, as though waking from a dream, and studied her for a moment before he cleared his throat, moving her off his lap and quickly sending her the photo. "I think I got it."

She squirmed in her seat, squeezing her thighs together, and opened the photo. She was wrong. Sebastian wasn't just beautiful. He was stunning. And they looked good together, him in his suit and her in her silk blouse and pencil skirt. Better than good. They looked like they belonged together.

With a few swipes, the photo was posted, this time with the caption, "Missed you #StartingOver."

"I really did miss you, ya know," she said, showing him the post.

"Yeah?"

"Yeah. Do you remember that time we were waiting for Longfield Farm to make the produce delivery and we found that old Clue game in the break room?"

Sebastian's lip twitched. "It was missing all the weapon pieces."

Sabrina lowered her voice in a poor approximation of his. "It was Colonel Mustard in the billiard's room with the paperclip!" He laughed and her gaze caught on the way his Adam's apple bobbed in his throat.

As his laughter died away, their eyes met. He swallowed, his lips and throat doing all kinds of interesting things. "Yeah, wildflower. I remember."

Something settled inside her at the sound of the nickname he'd given her so long ago. She'd never thought she'd hear it again, yet here they were...

For a moment, it looked like he had something else to say, but then he took another sip of his drink instead—she'd lost count of how many they'd had at that point—as her phone buzzed in her hand.

"Ha! I knew it!" she crowed, swiping open the message from her sister.

"What does it say?"

She grinned as she read the message aloud. "*What the actual fuck?*" She glanced at Sebastian and they both burst out laughing until she was nearly doubled over the bar, his arm appearing across her back, fingers digging into her hip to hold her up.

"Mission accomplished?" he asked.

She lifted her glass, clinking it against his. "I'll drink to that."

Their laughter died as they returned to their drinks, his hold on her slowly loosening. When she thought he was about to pull away, he instead gripped the edge of her stool and spun her to face him.

"Want to really make her mad?"

"Vindictive Sebastian is fun," she giggled. "What did you have in mind."

He stared at her for a long moment, studying her eyes, and she started to wonder if he'd forgotten that it was his turn to speak. Or was it hers? She'd had more margaritas than she'd ever consumed in one sitting and it had to be long past dinner time by now. Maybe she was supposed to say something and she'd forgotten? She opened her mouth and he pressed a long, thick finger against her lips, his expression growing stern.

With his other hand Sebastian waved his phone towards the bartender. Phillip must have taken the phone because Sebastian's hand slid into her hair, pushing it behind her ear and trailing down the curve of her skull to grip the back of her neck. Her eyes darted between his, taking in the deep concentration there, the way his gaze flitted across her face, over the bridge of her nose, down the line of her jaw.

"Sebastian?"

"If you were really mine, I'd need your mouth on more than my neck," he said, the sound deep and low as it dragged across her skin, drawing her nearer. "I'd need to taste those pretty lips."

He pressed his lips to hers and her mind filled with static. The world tilted on its axis, and she reached up to grip his wrist, steadying herself with his solidness. He kissed with that same predatory grace she'd clocked earlier, slow and deep, like he was pulling her through water, drugging her with each movement of his mouth over hers. When his tongue slid against her own, a slow glide of velvet teasing her, she whimpered and leaned closer. The hand on her nape was firm, though, and he held her in place, kept her exactly where he wanted her as he obliterated her senses with his kiss.

She was drunk on him, on his scent and his touch and the expert movement of his mouth—or maybe that was the tequila talking. It didn't matter. She felt like she was floating, fizzy and bubbly and lighter than air, and at the same time she'd never felt more aware of her own body, of the tingling heat crawling up her spine and the deep, pleasant ache gathering between her legs.

When he pulled away, she leaned forward, chasing his lips. She would have fallen out of her seat if he hadn't still been holding her.

"Did you get it?" he asked, though he kept his eyes—and hands—on her.

"Oh, I got it alright," the bartender replied with a chuckle, setting Sebastian's phone down on the bar in front of them.

They stayed like that for what could have been seconds or hours—she didn't know. She'd lost all sense of time, of what was up and what was down. Finally, his lips pulled into a slow, sexy smirk, and she felt her mouth mimicking the movement.

She laughed, still holding his wrist, and delighted in the way his smile grew. She slid off her stool and stood between his thighs, watching in fascination as his eyes grew darker. "What next?"

# Chapter Seven

Baz's head felt like it was full of bees.

He'd only just woken up and already he wanted to go back to bed. Well, technically, he hadn't left bed yet, but that was beside the point. His dry mouth tasted like sweaty gym socks, his stomach lurched at the mere suggestion of sunlight coming through the opening in the curtains, and the left side of his body was unreasonably heavy.

*Wait.*

He opened one eye a sliver, barely enough for the sunlight to shoot spikes through his skull. His left side wasn't heavier than usual—it was serving as a body pillow for the tempting redhead in bed next to him. A very familiar tempting redhead wearing nothing more than a plush hotel bathrobe and last night's smudged makeup. At this angle, the generous curves of Sabrina's breasts threatened to spill out of her loosely tied robe. She sighed happily in her sleep and snuggled closer, the movement shifting the opening of her robe.

How had he ended up in bed with Sabrina Page?

He remembered finding her in the bar, the conversation, too many glasses of Scotch. The feel of her wiggling in his lap, her breath on his neck, the little sounds she'd made against his lips when he'd kissed her.

*Christ, I kissed her.*

He remembered wanting to kiss her again, wanting to do more than kiss her. At some point they'd left the bar. Flashes of holding her hand as they stumbled down the sidewalk, the bite of concrete beneath his hands when he'd pushed her up against a wall and kissed her again just to hear more of those goddamn noises.

But he didn't remember a thing after that.

How had they gone from the sidewalk to twined together in bed?

And what had happened to her clothes?

He was 96% sure he hadn't fucked her…or maybe 83% sure. Not that he hadn't wanted to. He remembered that hunger clear as day, the way he'd ached to touch her, to taste her everywhere, to feel her move beneath him…

And now he was hard. *Fucking hell.*

Warily, he lifted the sheet draped over his lower body, even though he was 75% certain they hadn't done anything more than kiss. His belt was gone, as was his shirt and suit jacket, but his pants had stayed on.

How much trouble could they have gotten into with his dress pants on, really?

He fought the urge to stroke her hip through the terrycloth of her robe, to bury his nose in her hair and shift her closer so she could feel his hard on through their clothing. They may have reconciled, but the fact remained that he had been engaged to her sister. It was one thing to kiss Sabrina in a drunken haze, but he was pretty sure there was a rule against sleeping with your almost-sister-in-law.

Across the room, his phone, still in his suit jacket pocket slung over the arm of the pull-out couch, chimed with a series a notifications. Cursing under his breath and swearing to all gods that had ever existed that he would gut whoever had the audacity to text him at—he glanced at the alarm clock and grimaced—seven o'clock in the morning, he dragged himself out from under Sabrina's koala grip.

Rubbing the sleep from his eyes, he shuffled across the room and dug his phone out of the pile of discarded clothing. Beneath his suit jacket, a bright red, lacy bra lay accusingly atop his crumpled button-down shirt. He glanced back at the sleeping woman.

He would have remembered if he'd seen her naked, right? There was no way he would have forgotten something like that.

Baz swallowed down the illogical urge to climb back into bed beside her, to curl himself around her and hold her a few minutes longer. His phone chimed again as he finally opened up the group text with his friends.

**Jamie:** What did you do?

**Gavin:** Me?

**Jamie:** Not you. Baz.
**Jamie:** Are these pictures real?

**Ethan:** What pictures?

**Gavin:** There are pictures?

**Jamie:** At least a dozen of them.

**Gavin:** Pictures of what?

**Ethan:** Where are you seeing pictures?

**Jamie:** Tessa found them on Sabrina's Instagram page.

**Ethan:** How does Tessa know Sabrina?

**Jamie:** They met at St. Anthony's Bazaar.
**Jamie:** That's not the important part. The important part is the pictures.

**Gavin:** Oh, shit. There are pictures alright.

**Ethan:** What pictures? I don't have Instagram.

**Jamie:** [link to Sabrina's Instagram page]

**Ethan:** Holy shit.

**Jamie:** That's what I'm saying!

**Gavin:** Baz!
**Gavin:** Wait, is this a good thing, or a bad thing? Are we supposed to be excited or worried?

Scowling at his phone, he clicked the link to Sabrina's Instagram page and was immediately hit with a wall of photographs of the two of them from the night before. It started with an innocent-enough photo of her perched on his lap, #Reunited. The next one showed her kissing his neck, #StartingOver. In the next, they were kissing, his fingers twined in her hair and her hand wrapped around his wrist, #HeatingUp. Photo after photo of them, each one bringing back flashes of the night before, fuzzy and muted.

Their clasped hands, #BetterTogether.

A blurry selfie on the sidewalk outside the hotel, his arm looped around her neck and lips pressed to her temple, #CoupleGoals.

His hand on her thigh, right above her knee, his pinkie disappearing beneath the hem of her skirt, #Scandalous.

Then a series of photos that had obviously been taken by somebody else: Sabrina wrapped in his arms, her head thrown back in laughter and his hands low on her back, tugging her towards him, his eyes focused on her, #NewBeginnings.

Another one of them kissing, this time accompanied by a bundle of fake, faded flowers in Sabrina's hand, #Perfect.

It was the last photo that made him nearly drop his phone.

Sabrina's hand in his, his lips brushing her knuckles, and shiny gold bands on both of their left hands, #HusbandMaterial.

*What the fuck?*

He glanced down at his left hand. Why the fuck was he wearing a wedding ring?

He sank down onto the couch, digging his hand into his hair.

*Holy shit.*

He had married Sabrina.

**Baz:** Who else knows?

**Ethan:** That's the first thing you say to us? You got married without any of us there!

**Jamie:** Who else knows? Anyone with an Instagram account, that's who!

**Gavin:** I'm guessing that means we aren't supposed to be congratulating you.

**Jamie:** I thought you hated Sabrina.

**Gavin:** Doesn't look like he hates her anymore.

"Hey."

Baz slid his phone into his pocket and shot to his feet, his eyes locked on Sabrina as she stretched and turned her sleepy gaze on him.

"What time is it?" she asked.

He dug his hands into his pockets and glanced at the clock. "A little after seven."

She blinked away the last bits of sleep from her eyes and stifled a yawn behind her hand. She froze, her eyes going wide, and slowly pulled her hand away from her mouth, her gaze locked on the gold band around her finger.

"Sebastian? Why am I wearing a wedding ring?"

He held up his own left hand. "Probably the same reason I am."

She leapt out of bed and was at his side in a second, taking his hand in hers and holding it in front of her face. "Why are *you* wearing a wedding ring?"

He stared at her, at the sleep-rumpled cloud of auburn hair and the soft pillow lines along her cheek, the freckles over the bridge of her nose and across her clavicle, the creamy skin visible through the opening in her robe, daring him to look at her in a way he had no right to. Even if he had married her.

She met his gaze with a wide-eyed look. "We got *married*?"

He gave her a tight nod and tried to ignore the lick of hurt at her disbelief, but that incredulous look had released something wild in his chest. Some primal urge to show her how it would be if they were really married, to make her his in truth and not just in name.

"Holy shit. Did we…" She dropped his hand and pulled the robe around herself tighter, flitting her eyes back to the bed. "I mean…Did we?"

"Did we fuck?"

She winced at the harshness of his question. It was a good reminder for them both. One drunken mistake didn't change anything. She was still the youngest daughter of one of Boston's wealthiest families, and he was still the man who hadn't been good enough for her sister. A set of cheap gold bands couldn't change that.

Neither would touching her. But it didn't stop him from wanting to. Something about seeing that ring on her finger and knowing he put it there (even if he didn't remember doing it), something about the way her pupils dilated and her breathing grew shallow when he was near made him want to see how messy he could make her. He was no stranger to having beautiful women in his bed, but this feral feeling, this desire to mark her, to claim her, like the monster dragging the princess back to his lair, that was something new.

He liked it far too much. And judging from the heat in her eyes when she looked at him, she liked it too. Even if she shouldn't.

He stepped closer to her, crowding her, and a thrill shot through him when she didn't back away. Instead, she tilted her face up to him, holding his gaze with those deep green eyes.

"If we'd fucked, you'd remember," he said, his voice low and gravelly as he dragged his gaze over her face, down the curve of her neck, to the shadow of her breasts and back again. "If we'd fucked, you'd still be able to feel me."

She sucked in a breath, the sudden inhale pressing her terrycloth-covered chest against his. His hands fisted at his side, keeping himself from pulling her against him, to make sure she knew exactly how much of him there was to feel. She swayed closer, lips parted. It would be so easy to kiss her, to give her what they both wanted...

Except she didn't want him. Not really. What was it she had said at the bar? Something about making her sister jealous? This was all a game to her, one he couldn't win.

*Then it's time to stop playing.*

He stepped away, turning his back on her before he could give in to the fantasy of it. He might want to kiss her, to fuck her until neither one of them could remember their names, but at some point, she'd call an end to this charade.

He'd just have to end it first.

He would not be rejected by another Page woman.

"Get dressed." He didn't look at her as he gathered his shirt and suit jacket and stormed off to the bathroom to change. "I don't want to miss our flight."

# Chapter Eight

Sebastian hardly spoke to Sabrina in the hours after they left the hotel, sitting next to her in the airport terminal in stony silence. Sure, he'd grunted in the affirmative when she asked if he wanted a coffee and managed to grate out a word of thanks when she'd handed him his Starbucks, but that was the extent of it. His gaze hardly lifted from his phone screen.

Meanwhile, Sabrina couldn't bring herself to look at her phone at all. When the buzzing and pinging of the incessant notifications and missed calls reached a fever pitch, she'd simply turned it off. Which meant she couldn't play any of her favorite match-three games during their interminable wait for their flight home, but it also meant she didn't have to see her mother's name flashing across the screen every three minutes or the nonstop string of text messages from Holly, each one more incensed than the last. If she'd thought her family had been disappointed in her when she'd filed for divorce, she could only imagine what they must think of her after a quickie Vegas wedding to her sister's ex-fiancé.

But who had time to deal with her family's total meltdown over her Vegas misadventures when there was a whole flight, complete with possible impending death, to obsess over?

When at last it was time to board, Sebastian grabbed her

bag without a word, hauling it down the jetway along with his own and hoisting it easily into the overhead bin. Sabrina didn't know what to do with this grumpy chivalry. Now that she knew how he kissed, the way he tugged on her hair as he positioned her exactly where he wanted her, now that she knew how it felt to sleep in his arms, she found herself reading into every word, every gesture.

And when the plane jolted as it began taxiing down the runway and her hands gripped the armrests for dear life, she didn't know how to feel about the fact that Sebastian pulled her hand into his own, twining their fingers together. He didn't say a word, didn't even look at her, but the reassuring strength of his grasp combined with the almost absent-minded way his thumb skated over the wedding band on her finger twisted her up inside more than any cross-country flight ever could.

They sat that way for hours, her hand in his, until she could no longer take the silence.

"Sebastian?"

"Hmm?"

"We're married," she whispered.

Strange how that word set off an avalanche in her brain, burying her beneath all the promises she'd made to herself when she filed for divorce from Jordan, all the things she swore she'd never do again.

"Oh, God, what were we thinking?"

He glanced at her, his eyes scanning her face for…she didn't know what. "I'll take care of it," he said, looking away.

"What does that mean? Take care of it?"

"I'll call my lawyer when we get back to Aster Bay. With any luck, it'll be annulled by the end of the week."

She blinked helplessly as his words settled between them, her stomach lurching. He was going to walk away, just like that.

*What did you expect? This was some stupid ploy to piss off Holly that got out of hand. You were never supposed to end up married to the guy.*

She knew it wasn't a *real* marriage, not like the one he had wanted with her sister, not like the one she'd thought she had with Jordan. Her breath caught, lungs burning as she willed herself not to cry at the sudden realization that he may have married her, but he never wanted her. It was all a mistake, a stupid, drunken mistake and, despite his confusing as hell chivalry, none of it was real. Not the kissing or the moments when he'd looked at her like…well, it didn't matter what she'd thought she saw in those looks. It wasn't real, and in only a few days it would be like none of it had even happened.

Why did that thought hurt so much? It's not like she had planned on marrying him. It's not like they were in love. They didn't even know each other anymore.

*Oh, God, I'm going to be twice divorced before I hit thirty-five.*

Could she even survive another divorce? The last one had left her barely scraping by, a hollowed-out shell of her former self, without a husband, without a home, without the studio she'd worked tirelessly to build. What would she lose this time? Did she even have anything left to lose?

"Breathe, Sabrina." His voice was soft, like the whisper of distant thunder. Her eyes went to his, darting between them as she felt the edges of her panic beginning to close in again, and this time it had nothing to do with the airplane. "Breathe," he commanded.

She drew in a breath, her ribcage aching, as though more than her pride was bruised, as if her skin would turn purple and green in the days to come, painting her with the proof of a pain she couldn't explain. His hand tightened in hers, his icy blue eyes holding her rapt.

"I promise, it'll be like it never happened." His thumb drew circles on her palm between their clasped hands.

A startled burst of laughter pushed through her lips. He thought she was worried they *wouldn't* get an annulment? That the idea of staying married to him had made her forget how to breathe, when all she could think about was how little she had left, how much harder it was going to be to lose him a second time around.

*He was never yours to begin with, idiot. Not then and not now.*

It's not that she wanted to stay married—signing away half her life to another person wasn't something she'd ever intended to do a second time. Of course, they would get an annulment or a divorce or whatever else people did in these situations. It's not like he was actually her husband.

She wasn't sure which hurt more: the fact she'd been reckless enough to get married again, despite all her promises to herself to stay single, or the idea of no longer being Sebastian Graham's wife. Either way she was screwed. If they stayed married, she'd always wonder when it would fall apart, when the rug would be pulled out from under her and she'd lose everything all over again. And if they didn't...

She tugged her hand out his grasp, folding her hands together in her lap and leaning against the wall of the plane to put a few inches of distance between them. Something flashed in his eyes that she couldn't read, and he clenched his jaw as he pulled his own hand back, adjusting his suit jacket. The wedding ring felt heavy on her finger as the matching band of gold on Baz's left hand glinted in the sunlight streaming through the plane window.

"You're still wearing your ring." A pathetic flutter of hope gasped for air in her chest.

He glanced at his hand as though it were a surprise, his lips pressing together in a tight line. He clenched his fist and turned that cold stare her way. "So are you."

"Where did we get wedding rings?"

He looked at her as though she were stupid. "Typically, when you marry someone—"

"No, I know that. But I mean, people usually buy the rings

before the ceremony, like at a jeweler's or something. Where did these rings come from?"

He looked at the ring on his own hand again before glancing at hers, huffing out a laugh. "Fuck if I know." A hint of amusement tugged at the corner of his mouth, tipping up his lips into an unfairly disarming smirk.

She laughed, an uncontrollable wave of mirth that wrapped around her as the absurdity of the situation finally registered. He chuckled, as though her laughter was contagious, and relaxed back against his seat.

"The fuck were we thinking?" he asked with a barely concealed grin.

"I'm pretty sure we *weren't* thinking." She rolled her head to the side to get a better look at him, the humor slipping away. He really was the most beautiful man she'd ever known. "If I was going to wake up married to anyone, though, I'm glad it was you."

He met her gaze, his eyes holding hers. What she wouldn't give to be able to read the look in his eyes.

"Sebastian, last night, when you kissed me..." His eyes dipped to her lips as if he was considering kissing her again. "I'm really glad you did." He arched an eyebrow at her and waited for her to continue. "All those nights at the food pantry, when we'd stay late to finish stocking for the next day, I wondered what kissing you would be like."

"You did?"

Had his voice gotten deeper?

"Mmhmm. But then you met Holly..." She shut her eyes, forced herself to take a breath.

*Why did you bring up your sister?*

"I didn't know."

"I know. You were always nice to me, but you didn't look at me the way you looked at other women."

"How did I look at you?"

"Like I was an amusing kid."

She swallowed, wet her lips with her tongue, watched him tracking the movement of her mouth. He really did have the prettiest eyes.

"And how do I look at you now?" he asked, pitching his voice low.

"Like maybe you're glad about the kiss too."

He took a slow breath, his eyes focusing on her hand, on the ring there, as he gathered his thoughts. Maybe she'd gone too far. Maybe she'd been misreading all the little touches and glances.

"You are a beautiful woman," he said slowly. "And I am very attracted to you."

Hope fluttered to life in her chest—wild, reckless hope—

"And that makes this more complicated." Her heart sank. "The sooner we can get that annulment sorted out, the less confusing this will be. For everyone."

A staticky voice came over the speakers announcing their final descent to Providence, the crackling words saving Sabrina from having to agree with Sebastian. For a moment there it had almost felt like they were friends again, like they could maybe even be more than friends.

But that was a dangerous line of thinking. The last person Sabrina needed to develop feelings for was her husband.

Sabrina only took a few steps off the plane, dragging her bag behind her, before Baz pulled the strap from her grasp and slung it over his shoulder.

"I can get that," she protested as he strode down the jetway. "So can I."

She trotted after him, and he bit the inside of his cheeks to keep from smiling, though the warmth blooming in his chest was harder to ignore. He pressed the heel of his hand to his sternum under the guise of adjusting the strap of her bag, half convinced that he'd feel that warmth through his shirt.

"How are you getting back to Aster Bay? Do you want to split a cab?" she asked.

"Ethan's picking me up. We can drive you back to your aunt's."

They stepped onto the escalator that descended to the ground level where Ethan would be waiting. As his friend came into view, Baz got his first glimpse of the piece of cardboard Ethan held above his head, letters scrawled in black marker reading "Mr. and Mrs. Graham." Sabrina gasped, her hand flying to her mouth, where her eyes landed on her wedding ring and she let out a little squeak before shoving her hand into the pocket of her gray trousers. Baz was going to murder Ethan.

"Welcome home," Ethan said with a grin.

"Get rid of that thing," Baz barked.

Sabrina stumbled as she stepped off the escalator, and Baz's hand shot out to steady her. Ethan eyed the movement, his smirk growing wider.

"Shut up," Baz said. "We're giving her a ride home."

Ethan held out a hand to take Sabrina's bag from Baz, but Baz batted it away and strode past him towards the exit, Ethan's laughter following behind him.

"Where to?" Ethan asked once they were all settled in his truck.

"Mrs. Page's," Baz replied.

"Have you spoken to your aunt today, Sabrina?" Ethan asked.

"No," she said, shooting a wary glance Baz's way before asking Ethan, "Is she alright?"

"I'm sure she's fine, but I got a call from Gavin who got a call from Mrs. White who'd heard from Mrs. Greene that your aunt was looking for a way to move your things into Baz's condo before you arrived, as a sort of welcome home surprise," Ethan said as he steered the truck out of the airport parking lot and onto the highway.

"What?" Sabrina squeaked. "Why would she do that?"

Ethan glanced at Baz in the rear-view mirror. "I assume because newlyweds typically want to live together, and not with their elderly aunts."

"I'll kill him," Baz said, already firing off an incredulous text to Gavin.

"What was Gav supposed to do? Say no to Mrs. White?" Ethan scoffed. "Besides, you two *are* newlyweds, right?"

"That's no one's business but ours," Baz grated out.

Ethan laughed. "Hate to break it to you, man, but when you put shit like that on the internet, it's everyone's business. Especially in Aster Bay. You should know that."

The hell of it was, Baz *did* know. He knew better than anyone that keeping secrets in Aster Bay was futile. When he was seventeen, he'd skipped a shift washing dishes at the diner to take Cindy Parker on a date. Before he'd even gotten the chance to put his arm around her in the movie theater, half the town knew where he was. By morning he didn't have a job at the diner anymore. And Cindy hadn't posted a blow by blow of their evening online like Sabrina had.

Ethan caught Baz's eye again in the mirror, the laughter fading away. "You should call your mom."

*Fuck.* He hadn't even thought about that conversation yet.

Baz nodded. "Let's stop there first."

# Chapter Nine

Charlotte Graham lived in the same two-bedroom Cape a block away from the industrial park that she'd lived in all of Baz's life. Despite Baz's repeated offer to buy her something nicer, something bigger, something in a better part of town, his mother adamantly refused. "This house is my home," she'd say. "I don't need anything fancy."

What she never understood was that she might not have needed it, but *he* needed her to have it, to know he'd made her life better, that he'd provided the security and ease his father never did. But Charlotte Graham didn't care all that much for ease, as evidenced by the fact she continued to work as a hair stylist, completely ignoring Baz's repeated pleas to let him help her retire.

Ethan's truck pulled into the driveway along the side of Baz's mother's house and Baz made a mental note to send the landscaper by to trim the hedges. His mother might not have let him truly take care of her the way he wanted to, but she at least allowed him the small gesture of hiring a landscaper to look after the lawn and flower garden at the front of the house. She'd fought him at first, but all it took was one slip and fall on the icy front walk for her to relent and accept the help.

"Should I—I mean, do you want me to—I'd be happy to

come in and—" Sabrina stumbled through the words.

Baz shook his head sharply as he hopped out of the truck. "You go talk to your aunt."

She glanced uneasily at Ethan, before climbing out after Baz. She gripped his forearm so he couldn't walk away, lowering her voice to keep Ethan from hearing. "What are you going to tell your mom?"

"What do you want me to tell her?"

Her lips parted as though she would speak, but no sound came out. She blinked rapidly a few times, each flutter of her eyelashes winding some hidden coil in his chest, tighter and tighter with each moment she hesitated. "You should tell her the truth."

"What truth is that?" He stepped closer and dropped his voice low. "Should I tell her that I know the way you press against me when I kiss you, or how it feels to wake up with you in my arms?" He wasn't sure if the blush rising beneath the smattering of freckles across her cheekbones was a victory or another temptation. "Or that we got drunk in a bar in Vegas and lost our fucking minds? That this whole thing was a way to get back at your sister? Which truth are we telling today, Sabrina?"

He hated the flash of hurt in her eyes, but it was necessary. If he was going to survive this marriage—however brief it may be—he needed to remember that it was all a stupid mistake. Sabrina didn't want him, just like her sister hadn't wanted him. And the fact she made his dick hard didn't mean he wanted her either. Biology wasn't enough to build a marriage on.

He scraped his hand over his jaw. "I'll come get you when I'm done here and help you bring your things back to your aunt's."

He strode away from her, towards his mother's house. He didn't want to see any more of Sabrina's reactions. If she was upset that he was planning to send her home to her aunt, he didn't want to know. And, quite frankly, if she wasn't upset, he didn't want to know that either.

"Oh, good, you're home!"

They turned to see Sabrina's aunt and Baz's mother standing arm in arm on the front step.

Baz tilted his chin at Ethan, who waved his goodbye and got the hell out of dodge. *Lucky bastard.*

When Baz reached the front step, Sabrina right behind him, his mother pulled him down into a hug, hands pressed to his cheeks like she used to do when he was a boy. She practically bounced on the balls of her feet when she asked, "Did you just get back?"

*Fuck. She already knows.*

"You know?" he asked.

"Maybe, but tell us anyway."

Christ, her smile was wide enough to look like it must hurt.

He scrubbed his hand over his face, but barely got past his eyes before his mother gasped, taking hold of his hand and pulling it towards her to get a better look. "Jesus, Mary, and Joseph, it's true! You got married!"

"Mom, it's not—"

She squealed and threw her arms around him, jumping up and down while he stood frozen to the spot. "I can't believe it! Helen White said you'd done it, but I didn't believe it. Oh, honey, I'm so damn happy for you. And with Sabrina! Who would have thought?" she laughed. She released him and jogged down the front step, pulling Sabrina into a hug, swaying with her in her arms in the middle of the driveway.

Sabrina's aunt held out her arms to him and, despite his better judgment, he let her fold him into a hug of her own.

"Hi, Mrs. Page."

"Knock that off. It's Aunt Lucy." She squeezed him tighter. "Shouldn't you two be on your honeymoon?"

Then the two women switched and he was back in his mother's embrace as Aunt Lucy gripped Sabrina's arms, her eyes welling with tears. "You got *married*! Oh, dear heart, I couldn't believe it when your mother called!"

"Mom knows?" Sabrina's voice wobbled and she looked like she was ready to faint but her aunt didn't seem to notice.

"Of course, she does. She's none too happy she found out about it from your sister, but she'll come around." Her aunt pulled back, holding Sabrina by the arms. "Let me get a look at you, all grown up and married to such a handsome young man," she said, shooting a grin at Sebastian.

"It's complicated." Baz stuffed his hands in his pockets to keep himself from reaching for Sabrina.

"Well, of course, it's *complicated*," his mother laughed. "You almost married her sister! I imagine it's plenty complicated, but that doesn't make it any less wonderful." She squeezed his arm before pulling away from him and holding open the front door, urging everyone inside. "I've got a bottle of champagne somewhere, I'm sure of it, just waiting for a special occasion."

"Don't open the champagne, Mom," he groaned as they all filed into the kitchen.

"It's not every day my only child gets married! If I want to open the champagne, I'm going to open the damn champagne." Her top half disappeared inside the fridge for a moment, before she reappeared, bottle of champagne in hand and a triumphant grin on her face.

Baz sighed and took a seat at the kitchen table beside Sabrina as his mother twisted the cap off the cheap champagne and poured them each a glass.

"Helen White and I arranged for your things to be moved into your husband's condo. Now you two can get right into the business of married life, no need to delay for silly details," Aunt Lucy said as she handed Sabrina a glass of champagne.

"You really shouldn't have done that, Auntie." Sabrina leaned back in her chair, massaging a spot low on her stomach with the heel of her hand.

"It was no trouble at all. Gavin West—he's a professor over

at the university, and good friends with your young man here, you see—was happy to loan us his spare key. And Helen really can be quite convincing when she wants to be." Aunt Lucy laughed as she set a glass of champagne in front of Baz. "Thank heavens for us all she only uses her powers for good, isn't that right, Charlotte? We moved you all in but stopped short of putting your things away. I told Helen I didn't think Sebastian would appreciate us rummaging about in his drawers, even if it was for a good cause."

*Thank God for small miracles.*

"Oh! And I told Norm—he's the head of the Merchants' Association, you know—to leave your permits with me. I've got them right here." Aunt Lucy dug in her purse on the kitchen counter as she kept talking, Baz's mother looking at him and Sabrina with such affection he thought he might be sick. "Helen thought Sebastian might use a PO box for his mail and I didn't want them to get lost in some silly mix-up because I didn't know the right address. Speaking of which, I really must get your new address so I can update my book."

"Permits?" Sabrina asked, digging her hand harder into her abdomen.

"Are you alright?" he asked, his eye glued to the spot.

She gave him a tight nod, but he couldn't help the feeling that she was lying. Something was wrong—something other than their family members popping champagne to celebrate their drunken mistake.

"Your business permits. You see, once Ruthie Greene and I told Norm how you'd selflessly volunteered to go to the conference on the Association's behalf, he softened a bit towards your application. But then Helen told him that you and Sebastian had gotten married, so he had no doubt that you'd be staying in town long term." Aunt Lucy handed an envelope to Sabrina and took up a position leaning against the counter next to his mother. "And then Helen pointed out that we already have a lingerie shop and a boudoir photography studio in town—oh, and that adult store that I keep meaning to stop by—" Baz shuddered "—well, once she'd said all that, he could hardly deny your application simply because you teach people to make clay genitalia."

Baz's eyes snapped to the older woman. "Excuse me?"

"Auntie," Sabrina groaned.

"What? That's what they are, dear heart. A clay penis is still a penis."

Baz surveyed his mother, who didn't seem the least bit phased by this insane conversation.

"Oh, don't look so surprised, darling," his mother said, clucking her tongue. "There's no need to hide it from me. Lucy and I have been getting to know each other all morning waiting for you two to return. I know all about my daughter-in-law's business."

*More than I do, apparently.*

"I believe the only stipulation is that you don't display the penises in the store window," Aunt Lucy concluded.

Sabrina shifted in her seat, wincing as she did. *What the hell is going on?*

"I don't display the penises anywhere," she said through gritted teeth. "I smash them."

Aunt Lucy froze. "Well, that seems a bit harsh."

"Enough about the penises," Baz's mother said, taking up the seat on the other side of him and gripping his hand. "Tell me how this happened."

"Seems like a waste of a perfectly good penis," Aunt Lucy muttered to herself as she took another sip of her champagne.

"There's not much to tell," Baz hedged.

"Oh, don't be coy with me," his mother said with a knowing look. "You left here a few days ago a confirmed bachelor and now I have a daughter-in-law!"

What could he say? Sabrina liked margaritas and didn't get

along with her family. She wore skirts that drove him out of his damn mind and was afraid of flying. She still smelled like wildflowers and he couldn't stop thinking about the freckles on her clavicle and she'd only married him because they were both drunk off their asses and she wanted to get back at her sister.

Christ, what had he gotten himself into?

How could he look his mother in the eye and tell her that his marriage was a mistake, that it wasn't real?

"There's quite a bit of an age difference between you two, isn't there?" his mother prompted.

"Twelve years," Sabrina said with a slight grimace as he said, "She's not as young as Tessa or Kyla."

His mother laughed. "Well, no, I suppose she isn't. Gavin and Jamie did fall for lovely young women, though. I'm sure your wife will get along perfectly fine with them all."

*My wife.* His mouth went dry. He'd long ago given up on the idea of ever calling someone by that particular title, but hearing his mother say it, hearing her speculate about how well Sabrina would get along with his friends, he couldn't deny how much he liked it.

*You stupid asshole.*

"How'd it happen?" Aunt Lucy leaned forward eagerly. "Did you see each other on the plane and old feelings came rushing back? You know, I always thought you protested a bit too much when Holly said you had a crush on him. And now, all these years later, to think you two were the ones who were meant to be together all along!"

A puff of air left Sabrina's lips as she dug her hand into her side.

*Enough.* He didn't know what was wrong, but there was no denying *something* wasn't right, and if Sabrina wasn't going to tell him in front of the welcome wagon, then he would have to take her somewhere she would.

Baz got to his feet, sliding his arm around Sabrina's waist

and helping her to her feet. "We're tired from the flight. If you'll excuse us."

"Oh, yes, you poor things," his mother said, getting to her feet. "All that excitement and travel."

"You must be exhausted," Aunt Lucy said. "Let me drive you back to Sebastian's."

"We'll call a car," Baz said, leading Sabrina to the front door.

She'd gone pale, her eyes hazy. As he placed the order on the app on his phone, he wondered if he ought to call an ambulance instead.

"You good?" he asked, his lips against her ear so only she could hear.

"Fine." She gave him that tight nod again, but her jaw was clenched, hand clasped to her side. The appendix was on the lower right side, wasn't it? Or was he thinking of the gallbladder? Some expendable organ known to cause dramatic emergency room visits, surely.

"Now, I know, you'll want your privacy as you settle in as newlyweds. I promise, I won't stop by unannounced." His mother followed behind them as they made their way to the door. "I think you'll agree we don't need a repeat of that time I came home early the summer before you started college and found you and—"

"Mom, please." Having his mother walk in on him with his head between Cindy Parker's legs had been bad enough, he didn't need to relive the experience.

His mother laughed. "You get my point. But maybe you two could come up for air long enough to join me for dinner next weekend."

"Maybe," he hedged.

"I have to go to Brookline next weekend," Sabrina said, but he wasn't sure if she was serious or just trying to shake the invitation.

"Alright, I won't push."

On the front step, Aunt Lucy snagged Sabrina's hand, pulling her off to the side of the driveway for a hushed conversation. Baz's eyes stayed on her the entire time, scanning for signs of— he didn't know what he was looking for, but he knew something was wrong.

His mother came up beside him, sliding her arm around his waist and resting her head against his shoulder. "I'm so happy for you, Sebastian. You know, after everything that happened with Holly, I thought you'd given up on finding true love. And you seemed happy enough, but I'd be lying if I said I didn't want more for you."

He glanced at his mother before returning his attention to Sabrina. "What do you mean?"

"I wanted you to know the kind of love that changes you, the kind that lights a fire in your belly and keeps on burning, come hell or high water. To know what it's like to have someone look at you like maybe you're magic, and for you to feel the same about them. And now you have that."

His gut twisted, bile rising at the back of his throat as he swallowed down the truth and gave her a short nod. How could he tell her that he didn't have any of those things? All he had was a set of cheap wedding rings and the fuzzy memory of his wedding night to a woman whose family had already decided he wasn't good enough, a woman who he hadn't spoken to in ten years and who damn near had a panic attack at the mere idea of being his wife.

Across the driveway, Sabrina's eyes met his. Her face had gone gray, her brow crinkled as she winced again. He was across the pavement, pulling her into his side, before she could even lift her hand to press against her abdomen. She melted against him with a little exhale of relief that made him feel ten feet tall.

He pressed his lips to her forehead. "It's time to go."

"I guess at least they didn't also try to *unpack* my things." Sabrina nudged one of the boxes stacked neatly in the corner of Baz's living room. Her entire life crammed into a handful of boxes and old suitcases. If she hadn't finally gotten a reprieve from the period cramps from hell, she'd be inclined to feel sorry for herself, but as it was, all she wanted to do was figure out which box her aunt had packed her pads in before the cramps returned.

And Sebastian seemed to have calmed down now that she wasn't white as a sheet and two seconds away from cursing every female hormone in her body. But for a while there, as they'd driven home from his mother's house together in the back seat of some guy's Toyota Camry, he'd seemed rattled. Most people wouldn't have noticed the cracks in his stoic demeanor, but she'd clocked the way his eyes kept flitting to her, his lips pressed together into a flat line every time she shifted in her seat, the crease between his brows when she flinched as another cramp took hold.

Now, Sebastian stood in the middle of the living room, a good ten feet away from her, as though he were afraid of getting too close. A wild laugh bubbled up in Sabrina's chest and she clamped her lips shut to keep it contained. Her husband didn't want to get close to her—at least not when she wasn't on the brink of passing out from period pain. What the hell had her life even become?

He turned in a circle, hands on his hips, as though trying to decide what to do next, before letting out a grunt and gathering up two of the boxes like they weighed nothing at all. He took the boxes and headed down the hallway off the living room, Sabrina following on his heels. As they walked, he tilted his head towards a closed door on one side of the hall. "Bathroom's through there."

He pushed open a door on the other side of the hall, leading her into a sparsely decorated bedroom. He set the boxes on the floor and headed back out to the living room for more. The room was clean and bright, a large window overlooking the bay letting in plenty of natural light. The queen-sized bed in the center of the room looked like it had never been slept in, and the dresser drawers were, unsurprisingly, empty.

Sebastian returned, setting down another pair of boxes.

"You don't need to do that," she said. He arched an eyebrow at her and shook his head, turning back towards the living room. She followed after him. "I mean, if I'm not staying, there's no point in moving me into the guest room."

His step faltered, but he continued on moving the boxes.

Sabrina huffed out a frustrated breath and leaned back against the hallway wall, watching as he worked.

He dropped the box in his hands inside the door of the guest room and turned on her, planting his hands on his hips. "My mom and your aunt. They seemed…"

"Happy?" He grunted in agreement, and she slid down the wall until she was sitting on the floor. The cramps may have stopped for now, but they would be back. They always came back. And their brief, unexpected appearance earlier coupled with the insanity of that conversation at Sebastian's mother's house had drained any energy she had left. "Aunt Lucy is the only one who's never seemed disappointed in me, you know?"

She hadn't meant to say it out loud.

Sebastian stared at her for a long, silent moment, something working behind his eyes as a muscle in his jaw ticked. Finally he cleared his throat and looked away. "It'll probably take a few days at least for my lawyer to figure out the annulment. Maybe until then we could…"

"What?"

"Not tell them."

"You're serious? You want to pretend to be married?"

"We *are* married," he reminded her, taking a step closer. He reached his hand out to her and pulled her to her feet, leaving only a few inches between them.

She nodded, processing his proposal. "And I'd live here?"

"You stay here in the guest room. Bathroom across the hall is all yours." He tilted his chin towards the wall behind the guest bed's headboard. "I have an en suite in my room."

"So we'd be like roommates. Just for a few days?"

"Until the annulment is settled. Then we can tell everyone we realized we rushed into things."

"They'll still be disappointed. But maybe not as disappointed as they'll be when they find out this whole thing was the result of one too many margaritas."

"One?"

"Hey." She punched him lightly on the bicep, laughing.

The jostling of her abdomen sent another cramp shooting through her side and she pressed her hand to it, hissing. His brows pulled together as his eyes zeroed in on the spot on her side, his lips pulling into a frown.

She waved him off. "It's fine. I'm fine."

"You're not." He brushed the back of his hand over her forehead as though he were checking for a fever.

A shiver ran down her spine at the touch. "I will be," she said, busying herself with fluffing the curtains. As if she'd ever fluffed curtains before in her life. But she needed to do something with her hands. Caring, concerned Sebastian was a version of him she wasn't prepared for. "See? You don't want to stay married to me. I can't even laugh without falling apart," she joked.

"You don't have to tell me what it is, but maybe you should see a doctor about it."

She snorted. "If you know of one who takes self-pay patients without bankrupting them, let me know."

His stony silence was deafening. She glanced over her shoulder to find him scrubbing his hand through his hair, messing up all that coiffed perfection. "You don't have health insurance?"

"I will. As soon as I open my studio. And save up for a few months. Three months. Four, tops. Definitely by Christmas." *And now you're rambling. Great.*

He planted his hands on his hips and hung his head, sighing. When he looked back up at her, his jaw was tense but there was a softness to his eyes that raised goosebumps on her skin.

"I'll add you to my policy in the morning."

"What?"

"You're my wife, Sabrina," he growled, and oh shit, that growly thing did terrible, wonderful things to her.

"What about the annulment?"

"You'll stay on my policy until you can buy your own. Until Christmas. The annulment can wait until then."

"Why would you do that for me?"

He looked away, his Adam's apple bobbing with his swallow. "You're in pain. You should see a doctor."

"Thank you," she said, her voice choked with an emotion she was afraid to name. Gratitude and surprise and something dangerously close to letting herself feel things for this man she'd tried so hard not to feel anything for. She moved closer to him, but stopped short of hugging him, despite the way her arms ached to wrap around him.

He gave one small, tight nod, and adjusted a box, as though he, too, needed something to distract himself. "Next weekend. You're going to Brookline?"

"My mother has demanded that I attend her annual Labor Day party. She wants the whole family together to celebrate Hol—"

She swallowed the rest of the sentence. She wasn't sure if she should talk to him about her sister, which was ironic considering they wouldn't be married if she hadn't gotten drunk and babbled about Holly in the first place. His eyes scanned her face, settling on the gold chains around her neck. He hooked a finger beneath the longest chain, catching the small ceramic charm and moving it to the center of her chest, where he gently placed the cool pottery against her skin.

When he looked back up at her, his eyes were shuttered.

"What about Holly?"

Sabrina cleared her throat, suddenly all too aware of that charm lying in the dip of her clavicle, of how much she liked having his hands on the jewelry she'd made. On her.

"She made partner."

He looked as though he wanted to say something, and she found herself rocking towards him on the balls of her feet, hungry for whatever words he might give her.

Across the room, tucked in her purse, her phone rang. She closed her eyes, dropping back on her heels. "That's probably Mom now."

"Answer it."

"She's going to expect you to come to the party too. But I can skip it. It wouldn't be the first time I let her down," she said, forcing a chuckle.

"Answer it." He stepped away from her, putting distance between them as he dug his hands into his pants pockets. She hated every inch of that space, of the blank look in his eyes. "You can tell her I look forward to seeing her again."

# Chapter Ten

"We didn't order these." Gavin tried to hand back the round of shots as the bartender, Sam, set them on their table at The Rookery.

Sam quirked an eyebrow towards a table at the front of the room. "No, but they did." Baz groaned. He didn't need to look to know who had sent them drinks. Sam set the final glass in front of Baz with a shit-eating grin. "Congrats, man. Didn't even know you were seeing someone."

Gavin took a tentative sip of the drink. "Mm, it's fruity." He threw back the rest of the shot. "Is that cranberry?"

Jamie pressed his lips together thoughtfully. "I think so."

Ethan shoved the glass away from himself and held up his beer. "I'll stick to my Sam Adams."

"Now is that any way to show your gratitude? Ethan Hart, I know your mother taught you better than that," Mrs. Blumenthal said with mock offense as she and her gang of meddlesome friends appeared at their table.

"I'm a simple man, Mrs. B, with simple tastes." Ethan took another sip of his beer.

"And now you're the only bachelor in the bunch," Mrs. White mused, running her assessing gaze over him. "Pity. I really did think you would be next to tie the knot."

"She lost twenty bucks on that bet," Mrs. Kemp announced.

"You're betting on our love lives now?" Baz might need that shot after all.

"Only a bit of harmless fun," Mrs. Blumenthal said.

"Does this mean you'll be next to join the fatherhood club, Sebastian?" Mrs. Greene said.

Baz choked on his Scotch, slamming a fist into his sternum as he coughed.

Mrs. White laughed. "Go easy on him, Ruth. He hasn't even gone on his honeymoon yet."

"Where are your lovely ladies tonight?" Mrs. Kemp craned her neck around the bar as though Tessa and Kyla might pop out of thin air to surprise her.

"They're having a girls' night," Jamie said. "Tessa wants to get a few more in before the baby comes."

"Good, then we won't embarrass Sebastian in front of his new wife when we whoop your behinds tonight," Mrs. Greene laughed.

"One of these days, we're going to win," Gavin said.

The grandma gang laughed at that, Mrs. Blumenthal patting Gavin patronizingly on the shoulder.

"Alright, it's been over a week since you got home. Time to tell us the truth," Jamie said once Mrs. White and her friends had returned to their own table on the other side of the room. "Did you lose a bet? Is one of you dying?"

Baz shot him an unamused look. "The fuck are you talking about?"

"I'm trying to figure out how you left here four days ago a single man and now you're married to a woman you haven't even seen in ten years."

Baz glared at him.

"Are you in love with her?" Gavin asked. "What I mean is… have you been in love with her this whole time? I wouldn't judge you if you have. I mean, look at how long I was in love with Kyla before I even knew it."

"*We* all knew it," Jamie said.

"It would explain why you haven't had a single serious relationship with any other woman in the last decade," Ethan said, steering the conversation back to Baz.

Gavin nodded. "We would understand why you were so impulsive if you've been harboring feelings for her—"

"Jesus Christ, we went to Vegas. Shit happened, alright?"

"Are you saying you didn't mean to get married?" Jamie asked.

"I didn't say that."

"Then you're staying together?" Ethan asked.

"Of course, they're staying together. They just moved in together," Gavin said.

"Thanks for that, by the way," Baz said, narrowing his eyes. "That's not what your spare key is for."

"That's right. It's for stealing pieces from Baz's board games," Jamie said.

"I knew that was you!" Baz threw a handful of popcorn at Jamie across the table, swearing under his breath when his friend caught a piece in his mouth. "I tore apart my apartment looking for that fucking dog."

"Relax. I know exactly where your precious Monopoly dog is," Jamie said. "He's in the top drawer of my desk at the restaurant."

"He's in your fucking desk?"

"*He's* a hunk of metal mass produced for a children's board game," Jamie teased. "And you can have him back when you tell us what's really going on with you and Sabrina."

"There's nothing to tell."

"You went to a conference and ended up married," Jamie said.

"I wouldn't have even been at that fucking conference if you hadn't promised Norm one of us would go," Baz shot back.

"Well, then, apparently, you're welcome." Jamie grinned.

"He's salty that he lost at Scrabble," Ethan said. "Don't worry.

We can rematch this weekend."

"Not gonna be here this weekend," Baz said, straightening his jacket to have something to do with his hands.

"Since when? I thought we were all going to the carnival on Sunday. Like always," Gavin said.

"I don't think we've missed a carnival closing night as long as I've lived here," Jamie added.

"Longer," Ethan said. "Not since Gav broke his arm in fifth grade and Mrs. West wouldn't let him go."

"I'm busy," Baz said.

"Doing what?" Jamie asked.

"Sabrina and I are needed in Brookline."

His friends fell silent, sharing glances that were either concerned or shocked, he couldn't decide.

Gavin leaned across the table, lowering his voice. "Are you sure that's—"

"Are we gonna play trivia, or what?" Baz swung around on his barstool, trying to get a line of sight to Mike Greenhall at the front of the bar. The asshole was still arranging his index cards, like he was preparing for a student council speech or something.

"Let it go, guys," Ethan said, digging his hand into the bowl of popcorn in the center of the table. "I'm sure Tessa and Kyla will get the whole story from Sabrina tonight."

"What the fuck are you—" Baz froze. He exhaled harshly through his nose. "Girls' night."

The incessant buzzing of the doorbell pulled Sabrina from sleep. She sat up on the couch, staring out through a wall of glass at the most gorgeous sunset over the bay.

*Where the hell am I?*

She wiped sleep from her eyes and glanced around at

the minimalist space. Chrome and steel and leather in stark contrast to the driftwood accent wall, the waterfall of white marble serving as a kitchen island, the emotionless beachy landscapes hanging in shiny copper picture frames.

*Right. Sebastian's condo.*

She didn't remember lying down—just that by the time she'd gotten off the phone with her mother she'd been exhausted and alone in the condo—but the nap had done wonders. It seemed her uterus was done trying to murder her for the night, and—miracle of miracles—she hadn't actually gotten her period two weeks early as she'd feared. Must have been the stress of the last week turning her stomach into knots.

A niggling warning at the back of her mind reminded her that it was likely more than stress. And if Sebastian meant it, if he actually added her to his insurance policy, she could finally see a doctor. She wouldn't need to wait another four months—realistically more like five—to buy her own insurance. Not that having the insurance itself would stop her ovary from producing cysts the size of grapefruit or keep the endometriosis from spreading, but it would mean she could find a new gynecologist, get the medication she needed to keep the cysts under control, maybe stop living in fear of the ever-more-frequent flare-ups.

The doorbell buzzed again. "Hello?" she asked into the speaker mounted on the wall beside the front door.

"Sabrina? Let us up! It's Tessa and Kyla—we met at St. Anthony's Bazaar two weeks ago," the staticky reply filled the condo.

Sabrina pressed the button at the bottom of the intercom. A few moments later, a sharp knock came at the front door. She pulled the door open, but before she could say anything, a very pregnant Tessa pushed past her. "Sorry, gotta pee!" Tessa called as she waddled down the hall towards the guest bathroom.

"Don't mind her. The baby's been sitting on her bladder all

week. I'm Kyla. I'm not sure if you remember me," the curvy blonde in the doorway said with a sheepish smile.

"Kyla, hi. Yes, of course, I remember you. Come in." Sabrina stepped back and ushered her into Sebastian's living room. "What are you guys doing here?"

"We're the welcome wagon. Tessa is married to Jamie, and I'm engaged to Gavin and now that you're married to Baz…" She shrugged with a smile. "Welcome!"

"I'm sorry, Jamie and Gavin are…?"

"Your husband's best friends," Tessa called from the bathroom down the hall. She emerged a few minutes later. "My dad, Ethan, is the fourth."

"I met Ethan. He picked us up from the airport." Sabrina paused, running back Tessa's words. "Wait, your dad is friends with your husband?"

"Best friends," Tessa confirmed. "We're one big, modern family."

"And now, you're one of us." Kyla beamed. "So while the boys are out playing trivia—"

"Losing trivia," Tessa corrected. "You should be prepared for that when Baz gets home. They always lose to Mrs. White and her friends. Baz takes it the hardest."

"Yes, while they're losing, we're having girls' night." Kyla reached into the giant bag on her shoulder and produced a bottle of sparkling cider. "I'm thinking pizza and a corny romcom."

Tessa sank into the armchair at one end of the living room. "Only if we get cheesy bread too, with that garlic butter dipping sauce. But no pepperoni. This kid is giving me awful heartburn."

"Right, it's the baby and not the mountain of buffalo wings you've been having for lunch every day," Kyla said with a smirk as she rummaged for glasses in Baz's cabinets.

"The baby likes spicy food. What can I say? At least we're done with the Indian cravings. Our house smelled like curry for a month."

"Tessa's husband is a chef," Kyla explained. "When she has a craving, he doesn't order take out. He cooks."

"The food is amazing, but the smell lingers," Tessa said, resting her hand absent-mindedly on her baby bump.

Sabrina smiled, though the easy conversation and friendly banter had her off kilter, like she'd been dropped into the middle of one of those supportive, funny, female friend groups people always had on TV but no one actually had in real life. At least, she'd thought no one actually had them in real life. But here Tessa and Kyla were—funny, supportive, female, and determined, it seemed, to be her friends.

"What'll it be?" Kyla asked, handing Sabrina a glass of sparkling cider and making herself at home on the couch. "90s, 2000s, or made for a streaming service?"

"90s," Tessa and Sabrina said at the same time.

Kyla fumbled with the remote to Sebastian's oversized television. After a minute, she held it out to Sabrina. "How do you work this thing?"

"Don't ask me," Sabrina laughed. "I only just moved in."

"That's right! Mrs. White's little welcome home gift," Tessa said with a smile. "Personally, I would have preferred a dozen cupcakes to having Mrs. White digging through my things. Oh! Or a cheesecake. Or a carrot cake." Her eyes lit up. "A carrot cake cheesecake!"

Kyla laughed and dug into her bag again, producing a bar of expensive chocolate. "Best I can do on short notice."

Tessa accepted the bar of chocolate with a happy sigh. "You're too good to me." She peeled back a corner of the bar and took a bite, her eyes falling closed and a look of pure bliss crossing her face. "Maybe I'll have the crew at the bakery make me a carrot cake cheesecake tomorrow."

"Have them make whatever you'd like. You own the place," Kyla said.

Fortified by her chocolate bar, Tessa turned her attention

back to Sabrina. "Well, if we can't watch a romcom, we'll have to talk. Tell us everything about yourself."

Sabrina laughed, startled. "Everything is…a lot."

"Let's start with how you met Baz," Tessa said between bites of chocolate. "Jamie said you guys had history."

Sabrina opened her mouth but found she didn't know where to begin. *We met while volunteering?* True, but probably not what Tessa was looking for. *He almost married my sister?* Also true, but too complicated. *He's the one I always wondered about, my 'what if' guy.* Oof, definitely not something she was ready to share with these women, no matter how friendly they were.

Kyla reached across the couch and placed a calming hand on Sabrina's arm. "No need to dive into the deep end right away. How about something easier? Tessa owns the best bakery in the state. I have a boudoir photography studio in town. What do you do?"

"I'm opening a pottery studio," Sabrina said, flashing a grateful smile Kyla's way.

"Like mugs and vases?" Tessa asked.

"Sure, and…other things." Sabrina glanced between the women. If anyone would understand Sabrina's specialty, surely it was the owner of a boudoir photography studio and a woman who'd married her father's best friend. "I had a studio in Maine before I moved here. We were mostly known for hosting break-up parties."

"What's a break-up party?" Kyla asked.

"When people want to get together with their friends and wish their ex good riddance—metaphorically, of course—they can book a break-up party. There's wine and a safe space for the airing of grievances." She steeled herself in case she'd misjudged these women and powered through. "And I teach them how to make a clay penis to represent their ex. I fire it in the kiln overnight, and the next day they come back, and we have a smashing party."

"Where you smash the penises?" Tessa asked, leaning so far forward in her seat that Sabrina was almost afraid she'd fall.

"Yes. Where we smash the penises."

Tessa and Kyla looked at each other, slow smiles spreading across both of their faces.

"I *love* that," Kyla said at last.

"That's brilliant!" Tessa leaned back in her chair with a laugh. Her eyes sparkled in a way that made Sabrina sure Tessa had been the friend in high school who convinced you to cut class and spend the day at the beach instead of learning trigonometry. "What if someone doesn't want to smash it?" she asked.

"Then I guess they don't have to. It hasn't come up before. Why?"

"What if someone wanted to…I don't know…make use of their new clay dick?" A surprised laugh burst from Sabrina's lips. "I mean, theoretically, of course, if someone were to spend all that time crafting the perfect pottery penis, they might want to give it a test drive. Could someone do something like that? Theoretically?"

"Sure, theoretically," Sabrina said. Dammit but she liked these women. "I'd have to do a little research to be sure, but I think that with a food grade glaze and the right firing the pottery would be body safe."

"Hmm," Tessa said, popping the last bite of chocolate bar into her mouth. "Food for thought."

# Chapter Eleven

In all the years Baz had lived in his condo, he'd never had a guest in his guest room. He knew that was the room's purpose, had furnished it accordingly, and yet there was something unsettling about hearing the muted sounds of movement on the other side of his bedroom wall. When he'd toured the condo before buying it, the bed in the master had been on the opposite wall, and now he knew why. With his headboard up against the wall he shared with the guest room, he could hear every time Sabrina tossed and turned in bed, and he had no doubt she could hear each of his frustrated exhales in return.

This wasn't working.

He reached above his head and rapped his knuckles against their shared wall. The movement on the other side stilled. "You up?" he asked, barely raising his voice.

Another frustrated harrumph through the wall.

"I can't sleep." Then, quieter, to herself, "Stupid nap."

"On the couch?"

"Yes! Why is that thing so comfortable? A couch has no right to be that comfortable."

He chuckled to himself and climbed out of bed. A moment later, he was knocking on her door. At her startled gasp, he leaned his shoulder against the wall beside her door, crossing his arms over his chest, and waited through the shuffling and muffled curse when she tripped over something before she pulled the door to her room open.

She wore black bike shorts that made her legs seem even longer than he'd thought possible and a worn Rhode Island School of Design t-shirt that was two sizes too big. Her hair was pulled up in a messy bun on the top of her head and her face was clean, her usual eye makeup washed away. He let his gaze trace the long lines of her legs, over each toe dug into his carpet, over the flared curve of her hips. As beautiful as she was in pencil skirts and heels, Baz thought this might be his favorite version of her—a little undone, a little less polished, a little more...her.

As she made her own perusal of his body in the gray sweatpants that left little to the imagination, he bit back the irrational burst of satisfaction at the awareness in her eyes taking in the sight of him.

With a tilt of his head, he said, "Come on," and led her into the kitchen.

"It's two o'clock in the morning," she protested, but she padded after him.

In the kitchen, he dug through his silverware drawer until he located the good ice cream scoop that Tessa had bought him for Christmas last year and used it to gesture to a seat at the marble island. She huffed but sat, and he turned away before she could see his smile.

"What are you doing?"

He opened the freezer and pulled out two pints of ice cream in plain white containers. "Strawberry or mint chocolate chip?"

"You want to have ice cream? Now?" He eyed the containers and then looked back at her, waiting for her to realize what a ridiculous question that was. Finally, she said, "Strawberry."

He nodded, placing both pints on the counter. He filled a white ceramic bowl with strawberry before filling his own bowl with mint chocolate chip and returning the pints to the freezer. "It's local," he said, as he retrieved a jar of Tessa's homemade chocolate sauce from the fridge. He held it up for her to see and she nodded enthusiastically. "Made with local strawberries. And mint." Each of their bowls topped with a suitable amount of chocolate sauce, he returned the jar to the fridge and brought the bowls over to the island. He slid onto the seat opposite Sabrina and set her bowl in front of her. "I'm out of whipped cream."

Sabrina brought a scoop of her ice cream to her mouth, her eyes falling closed as her lips wrapped around her spoon. "God, that's good," she moaned. "You can really taste the strawberry. I wouldn't have taken you for a fancy ice cream kind of guy."

"Strawberry's not fancy."

"Local strawberry is." She leaned towards him, her spoon hovering near the edge of his bowl. "Can I?" she asked, gesturing towards his bowl.

He nodded and watched with rapt attention as she scooped up a bite of his mint chocolate chip and slid it into her mouth.

"Oh, fuck," she groaned, her tongue darting out to wipe away a drop of chocolate from her lip.

He forced his eyes back to his bowl of ice cream and shifted in his seat, willing his cock to stand down. Had it been that long since he'd been with a woman that he was getting hard watching Sabrina eat ice cream?

"That's a freaking religious experience in a bowl." Another bite. Another moan that his cock definitely noticed. "That's it. You've ruined me. I am ruined. I can never eat grocery store ice cream again."

"You're welcome."

"Where would one get local ice cream? You know, if one were to run out and need to restock the freezer," she asked between bites.

He bit the inside of his cheeks to keep from smiling. "There's a stand at the farmer's market."

She stared at him. "*You* go to the farmer's market?"

"Fuck, no. Jamie gets it delivered to the restaurant. He always gets a few extra pints for me."

"That's Tessa's husband?"

He nodded. "She made the chocolate sauce."

"I'll have to thank her next time I see her then."

Right, because Sabrina was friends with Tessa now. He wondered how their girls' night had been, Knowing Tessa and Kyla, they would have welcomed Sabrina with open arms into their little club of wives and girlfriends, the newest addition to his group of friends. He wasn't ready to examine how much he liked the idea of including Sabrina in that group.

The sound of their spoons scraping their bowls filled the silence between them. After a while, Baz chanced a glance at her to find her dancing happily in her seat as she spooned bites of ice cream into her mouth. She licked the last of the chocolate sauce off her spoon and set it down, resting her forearms on the countertop as she leaned forward.

"You seem like you're feeling better," he said, his voice turning up at the end like he wasn't quite sure if it was a question.

"Oh, that." She took her time gathering another bite of ice cream, and for a minute he thought she might not say anything else. "I have PCOS." She glanced at him, and his lack of understanding must have been written all over his face, because she smiled wryly and continued. "It means my ovary creates cysts when they shouldn't. Sometimes they're really big."

"Your reproductive organs are overachievers?"

She huffed out a laugh. "Pretty much the exact opposite actually. When the cysts get too big, the ovary twists under its weight."

He knew he was staring, but he couldn't look away. One of her organs was *twisting* and she hadn't seen a doctor because somehow, despite being the youngest daughter of an insanely wealthy family, she couldn't afford health insurance. He hated everything about this.

"Sounds serious."

"It can be." She wouldn't look at him, her gaze focused on the last bits of her melting ice cream, and he gripped his bowl harder to keep himself from going to her. "Most of the time it's no worse than what you've seen this past week."

"And the rest of the time?"

"The rest of the time I get real friendly with the nurses in the ER." His shoulders went stiff, his jaw clenched, and her face softened. "That hasn't been necessary in a while."

"But it could be."

"It could. But there are drugs that can help lessen the symptoms. Birth control," she said, her false brightness chafing at his skin. "Which, thanks to you and your handy-dandy insurance, I'll be able to get back on soon. So, thanks for that."

"Lessen but not cure."

She sighed and, for the first time that night, she looked tired. "There is no cure. Not unless the thing twists long enough to require surgical removal. But that's the worst case scenario."

"How close have you come to that worst case scenario?"

She smiled a sad sort of smile. "Lately? Not that close."

"And that," he gestured back towards the guest room where he'd last seen her wincing in pain, "was—what? A medium case scenario?"

She chuckled and shrugged one shoulder. "That was a Monday."

"Jesus." He scraped his hand over his jaw. She was so cavalier about it, so accepting that she was going to be in pain.

"It's not always like that. I have plenty of days where I'm not in pain at all."

"And then you have others where you land in the ER."

She tilted her head in agreement.

"How will I know? When it's just a Monday versus when I

should take you to the ER?"

She cocked her head to the side, her face scrunched up in question. "It's not something you need to worry about, Sebastian."

"But I do. Worry about it." He hadn't realized he'd taken a step closer to her, and it suddenly felt too close, even though there was half a room between them. He forced himself to ease back towards the safety of the counter.

She studied him for a minute, the surprise on her face melting into something shy. A retreat. The back of his neck itched with the suppressed desire to tear down all her walls. But that wasn't what they were doing here. A few weeks together didn't make them the kinds of friends who had to let each other all the way in, even though the glimpse of herself she'd given him was enough to make him want to bust down the door. It was a reminder of how little they actually knew of each other.

"Why couldn't you sleep tonight?"

He busied himself with scraping up the last of his ice cream, gathering the melted bits into a final bite, and tried to brush off the lingering sense that he'd let her down somehow. "Just couldn't."

He could feel her eyes on him and, for a moment, he wished he had more to say. She'd shared so much, and he knew he should be able to offer her something in return. But he didn't know why he hadn't been able to sleep—other than the new noises coming through his wall, that is. All he knew was he had a ball of knotted up…something…lodged behind his sternum. Gavin had called it emotional constipation, but that wasn't an image he particularly wanted in his brain.

"I haven't slept well since I was a kid. My mom's house is old. Half the floorboards creek and in the winter you can hear the air in the pipes." She looked at him as though she were eagerly awaiting his next words, and despite himself, he found himself telling her more. "I used to lie awake and wait until Mom went to bed, too, and the noises stopped."

"Why?"

He shrugged one shoulder. He didn't like being on the receiving end of the questions. "I don't think I could relax until I knew she was safe."

"And tonight you could hear me."

He shrugged again.

She looked as though she were about to ask something else, but no good could come from continuing this game of twenty questions with Sabrina in the middle of the night. He wasn't even sure why he had initiated this midnight snack in the first place. It was better if he maintained at least some semblance of distance. This was a practical arrangement. Nothing more.

*Liar.*

He swept up their bowls and moved them to the counter by the sink. "Do you want any more?" he asked, his back to her as he rinsed out his bowl.

"No. One bowl of ice cream is probably enough for now. But don't hold me to that later. Especially if all the other flavors are as good as the strawberry."

He chanced a glance at her over his shoulder for a second to catch the way the corner of her lips quirked up in a smile. "Noted." He set the rinsed bowls in the sink and washed his hands, taking an inordinate amount of time to scrub the dish soap into his skin. "I heard you on the phone with your mom again earlier. How'd that go?"

"Awful," she said with a huffed laugh. "But no worse than I expected. She didn't really want to talk about us. She just wanted another excuse to remind me how important this party is. She only ever calls this often when she wants something." She paused, but he kept his attention on carefully drying the space between each of his fingers with a dishtowel. "I'm going to drive up Friday evening, stay the extra night. She can get the worst of her questions out of her system before all the guests arrive on Saturday."

He nodded, turning around to face her as he leaned against the counter, keeping the kitchen island between them. "What time are we leaving?"

"You don't have to do that, Sebastian. Really. I appreciate the offer, but—"

"Will it make it easier for you if I'm there?" She paused, opened her mouth as though she might speak, and then pressed her lips together and nodded. "What time are we leaving?"

"Six? We'll get there with enough time to talk, but not too much before we can excuse ourselves to go to bed."

Heat flared in her cheeks at the mention of a bed and he wondered if she was remembering the way they'd slept curled around each other in Vegas, if she knew he'd woken harder than stone and dying to kiss her again. He had the strangest desire to press his lips to that pretty blush climbing up her throat, to see if her skin tasted different because of it.

Her voice was thready when she continued. "They'll expect us to share a room. Since we're married."

"I figured."

"And to act like a couple."

"Since we're married."

"Right. Since we're married."

He pushed off from the counter and moved around the island, stopping in front of her. Her eyes widened as she tilted her chin up to meet his gaze. "And how would a married couple act?"

Her eyes dipped to his lips. "Maybe we could hold hands, or do that thing where you put your hand on my back when we're walking."

He hummed in thought, noting the way her breathing grew heavier in response, and for a moment the wondered what it would feel like to have her pressed against him when she breathed like that, to feel the rise and fall of her chest against his. "Maybe I could kiss you when you come into a room. Or before you leave."

"That is something a married couple would do." Her eyes flickered to his lips. "Or you could kiss me just because. Since we're married."

"We are that."

Without thinking it through, he tugged the elastic from her bun, her hair falling in messy waves around her face. He set the elastic on the counter, covering it with his palm as he leaned forward until they were eye to eye. Her breathing stuttered, but still she held his gaze.

He fucking loved it.

"Time for bed, wife."

She sucked in a breath, her little gasp shooting like an electrical current down his spine.

*What the fuck am I doing?*

He stepped away from her and scrubbed a hand over his jaw. Christ, he'd almost kissed her. The memory of the last time he'd kissed her, of her little sighs and his hands in her hair and her nails on the nape of his neck, mingled with the vision of hauling her onto his pristine marble countertop and burying his face between her thighs.

"Sebastian?"

Her breathing was still shaky, her ample chest rising and falling visibly with each breath, even as her eyes searched his for answers he didn't have.

He broke their staring contest and moved down the hall, only pausing once he'd reached the safety of his bedroom door. When he glanced back at her, still sitting at his kitchen island, her brows pulled low in confusion, that lump behind his sternum grew and twisted.

"Goodnight, wildflower."

# Chapter Twelve

"No, I don't fucking understand." Baz pinched the bridge of his nose and tried to remember not to swear like a sailor in the parking lot of a church. "Explain."

"Annulment isn't a thing in Rhode Island," came the reply from the other end of the phone. "In special circumstances you can ask a judge to rule that the marriage never legally existed, but I can tell you right now, getting drunk in Vegas is not one of those special circumstances. Especially when you're in the process of adding her to your health insurance."

"Then what the fuck am I supposed to do?"

"You can get a divorce like every other person in the state who wishes they never got married."

Was that true? Did Baz wish he'd never gotten married? The sentiment didn't sit right, like an oil slick on his skin that he wanted to scrub off. It wasn't that he wished the last few days had never happened, just that he needed it to stop. The other night he'd come way too close to treating her like she was actually his wife and not...whatever the hell she actually was to him. The only way he could see to getting out of this with his sanity intact was to no longer be married to the redhead who'd invaded his home and his thoughts.

"I can start the paperwork today."

The door at the side of the church opened and Sabrina leaned out. "Sebastian?"

She was always beautiful, but when she wore a pencil skirt and heels, she was absolutely breathtaking. The gold chains of her necklace fell beneath the neckline of her floral blouse and her hair fell over one shoulder, fluttering in the late summer breeze. He knew what was on the end of that chain now—a delicate ceramic curlicue doubling back on itself in an intricate pattern. Knowing felt intimate somehow.

She smiled, red-painted lips pulling into a tantalizing curve, and cocked her head to the side. "You ready?"

He ran his eyes over her, lingering on the place where those chains dipped into her cleavage, the flare of her hips, the smooth skin of her bare calves. "I have to go. Don't do anything yet," he said into the phone, ending the call.

"Everything alright?" she asked.

"Fine. Let's get this over with."

He followed her down the dark hall on the ground level of St. Anthony's to the large meeting room where the Merchants' Association held their monthly meetings. Tessa and Jamie hovered around the refreshments table at the back of the room, adjusting the display of mini pastries Tessa's bakery had provided. Kyla, Gavin, and Ethan sat off to one side of the bank of metal folding chairs, chatting happily with Natalia, the lingerie shop owner, and Lindsay, the owner of the fancy breakfast food truck. At the front of the room, Norm, still in his signature beanie and flannel despite the August heat, fiddled with a projector. He turned at the clicking of Sabrina's heels along the linoleum floor.

"Good. You're here. Let's get started." Norm held the remote control for the projector out to Sabrina. "How do you want to be introduced? Mr. and Mrs. Graham?"

"No," Sabrina and Baz said simultaneously and a little too quickly.

"We'll introduce ourselves," Sabrina said.

"Everyone already knows us," Baz pointed out.

Norm chuckled. "Suit yourselves." Then, to the assembled group, "Alright, let's get this thing started." The crowd settled into the folding chairs as conversation died down, turning their attention to the front of the room. "We're skipping our usual business tonight so we can come up to speed on the Vegas conference and make a plan for this year's Food and Wine Festival. Unless anyone has anything pressing."

A hand shot up on one side of the room and Jenny from the hair salon got to her feet. "When are we going to talk about the fact that wedding bookings are still down?"

"Temporary market dip," Norm said.

"Maybe, but I don't know how many years in a row my business can survive this *temporary* dip." A murmur of agreement rolled through the room. "You can't keep punting on this, Norm. We need a new plan. I don't much care if it's more weddings or something else entirely, but we can't simply keep wringing our hands and taking the hit."

Natalia chimed in, "The Food and Wine Festival has already proven there's a real market for bringing other kinds of tourism to town. Maybe we should explore ways to do that all year, and not only in the winter."

As the meeting quickly devolved into side conversations, Sabrina leaned close to Baz, whispering. "Do you think they'd notice if we left?"

He choked on the burst of laughter that tried to work its way past that lump in his chest. When he turned his head to look at her, she was close enough that he could count the freckles on her cheeks. He wanted to kiss each one, see if the freckles near her ear tasted different than the ones on her clavicle, see where else those freckles dotted her skin.

*Where the fuck did that thought come from?* He couldn't remember the last time he'd thought this much about *kissing* someone.

He swallowed hard and turned back to the chaos of the room. "Did you go to the seminar on gamification?"

"You know I did."

He did know. He'd spent half the lecture obsessing over the red mark that appeared on her knee when she crossed and uncrossed her legs, and the other half hating himself for even noticing it.

"Could be a solution."

He glanced her way and she nodded, that smile lighting up her face again. "It's at least more interesting than rehashing the workshop on public transportation and infrastructure."

Norm shouted over the growing conversations in the room as the assembled business owners splintered into smaller and smaller groups bemoaning the declining wedding industry in town. Finally, exasperated, he stuck his index fingers in his mouth and blew, the piercing whistle cutting through the noise.

"That's enough," he huffed. "Now Baz and Sabrina are here to tell us what they learned at that conference so we can make sure the Food and Wine Festival has its most successful year, even with Jamie and Tessa needing to take a back seat. That's the only thing on the agenda for tonight."

"We might be able to do both," Sabrina said, stepping to the center of the space at the front of the room. "There was a lot to learn at the conference, and we've sent all the slides from the various presentations to Norm. He can make those available to anyone who'd like to review. But I think we can do better than rehash hours of slides about dynamic pricing models." She reached forward and turned off the projector, the machine whirring as it shut down, before turning the full force of her smile on the gathered business owners. "If you really want to address the shrinking wedding market and increase alternative tourism streams, the town's festivals should be part of the plan, and we need to be talking about gamification."

"What's that?" Jenny asked skeptically.

"It's simpler than it sounds. It's just turning things into a game. There's all kinds of blah-biddy-blah in the slides about exactly what it means and complicated ways to do it, but what it boils down is, you decide what you want people to do, and then you figure out a reward system for when they do it. And it's even better if they can compete against other people, earn points over time, that sort of thing."

"It's a very common concept in marketing," Gavin chimed in from the back of the room. "Like when you see those online crowdfunding campaigns and people team up to see which team can raise more money."

"Exactly." Sabrina beamed. "But instead of getting the tourists to raise money, we want them to make reservations at local restaurants and hotels, buy tickets to a museum, rent a kayak, come to a festival. That kind of thing. When I had my studio in Maine, the other local businesses and I did something really similar one summer. We made a passport of sorts that encouraged people to visit all the arts businesses in the area— the galleries and the art museum and the bead shop. And if you visited all the businesses on the list, you were entered into a raffle for a cash prize. We all saw more business that summer."

Baz leaned back against the wall of St. Anthony's listening as Sabrina—with some help from Gavin—helped the association brainstorm lists of ways they could gamify their tourist experience: a passport of local businesses that, when completed, would enter the visitor in a drawing to win a prize; a repeat visitor program that rewarded tourists who came back year over year; ways to earn extra points for leaving reviews online and referring friends to book their own Aster Bay vacations. The list went on and on. By the end of the meeting, they'd developed a rough plan for testing out gamified promotions at the Food and Wine Festival and Sabrina was swarmed with members of the association, eager to continue the conversation.

Through it all, he couldn't take her eyes off her. She was magnetic, weaving a spell that captivated everyone in the room with each open-hearted laugh and nod of encouragement, and blossoming under their reflected appreciation. She practically glowed with it.

"She's got them eating out of the palm of her hand."

Baz turned to see Ethan leaning against the wall beside him. He'd been so caught up in watching Sabrina, he hadn't even noticed his friend approach.

"She's good with people," Baz said.

"Unlike your grumpy ass."

Baz shot him a look. "And she knows how to run a business."

"Why'd she leave her studio in Maine?"

Baz shook his head. "I don't know."

Ethan tilted his head towards Baz's hands. When he glanced down, he realized he was turning his wedding ring on his finger. He hadn't even noticed he was doing it. He shoved his hands in his pockets.

"Did I ever tell you I asked Stephanie to marry me the day I turned eighteen. I wanted to do what you two did, run away to Vegas and get married before our parents could talk us out of it." Ethan said.

He hadn't told him. Not that Baz was surprised. Ethan had been head over heels in love with his childhood sweetheart. Even when she'd gotten pregnant with Tessa at sixteen, Ethan never wavered.

"What happened?"

"She didn't want to marry me."

Ethan looked at Sabrina and Baz followed his line of sight to where she stood, surrounded by their friends and neighbors, like she'd been one of them all along. As though she could sense his eyes on her, Sabrina turned to meet Baz's gaze, flashing him a bright smile that made his skin feel too tight.

"I know you don't want to talk about how you went from

hating her for ten years to marrying her, but that woman—" Ethan tilted his chin towards Sabrina, "—she's something special. And it seems like she thinks you're not half bad either." Baz shoved Ethan's shoulder without ever taking his eyes off Sabrina. Ethan laughed. "Don't overthink it."

"I'm not—"

"I could see those gears turning in your head from all the way across the room."

Baz exhaled through his nose, watching as Sabrina added more notes to the whiteboard from the group excitedly chattering around her. "Just can't figure out why she came back in the first place."

"Does it matter?"

Baz shrugged. Maybe it shouldn't matter, but he couldn't shake the feeling that it did. That maybe it had something to do with that pain she was in the other day, with the fact that she didn't have—and clearly needed—health insurance.

"Then ask her about it," Ethan said.

Right. Ask her about it. He could do that. Provided he could stop thinking about kissing her again long enough to have the conversation.

# Chapter Thirteen

Sabrina had tried counting sheep. She'd tried doing yoga on the floor of the guest bedroom, focusing her gaze on the water of the bay rippling in the moonlight. She'd even tried reciting the state capitals to herself, but nothing had worked. It was after midnight, she was still wide awake, and now she couldn't remember the capital of Missouri.

Tentatively, she reached her hand above her head and tapped against the wall behind her bed.

"What?" Sebastian's gruff reply came as clearly as if he was in the room with her.

"Are you awake?" No answer. She let out a huff that sent the strands of hair hanging about her face fluttering. "I mean, obviously you're awake since you spoke, but are you *awake* awake?"

"What does that mean?"

"I don't know. Are you half asleep, barely keeping your eyes open, or are you actually awake, like mind and body?"

There was a long pause, then, "I'm awake."

Sabrina sat up in bed, leaning back against the wall that separated them and listening to the rustle of Sebastian's movements on the other side of the wall. "Still having trouble sleeping?"

"My only trouble is you banging around in there."

"I was not banging around," she said, trying not to laugh. Because really, what else could you call it when you accidentally fall out of tree pose and almost knock over everything on top of the dresser?

"Like you're a goddamn crash test dummy."

The laugh burst out of her, and she tucked her knees up against her chest, resting her chin on her folded hands. "I was doing yoga."

She could practically hear his incredulous eyebrow raise from the other side of the wall.

"I always have trouble sleeping," he said.

Something warm melted through her at the softness of his voice, the quiet admission, like he was sharing a secret with her. Sharing some hidden part of himself. And she suddenly felt compelled to do the same.

"Me too."

"What's keeping you up tonight?"

"The grumpy guy at the meeting tonight—with the flannel?"

"Norm."

"That's right. Norm. He asked me to join the Food and Wine Festival committee."

"That's how they get you."

"Who?"

"This town. Ask Tessa."

She liked the idea of the town 'getting' her, of them drawing her into their inner circles and keeping her there, of finally being claimed by this place the way she wanted to claim it.

"Are you going to do it?" he asked.

"I think I am."

A few moments later, there was a soft knock on her bedroom door. She climbed out of bed and pulled open the door to find Sebastian leaning in the doorframe. He wore those gray sweatpants again, slung low on his hips and offering a teasing glimpse of the carved muscle of his Adonis belt. Her eyes snagged on his bare chest, the broad expanse of defined muscles with a smattering of dark, coarse hair between his pecs.

She met his eyes as all the filthy things they could do to sate her hunger flashed through her mind. From the way his lip quirked up, he knew exactly what she was thinking. The bastard.

"C'mon." He tilted his head towards the kitchen and started down the hall.

In the kitchen, Baz set about retrieving bowls and spoons. "I ate the last of the ice cream this afternoon," she confessed as she hopped up onto the kitchen island, the marble cool beneath her bare thighs.

Sebastian paused in his movements, his eyes raking over her, lingering on her legs with such focused attention that heat wound its way down her spine. He dragged his gaze back to her face, his eyes pools of black ringed with the thinnest band of ice blue. Without saying anything, he pulled open the freezer door and retrieved another container of ice cream that hadn't been there earlier.

"I bought more," he said, as he scooped ice cream into the bowls. "Black raspberry."

He handed her a bowl and took up a place beside her, leaning against the island as they ate. He kept his attention focused on his bowl but shifted his weight so her dangling calf brushed against his thigh.

"What happened in Maine?" he asked, keeping his eyes focused on the melting ice cream.

She popped another spoonful into her mouth, letting it coat her tongue. She struggled to find the words to explain. How much did she want Sebastian to know about why she'd given up her life in Maine, really?

"It was time for a change."

He exhaled through his nose, a sound she was coming to understand signaled his frustration. "You had a studio there."

It wasn't a question, but she still found herself nodding.

"You sold it?"

"I let myself be bought out."

"Why?"

She scraped her spoon against the edge of the bowl and let her calf swing back and forth enough to stroke his leg through his sweatpants. "I needed to start over. Somewhere new."

"Aster Bay isn't new for you."

"Somewhere I wouldn't feel like such a failure."

He froze, every line and plane in his body going hard, as though he were bracing for a physical blow. *Shit. I said that out loud.*

After a long moment, he shifted a hair closer, the muscles of his body relaxing even if his jaw still ticked.

"You're not a failure." His voice was low and dark, and she could feel the vibration of it through the few inches where his hip was pressed against hers. She shrugged, scraping up the last bits of melted ice cream. "All those people tonight were hanging on your every word."

"Tonight felt really good." A smile pulled at the corners of her lips. She thought for a minute and, though he didn't say anything, she got the feeling that Sebastian was patiently waiting for her to continue, that he somehow knew she had more to say. "They wanted to hear my ideas," she said softly, like giving voice to the thought might make it untrue.

He took her bowl from her and set it alongside his on the counter. In one fluid motion, he boxed her in against the counter, his hands flat on the marble beside her hips, as he leaned down so they were eye to eye.

"Why does that surprise you?" he asked.

"Most people don't want to hear what I think."

"Meaning your parents."

She nodded.

"And some asshole in Maine who bought you out of your

own business?"

She nodded again.

"You know what I think?"

She shook her head, suddenly finding it incredibly challenging to speak when he was looking at her with such intensity, when the heat from his bare chest was radiating off him.

He leaned closer, his lips brushing against the shell of her ear. "Fuck 'em."

A surprised laugh bubbled past her lips and she thought she saw something like satisfaction flicker through Sebastian's eyes. "Is that what you'll say when my parents are awful this weekend?"

All humor fell from his face and one of his hands slid from the counter up over her hip, resting on the curve of her waist. She felt that touch everywhere, the heat of it burning through her thin t-shirt and pulsing low in her abdomen.

"Why would they be awful?"

"Because I'm not like my sister."

His gaze darted across her face like he was memorizing her, until finally he met her eyes, studied her like he could hunt out her secrets if he looked at her closely enough. Maybe she wanted him to.

"Do you want to be?"

"Sometimes."

"Would it help if I told you that I'm glad you're not like her?"

"Only if you meant it."

His other hand slid into her hair, curling around the nape of her neck and tilting her chin up to meet his eyes as he stepped closer. Her thighs parted for him and he stepped between them without hesitation as she rested her own hands on the bare skin at his sides.

"I mean it."

She wasn't sure who leaned in first, and she didn't suppose it mattered. All that mattered was the movement of his lips over hers, the way his hand bunched in the fabric of her t-shirt while the other used his hold in her hair to bring her face closer, to angle her the way he wanted. His tongue teased at her lips and she parted for him eagerly, welcoming him closer as she slipped her hands around his back and pulled him against her.

He kissed deeply, with his whole body. How had she not noticed that the last time he'd kissed her?

*Because you were drunk.*

But they weren't drunk now.

He held her still, like he was afraid she'd disappear if he loosened his grip on her, and she loved it—the idea that he wanted to keep her close, the way he molded himself against her, the push and pull of it. She loved it all.

His lips pressed to the delicate spot on the underside of her jaw, trailed down her throat and across her collarbone.

"These goddamn freckles," he rumbled against her skin, his tongue darting out to flick at the offending marks.

She laughed, the bubbly sound dissolving into a moan as he dragged his teeth over the sensitive skin where her neck met her shoulder. "I've always hated my freckles."

He nipped at her again, harder this time, and she yelped in surprise. "I fucking love them," he growled.

She was lightheaded, whether from the lack of oxygen—that happened when you breathed too hard, right?—or from his words, his cardamom scent surrounding her, she wasn't sure. And she didn't care. He loved her freckles. Sebastian Graham *loved* her freckles.

His lips returned to hers, and the hand on her waist slid around to her lower back. He guided her back, his weight pressing her down over the marble countertop as though he'd crawl on top of her right then and there. She wrapped her legs around his hips, locking her ankles behind him. It was all happening too fast and not nearly fast enough, and the marble was cold but Sebastian was delightfully warm. He rocked against her and swallowed her moan as the rigid length of his erection ground between her thighs.

A loud crash cut through the haze of her thoughts and they pulled apart, breathing hard. Sebastian scrubbed his hand over his kiss-swollen lips and stepped back until he was leaning against the counter on the opposite side of the kitchen. On the floor beside the island where Sabrina sat trying to catch her breath were the shattered remnants of their bowls.

"Shit. Where's the broom?" she asked, sliding off the island.

He shook his head, his eyes locked on the mess on the floor. "I've got it."

"I can help. If you tell me—"

"I've got it."

She took a step towards him, but stopped short when he looked like he'd plaster himself against the wall to preserve the distance between them. Cold fingers of dread wrapped around her throat. "Sebastian?"

He shook his head again, almost as though he were clearing it. "We shouldn't…" He met her eyes for a moment, a wild, haunted look that she didn't recognize greeting her. "It's not a good idea."

All the air rushed from her lungs at the rejection, the finality of it. "Why not?"

"Sabrina." The word was half plea, half chastisement.

She blinked back the stinging in her nose and turned away from him, determined not to let him see how badly he'd hurt her.

"I'll find the broom." Her voice broke on the last word as she turned the corner out of the kitchen.

He called after her but she didn't stop. As her name echoed in the dark apartment, she abandoned any intention of finding the broom, and instead slipped back into the guest room, leaning against the door as soon as it closed. She heard his footsteps in the hall, heard them stop in front of her door, and she held her breath, but it only took a moment for him to move on, the footsteps retreating back towards the kitchen.

Sebastian Graham may have loved her freckles, but he didn't love *her*. A small, but important distinction she needed to remember.

# Chapter Fourteen

"Knock, knock!" Aunt Lucy stuck her head through the propped-open front door of Sabrina's new studio. "I come bearing cookies."

Sabrina set the last jar of glaze on the shelf beside the others and turned to face her aunt, wiping her hands on the navy blue apron she wore over her jeans and t-shirt. "You didn't have to do that. You know you're welcome to visit without bringing baked goods."

Aunt Lucy smiled and set the overflowing tray of cookies loosely covered in plastic wrap on the worktable at the front of the studio. "Jam thumbprints. Both your and Sebastain's favorite." She glanced around the studio, her smile widening. "It looks wonderful in here, dear. You didn't waste any time getting set up."

"Only thing left to do is put up the sign."

"When is the grand opening?"

"I'm not sure." Sabrina focused her attention on straightening the jars of glaze on the shelf, making sure all the labels faced forward.

"Looks to me like you're ready to open tomorrow."

"Not quite. I want it to be perfect."

"Nothing's perfect, dear heart." Aunt Lucy lay a hand over

Sabrina's, stilling her nervous arranging. "But this place comes pretty darn close."

"Thanks, Auntie." Sabrina looked away, clearing her throat. She wasn't sure exactly why her aunt's praise should lodge a lump in her airway.

"Come on. We're going to lunch. My treat."

"You don't have to—"

"I want to! It's not every day I get to celebrate with my favorite niece. Besides, I've had the worst craving for one of Lemon and Thyme's lobster rolls. Indulge me."

Before Sabrina could protest, she found herself sitting at a table overlooking the water, eating lobster rolls and the best French fries she'd ever had while her aunt shared bits of gossip about people Sabrina had never met.

"When are you going to tell me what happened in Las Vegas?" Aunt Lucy asked.

Sabrina stiffened as she dragged a fry through the puddle of ketchup on her plate. "What do you mean?"

"Don't play coy with me, young lady. I had to practically twist your arm to get you to go on that trip."

Sabrina eyed her aunt carefully. "Did you know Sebastian was the other person going?"

"I honestly did not. Ruthie seemed to think it would be Ethan Hart—the one that lives at the vineyard. Ruthie and his mother are friendly and she and her friends have been trying— to no avail, mind you—to set that boy up with a nice girl for years now."

"I knew it was a set up."

"Yes, but not with *Sebastian*. Even *I* didn't think—" Aunt Lucy cut herself off and tried to hide it behind a sip of her iced tea.

But Sabrina had already heard. She twisted her hands in the cloth napkin on her lap. "Even you *what*, Auntie? Even you didn't think I'd stoop low enough to marry Holly's ex-fiancé?"

"That is not what I said."

"But you were going to."

"I certainly was not!" Aunt Lucy reached across the table, capturing one of Sabrina's fidgeting hands with her own.

"I'm sorry," Sabrina said. "I'm nervous about what Mom and Dad are going to say when I see them this weekend."

"I've always liked Sebastian, and I know how much you cared for him, even back then."

Heat rushed to Sabrina's cheeks. Had everyone known she had a crush on her almost brother-in-law? Had *he*?

"Now, I was as surprised as anyone when I heard the news of your marriage, but never for a second did it make me think any less of you."

*You'd think less of me if you knew the truth. You'd be disappointed if you knew this all started as a way to get back at Holly for being the perfect daughter. And now I'm lying to you, to the insurance company, to everyone! Petty, stupid, childish plan gone wrong.*

"So tell me, how did you go from not wanting to go on that trip to marrying one of Aster Bay's most eligible bachelors? I didn't think we'd ever see you walk down the aisle again. Though, I suppose, we didn't see it at all, now did we?"

Where to begin?

*He held my hand on the plane and didn't make fun of my morbid mantras. He looks so ridiculously sexy in a suit it's not fair. We were drunk and impulsive, but really I think we both wanted an excuse to give in to the sexual tension between us. Or maybe that was just me.*

"I imagine," Aunt Lucy said carefully, "there was a great deal of alcohol involved?"

Sabrina's eyes flew to Aunt Lucy's. "How did you know?"

Her aunt laughed. "Dear heart, you are hardly the first woman to find herself making rash decisions in the company of an attractive man, especially when the wine is flowing."

"It was margaritas," Sabrina said with a begrudging smile.

"Even more deadly!" Aunt Lucy leaned back in her seat. "Then, a grand elopement it was not. And yet, you don't seem to be in a rush to rid yourself of your new husband."

"We have a…practical arrangement."

Aunt Lucy hummed in understanding. "Not a love match, then." Sabrina shook her head. "Well, I must say that I was hoping there was a bit less…*practicality* in the mix, but I am perhaps more relieved than I should admit to."

"Relieved?"

Aunt Lucy's eyes softened, and somehow Sabrina knew her aunt could see how impractical Sabrina's feelings for Sebastian really were. "He is a wonderful young man. Kind, generous, loyal, even if he does try to hide all that behind his brooding and his suits. But he's also closed off. Solitary. I would imagine it would be quite hard to get beneath that grumpy exterior of his, especially when he doesn't seem inclined to let anyone in. You've been through so much over the last few years. I would hate to see you get your heart broken."

Sabrina's heart squeezed in her chest. "Don't worry, Auntie. No hearts involved."

The lie was bitter on her lips, but it seemed to appease her aunt, who smiled broadly. "Good. Now, what shall we get for dessert?"

"Tell me again why you called me instead of Gavin?" Ethan leaned over the jewelry case in the small store on the edge of town, eyeing the display of gold rings.

"Gavin's too much of a romantic," Baz said, pointing out a set of simple platinum wedding bands to the man behind the counter.

"Too much of a romantic to pick out wedding rings?"

When Baz didn't respond, Ethan made his way over to where the attendant was showing Baz the platinum set. "Didn't you already buy rings?" He tilted his head towards the cheap gold band on Baz's finger.

"Vegas rings. I can't take Sabrina home to her parents' house wearing dime store jewelry. What do you think of these?"

Ethan looked at the platinum rings. "They're nice."

"That's what you've said about every ring we've looked at," Baz complained, picking up the delicate women's band to examine it more closely.

"I don't know anything about wedding rings, Baz. Never worn one, never picked one out. You really should have called Gavin or Jamie, or—"

"I'll take these," Baz said, handing the ring back to the man behind the counter, along with a folded piece of paper he withdrew from his blazer's inside pocket. "These are our sizes. I'd like to pick them up tomorrow afternoon."

The man smiled the wide grin of someone who was about to make a killing on commission. "Of course, sir. There will be a small rush service fee."

"Fine." Baz pulled his wallet out and slapped a credit card down on the counter. The man snatched it up with an avalanche of obsequious chatter and disappeared into the back room to run the card.

"What really happened in Vegas?" Ethan asked when they were alone.

Baz pinched the bridge of his nose, a headache gathering behind his eyes. He had hardly slept last night, too busy berating himself for being an insensitive jackass who couldn't control his hormones and too afraid to go to bed and hear Sabrina through the wall.

"Come on," Ethan prodded. "You go to Vegas and get married, without bothering to tell any of your closest friends—or your mother—that you were even interested in someone, then you come home and it's like you're doing everything you can to avoid talking about this huge thing that happened in your life. And now you're dropping a small fortune on new wedding rings to impress her family, but you didn't want to bring the one person who actually *likes* this kind of shit—"

"It's not real," Baz blurted out. "We didn't mean to get married."

Ethan blinked, his forehead wrinkling. "I'm sorry, how does someone get married if they don't mean to get married?"

"We were drunk and I'm a fucking idiot, that's how."

"Okay," Ethan said, drawing out the word. "Then why not get it annulled or get divorced or whatever? Why pretend?"

Baz sighed, rubbing his thumb and index finger over his eyes as though that could ease the pounding in his skull. "It's complicated. Sabrina needs health insurance."

Ethan's face dropped. "She alright?"

"I don't know," Sebastian said helplessly, guilt and worry and frustration twisting in his gut into a tangled mess.

"Okay, forget why. How long are you intending to lie to everyone—"

"It's not technically a lie." Baz avoided his friend's disapproving glare. "We *are* married."

"But you don't want to be."

Baz shot him a look. Why had he brought him again? *Next time you get accidentally married, buy the damn rings yourself.*

"I still don't understand why you're buying new rings," Ethan continued as the salesman returned with Baz's credit card and a slip for him to sign.

Baz signed the receipt and took his copy, tucking it into his wallet alongside his credit card. He thanked the salesman, promising to return the next afternoon to pick up the rings, and led Ethan out of the shop. This part of town had little foot traffic, the street lined with real estate and insurance offices rather than the shops and restaurants that were more common in the center of town. The two friends walked nearly two blocks in silence before Baz finally stopped in front of his car, turning to face Ethan.

"She deserves a real ring," Baz said, that knot behind his sternum hot and growing by the second.

"She deserves a real marriage," Ethan countered.

"I can give her the ring." Ethan stared at him, his gaze boring into Baz like he'd excavate that burning knot from his chest with a look alone. "Don't say anything to Gav and Jamie, alright? They wouldn't get it."

"Alright." Ethan stood back as Baz climbed into his car, but he leaned down to speak to him through the open window. "For the record, you deserve a real marriage too."

# Chapter Fifteen

"Sabrina?"

Sebastian's voice pinged through the condo, bouncing off all the metal and hardwood until it knocked at the door to the bathroom where Sabrina stood on the bathmat, naked, massaging lotion into her legs, her wet hair twisted on top of her head in a towel.

"In here!" she called back.

Heavy footsteps drew nearer, each one coiling something hot and tight low in her belly. Sebastian was mere steps away and she was naked, her skin still damp from her shower, her hands gliding over her thighs and calves as she methodically applied the lotion. If he were to open the door, if he were to lean on it too hard—he was always leaning in doorways, as if he didn't know how gorgeous it made him look, or maybe because he did know?—the latch on the bathroom door might give way. He might catch a glimpse of her, naked in his condo—*their* condo. Her nipples tightened at the thought, the way she imagined his eyes would darken, the tick of his jaw, the heavy outline of him in those flimsy sweatpants he always slept in.

*Stop. He doesn't want you.*

That's what he'd said the night before, wasn't it? Not in so many words, but that's what he'd meant. And after Aunt Lucy's warning… Definitely best to shut down any fantasy she still harbored that her fake husband might turn into her real lover.

His footsteps paused outside the bathroom door. "You almost ready to go?"

"Five minutes." *More like ten, but who's counting?*

She rinsed her hands in the sink, washing away the excess lotion, and wrapped one of his oversized, fluffy towels around herself, tucking the end into the top between her breasts. She removed the towel from her head and scrunched the still-damp locks in the fabric, working out the last bits of water.

"So ten?" he asked from the other side of the door.

Her cheeks ached from trying to contain her smile. She set aside the towel she'd been using to dry her hair and opened the bathroom door. Sure enough, Sebastian was leaning against the door frame. His eyes slid down her body, leaving goosebumps in their wake.

"Ten minutes," she said. "You can time me."

He cleared his throat, his eyes darting away. "I have something for you."

"Is it an insurance card?"

"No. Well, yes. The temporary card is next to your purse." He tilted his head down the hall, towards where she'd left her purse on the kitchen island. "The permanent one will be here next week. But this is something different."

Sabrina wasn't sure what she expected when he reached inside his jacket pocket, but it certainly wasn't a jewelry box. A black velvet ring box, to be exact. He held it out to her.

She opened the box and sucked in a shocked breath. The light glinted off the large oval diamond solitaire nestled in the box beside a matching platinum wedding band, a trio of small diamonds embedded in the center. "What is this?"

"Can't take you to your parents' house without a proper ring." Sebastian reached for her left hand, but paused before he touched her. "May I?"

"Of course."

It wasn't until he was slipping the gold band she'd worn for the last few weeks off her finger that she realized he also wore a new band, platinum to match the rings he'd presented to her. She grabbed for the gold band as he moved to pocket it.

"I like our original rings," she said, a lump forming in her throat that she couldn't quite explain.

"They're cheap."

"Inexpensive," she countered.

"It'll probably turn your finger green."

"Hasn't yet."

He paused, meeting her eyes, and placed the gold band in her palm.

"Where's yours?" she asked.

"In my pocket."

"You didn't get rid of it?"

He swallowed hard, his Adam's apple bobbing. "Seemed wasteful."

"But buying new rings wasn't?"

His eyes darted up to hers and away, back to her hand as he carefully removed the engagement ring from the box and slid it onto her finger. "Maybe we needed real rings."

Her fingers clenched around the small gold band hidden in her palm. "We already had real rings."

He paused with the wedding band halfway down her finger. His eyes narrowed as he examined the new jewelry on her finger. "Are these..." He cleared his throat and started again. "Are these not good?" His eyes flicked to hers and then back to the rings, but in that flash she saw the insecurity scrabbling for purchase. Her chest ached at the vulnerability there, how young and unsure he seemed in that moment, this man who was always sure of everything. "The jeweler said—"

"They're perfect." His eyes flicked to hers again, the doubt written in the tension in his lips and the furrow between his brows. "Really, Sebastian. They're beautiful. But it wasn't necessary. That's all."

He exhaled hard through his nose and finished sliding the wedding band into place, his fingers lingering for a moment to trace the line of the two bands against her skin. "It was. For me."

His fingers drifted from the rings across her palm, settling against her wrist. Each stroke of his fingertips against the sensitive skin there sent tendrils of hope through her nerve endings, wrapping themselves around her heart and squeezing.

*Stupid traitorous heart. Add it to the list of treasonous organs.*

"Give me five minutes," she said, gently pulling her hand away and slipping past him to get to her bedroom.

"I'll give you ten," he said, turning to face her. His tone was joking but his eyes held hers with such weight she felt it drop into her belly, like a stone sinking into the ocean, cushioned only by the faint wrinkles at the corners of his eyes and the quirk of his lips.

*You will not kiss him again. You will not let yourself hope for more with this man who has already told you he doesn't want that.*

She slipped inside the bedroom, pausing before she closed the door. "Thank you, Sebastian. Not just for the rings, but for coming with me this weekend. For…for all of it."

He nodded, a barely perceptible dip of his chin, and held her gaze as she closed the door. She pressed her forehead to the door, forcing air into her lungs, willing those tendrils wrapped around her heart to loosen enough to ease the ache settling into her chest.

*You will not fall for your husband.*

The two-story, red brick home of Maryann and Richard Page sat at the top of a winding, tree-lined driveway, the paving stones meandering across the lush, green lawn until they came to a stop at the front entrance of the sprawling home. In the golden light of the late summer early evening, the house seemed to glow, as though the Pages had arranged for spotlights to highlight the most imposing angles of the gabled roof, to draw attention to the ivy and wisteria climbing one side of the structure. Baz wouldn't have been surprised if they had.

Baz had only been inside the monstrosity of a home once, on the evening of his and Holly's engagement party, when Maryann and Richard had gathered together all of their wealthiest friends to celebrate their daughter's impending marriage. He hadn't needed to stand on the gleaming hardwood floors in rooms decorated as though white were an entire color palette unto itself to know he didn't belong.

But that was before.

A lot had changed in the intervening years. His suit was no longer too large, hanging from the slight shoulders of a man who lost himself so thoroughly in his work that he forgot to stop for meals. Instead, he'd had this suit custom tailored to highlight the new breadth of his frame, the taut musculature he'd cultivated as carefully as he'd cultivated his new wardrobe. His shoes weren't damp from where the rainwater had slipped through a worn patch on the sole, but shined from their latest polishing, the leather supple and a perfect match for his belt.

*And now you're here with the other sister.*

Baz parked his car beneath the linden tree at the top of the driveway and waited. Sabrina had hardly said a word as they'd approached her family home, her spine stiffening, shoulders pulling back into the posture of a woman who had been frequently scolded for slouching. Her fingers closed around the new rings on her left hand, twisting the metal bands around and around, as her eyes fixed on the light spilling from the front windows of the house.

"How did we meet?" she asked, a strain in her voice that Baz didn't recognize.

He fumbled for an answer to her question, not sure how to say, *You knocked over a rack of donated produce at the food pantry and we spent the better part of the afternoon trying to sort twenty types of squash into their correct bins again—don't you remember?*

"I mean," she said, turning to face him, her back still perfectly straight, "how did we reconnect? They'll want to know how this happened." She gestured between them, then returned to twisting her rings.

"We could say your aunt—"

She shook her head firmly. "Aunt Lucy would have told my mom. Have you ever been to Maine?"

"Maine?"

"Kennebunkport, yes. Have you ever been there?"

"Maybe?"

"We could say we ran into each other when I was still living there. You were visiting friends, or on vacation. Six months ago, maybe? Does that seem long enough for us to have...for it to become...for—"

"For us to fall in love?" She gave a wide-eyed nod, the speed of her ring turning increasing. He knocked her hand away and laced his fingers through hers, suddenly overcome with the urge to touch her, to settle the constant hum of anxiety that seemed to surround her since they'd cross the state line. "I ran into you in a bar."

"Coffee shop," she corrected.

His lip twitched with the urge to smile. "A coffee shop, then. We exchanged numbers."

"We stayed in touch," she said, her gaze locked on the glide of his thumb back and forth over the back of her hand. "The occasional phone call turned weekly. Then daily. We stayed up talking until all hours of the night. Since neither of us could sleep anyway."

His gut twisted with longing for those late-night phone calls they'd never have, for the hours of making her laugh, listening to her ramble. For falling asleep with the phone pressed to his ear. For the easy courtship, the morphing of friends to something more. For the inevitability of it, the security of it.

He'd never considered himself a romantic, but he could picture it, how it would be to fall for Sabrina. It would be as easy as breathing, a slow slide into a warm pool and, before he could realize he didn't know how to swim, he'd already be floating. He could imagine how it would feel to spend his day waiting to crawl into bed so he could hear her voice. It wouldn't be all that different from the way it felt now to crawl into bed and hold his breath so he could hear each shift of her skin beneath the sheets on the other side of the guest room wall.

When was the last time he'd *wanted* the way Sabrina made him want?

*Careful...*

"And then you moved back to Aster Bay," he said.

"To Aunt Lucy's at first. I wouldn't have wanted to put any pressure on you. I mean, what if we met again in person and this...what if it wasn't as good as it had felt from a distance? But it would have been a silly thing to worry about."

"Not silly. Pragmatic."

She loosed a startled laugh. "As if any of this is pragmatic."

He grinned despite himself and let his thumb drift over the ring on her finger, straightening the diamond solitaire until it lined up perfectly with the tiny sparkling gems embedded in the matching band.

"And then Vegas?" he asked.

"The least pragmatic of all." A deep crease formed between her brows as she lifted her face to his. "Do you think they'll believe it?"

With his free hand he smoothed her furrowed brow, the back of his hand grazing her cheek as he lowered it. "Of course."

"Really?"

"I almost believe it myself."

Her eyes widened, a look somewhere between panic and pain swirling amongst the green of her irises.

*Shit. That was too honest.*

She opened her mouth to speak, but a sharp knocking on the drivers' side window cut her off.

They turned to see the exasperated face of Maryann Page peering through the window, her lips twisted into a purse that emphasized the pink lipstick seeping into the crevices around her mouth. Baz lowered the window and pasted on his most neutral smile, the one he used with new clients and customer service representatives.

"Are you two going to sit in the car all evening?" she demanded. "Your father and I are waiting."

"I apologize, Maryann," he said as Sabrina's hand tightened its hold on his. "We were just about to come in."

Maryann harrumphed, clearly annoyed that she couldn't continue scolding her daughter over the perceived slight. "Yes, well, come along then." She marched off across the flag stone without waiting to see if they followed.

"So it begins," Sabrina said under her breath.

# Chapter Sixteen

"What was that?" Sabrina whispered to Sebastian as they walked, hand-in-hand, towards her parents' front door.

"What?"

"*I apologize, Maryann,*" she said, lowering her voice in a poor imitation of his rich baritone.

He shot an amused glance her way. "That's not what I sound like."

"*Yes, Maryann. Of course, Maryann. May I lick your boots, Maryann?*" she continued.

He stopped, turning to meet her eyes, the corner of his mouth quirking up. What a rush, to make this man smile, even a half smile.

"May I *lick your boots*?" he repeated.

She shrugged and bit the inside of her cheeks to keep from laughing, "If you're into that sort of thing."

He chuckled and turned back towards the door where her mother now hovered, sighing theatrically, and pulled Sabrina along with him. Sabrina's smile broke free, the exasperated laughter in his eyes easing some of the tension that had wrapped around her spine on the drive to Brookline. She liked needling him, liked watching him try to pretend he wasn't amused by her, almost as much as she liked the feel of his hand in hers.

"Richard! Sabrina and Baz are here!" Maryann shouted as she turned away from the door and disappeared down the hall, continuing to shout her husband's name.

Sebastian mounted the first step, but Sabrina froze, like her mother's bellowing had brought back every time she'd ever visited this house and it had gone poorly. Why had she agreed to come? To bring Sebastian? She tugged on his hand until he stepped back down.

"Let's make a break for it," she hissed.

"What?"

"We could get back in your car and go. Before they come back. Dad's probably still mixing his gin and tonic. We could get gone before—"

"Get gone?" His eyes searched the sky above her head as though he'd find the answer for how to deal with her written in the stars. "I thought you wanted to come here."

"I didn't *want* to. I *had* to."

"Why?"

"Because—because I did. But this was a mistake. I shouldn't have brought you here."

He stiffened, his jaw going tight, and he pulled his hand from hers, stuffing it into his pants pocket. "If you didn't want me to come, you could have said something before we sat in traffic for two hours."

"It's not that I didn't want you to come."

"That's what it sounds like to me."

"*I* didn't want to come."

"What are you two standing out there for?" Sabrina's father's voice cut through the air as he appeared in the open doorway. "Come in, come in. Can't stand here all evening with the door open."

Sebastian turned to her father and extended his hand as he climbed the steps. "Richard. Good to see you again, sir."

"Baz." Her father shook his hand, the ice in the gin and tonic clutched in his other hand rattling against the glass. His voice was several degrees colder when he turned his attention to her. "Sabrina. I expect you to apologize to your mother. Running off and getting married without so much as a note to let us know you were even engaged." He shook his head. "Your mother was devastated."

"It was my fault, Richard," Sebastian said, his back ramrod straight and that muscle in his jaw ticking away. "We got carried away. You know how it is."

She hardly recognized this sanitized version of Sebastian, as though he were some kind of politician, scraping his rough edges smooth to fit until he could fit his entire personality into a soundbite.

She hated it.

Her father ran a wary look over Sabrina, the hardness of his gaze a clear repetition of his demand that she apologize, before returning his attention to Sebastian. "Women do know how to make a man behave irrationally. I can hardly blame you for that," he laughed, heedless of the way Sebastian's eyes narrowed. But her father was not one to be deterred. He clapped Sebastian on the shoulder and continued on, as though he hadn't accused his daughter of somehow confounding Sebastian's good sense. "I hear you've built yourself quite an impressive firm down in Rhode Island. Good for you, son."

"Thank you, sir."

He led Sebastian into the house, barely sparing a glance for Sabrina. "Can I get you a drink? Maryann's stocked the bar cart with the best for tomorrow's shindig."

Sebastian glanced over his shoulder at Sabrina as she trailed behind them, closing the front door with a soft click. She tried to send him a reassuring smile as her father led him down the hall towards the study where Sabrina knew a small fortune in alcohol waited to impress the guests her parents entertained, but she barely managed a strained tip of her lips. Sabrina's mother reappeared in the large entrance hall, skidding to a stop a few feet from her daughter.

"Where are your bags?" her mother asked, holding her hands out as though her daughter's luggage would magically appear.

"Hi, Mom. Good to see you."

Her mother rolled her eyes. "Did you leave them in the car? We'll have to send Baz out to fetch them later. Your father has already corralled him for a drink, I'm sure, and you know how he hates to be interrupted while he's enjoying his gin and tonic."

Sabrina did know. Once, when she was about eight, she'd made the mistake of bursting into her father's study after returning home from a week at sleepaway camp, desperate to show him the collection of pinch pots she'd made. She'd had visions of him displaying them in his office alongside the photos of him and his clients on the golf course, the engraved knickknacks from various charities in recognition of his law firm's donations. "Sabrina, can't you see I'm busy?" he'd said instead. No greeting for his youngest daughter who hadn't seen him in seven days. No interest in the bits of pottery spilling from her small hands.

It was the last time she'd attempted to impress her father with her art.

"Well, let's see it." Her mother looked at Sabrina expectantly.

"See what?"

"The *ring*, Sabrina. What else?"

Sabrina lifted her left hand, allowing her mother to snatch at it and lean close, inspecting the bands on her finger. Her mother hummed to herself, tilting Sabrina's hand to see how the diamond caught the light. "Not bad," she said at last, releasing her hand. "White gold, I assume?"

"I think they're platinum."

Her mother's eyebrows shot up her forehead. "Not bad at all."

Was that *approval* in her mother's half smile? Surely not. Surely Sabrina wasn't seeing that look on her mother's face for the first time in years because Sebastian had picked a set of rings with a ridiculous price tag.

*To think, all I had to do to get my mother's approval was marry a man with money.* The thought left a bitter taste on her tongue.

"Come. The men will join us in the parlor when they're done with their little chat. I wanted a moment to speak to you alone." Her mother led her through the high archways of the front entrance hall to a formal sitting room decorated in shades of beige and cream. Her mother moved straight to the drink cart—a cart in every room, it seemed—and filled a glass with ice and vodka as she continued. "Your father had all the paperwork drawn up last week. All you need to do is sign."

"What paperwork?"

Her mother handed her a thick envelope. She peeled back the flap and her stomach sank. "Mom, Sebastian and I don't need a post-nuptial agreement."

"Like you and Jordan didn't need a pre-nup?" Her mother shot her a pointed look. "If you'd listened to us about that in the first place, you never would have lost your studio in Maine."

"I didn't lose it —"

"You wouldn't have been forced to sell because he never would have had his grubby fingers on your business in the first place. You're opening a new business, Sabrina, and suddenly you're married all over again. Don't repeat the same mistakes. Sign the papers and get Baz to sign too."

"Ah, there you are," her father said, appearing at the opposite entrance to the room with Sebastian in tow.

Sabrina shoved the envelope behind the bottles of liquor on the drink cart and scanned Sebastian's person for signs of distress, but found nothing more than a stilted posture and an untouched glass of Scotch. Her father ushered his new son-in-law into the room and joined her mother in a pair of armchairs opposite the settee.

*Right. So it's to be an interrogation.*

The last time Sabrina had sat on that settee with a boy was before her senior prom. JT Prindiville, who her father had insisted on calling Jeffrey, knew all the right things to say, when he should laugh, when he should nod along in solemn agreement. Her parents had been thrilled to see her with such a suitable prom date. Never mind that JT Prindiville had grabbed her ass when they posed for pictures on the curved staircase in the entrance hall, or that he'd flung himself on top of her in the limo as soon as they'd left her driveway, insisting that she owed him at least a kiss for picking out such an expensive corsage. She shuddered at the memory as she sank down onto the stiff cushion, Sebastian at her side.

"You alright?" he asked softly.

She nodded. "You? Dad wasn't too hard on you?"

"Grilled me on my projections for the next fiscal year." She sucked in a breath, and he turned inquisitive eyes her way. "It's fine. The business is solid."

"I didn't—I wasn't trying to imply—"

"Stop whispering, Sabrina. It's rude," her mother snapped.

Sebastian's eyes narrowed, his forehead creasing, but she gave him a tiny shake of her head. "Sorry, Mom."

"*That* she apologizes for," her mother huffed. "Not neglecting to tell me my youngest daughter got married. Not robbing me of the chance to help you pick out a dress or plan the wedding. We didn't even know you two were seeing each other." Her eyes darted to Sabrina's stomach and back to her face. "You're not pregnant, are you?"

It shouldn't have hurt so much, the implication that Sebastian had only married her because she was pregnant, the suggestion that she'd somehow made an even bigger mess of her life than they already suspected. And something darker. An old frustration twisting in her gut. Did her mother not remember the hours of doctor's visits, the ER trips, the prognosis handed down to her at sixteen, when she was too young to understand how deeply her PCOS would impact her life?

Sebastian's hand slid into her own, lacing their fingers together and squeezing tightly. "We're not pregnant," he said with a chuckle that sounded nothing like him at all. "Just impulsive."

"At least now it makes sense why you abandoned your business in Maine and moved back to Aster Bay," her mother continued, only slightly mollified by Sebastian's social graces.

"I didn't abandon it. Jordan bought me out." A storm gathered behind her eyes, and Sabrina imagined the scribbled clouds of twisting lines cartoonists added to thought bubbles to indicate consternation. She imagined one of those clouds forming deep in her brain, knotting together veins and tendons into a giant scribble of a headache.

"For a song, I'm sure," her father muttered. "If you'd gone to business school like you were supposed to—"

"Then I wouldn't have had the studio in the first place."

Sebastian's gaze ping-ponged back and forth between Sabrina and her parents, the crease in his brow deepening, as though he were trying to make sense of the hostility that thickened the air.

"Sabrina is a brilliant businesswoman," he said, squeezing her hand, though he held her father's gaze without wavering. "In fact, that's what we were doing in Las Vegas in the first place. She was chosen by the town's Merchants' Association to be their representative at a business conference." He looked at her fondly, tucking a strand of hair behind her ear. "She's been appointed to the Food and Wine Festival committee and she's already started teaching the other business owners in town how to use game theory to increase tourism. And her new studio will open very soon."

"Another studio," her mother humphed, as though she hadn't heard anything else Sebastian said.

But Sabrina wasn't listening to their muttered concessions. She was too stunned by Sebastian's praise. Did he really mean that? Did he really think she was…brilliant?

"How's your golf game these days?" her father asked Sebastian, shifting topics as if he and her mother hadn't just picked apart her life choices for the umpteenth time. "Sheldon and I have an early tee time tomorrow. I'm sure we could squeeze in another player."

If Sebastian was bothered by the mention of his former fiancée's husband, he didn't show it. "I'm afraid I'd only hold you back. Golf isn't really my game."

"You'll hardly want to stay here with the ladies." Her father laughed at the ridiculousness of the notion.

Sebastian glanced at Sabrina before raising their clasped hands to his mouth and brushing his lips over her knuckles. "Don't be so sure," he said to her father.

Her stomach swooped.

*You will not believe a word that comes out of his mouth tonight when he's turned into some kind of Stepford husband. You will not read into the heat in his eyes and the little touches. You will not believe your own lies.*

# Chapter Seventeen

The rest of the evening passed in a blur—Baz and Richard discussing the stock market, Maryann not-so-subtly reminding Sabrina to dress appropriately for the party tomorrow—and before Baz knew it, Maryann had shown them to the guest room in the south wing of the house.

Once they were alone, he toed off his shoes by the door and loosened his tie. Sabrina flopped backwards on the bed, spreading her arms and legs like a starfish—well, at least as far as the form-fitting skirt of her dress would allow. The fabric slid up her thighs as she stretched out on the bed, revealing another few inches of creamy skin. Taunting him. Tempting him.

"That was awful," she sighed.

"Not as bad as I expected."

She turned her head to face him, her eyes tracking the movement of the muscles beneath his shirt as he set aside his jacket and unbuttoned his vest. Christ, he liked her eyes on him too much.

"What did you expect? A literal firing squad?"

He slipped off his vest and set it on top of his jacket. "They were more welcoming than I thought they'd be."

"To you, maybe." She sighed and returned to staring at the ceiling.

"Your mom is put out she didn't get to plan the wedding. She'll get over it and—"

"She's always like this."

He sat on the bed beside her as he pulled his tie over his head, tossing it onto the pile with his other clothes. And then he waited for her to say whatever else was swirling through her mind, whatever it was that put that crease back between her eyes. She drew in a shaky breath, and when she spoke, she kept her eyes focused on the ceiling.

"When I said earlier that I shouldn't have asked you to come… That wasn't about you. They were always going to like *you.*"

"They didn't like me when I was engaged to Holly."

"That wasn't about you either."

"Then what was it about?"

She gave a little half shrug, her eyes still fixed on some unseen spot on the ceiling. Baz lay down beside her, nudging her over to make room for him, and fixed his own eyes on the ceiling. More white. Though Maryann probably had a fancy name for this particular shade of white. Ecru, or alabaster, or snow drift.

"When I said that earlier, what I meant was, you're already doing this amazing thing for me. With the health insurance. It was selfish to ask you to put on a show for my parents. To put you in a position to have to defend me. To tell them I'm a good businesswoman," she said with a self-deprecating laugh.

"I believe I said *brilliant.*" He turned his head to watch her.

"You only think that because you don't know me very well."

"I didn't say anything tonight that I didn't mean." Her eyes drifted his way, but only for a moment before she fixed them back on the ceiling. "What happened in Maine?" he asked softly.

Her lips contorted into a look of disgust, her eyes narrowing as they turned glassy. "My studio was thriving. People traveled from all over to book one of my break-up parties."

*Ahh yes, the infamous penis smashing parties.* He'd ask more about *that* later.

"I had a good life there. I had a regular coffee shop and the woman who cut my hair knew exactly how I liked it and I lived in a house where I could walk down to the beach to read at night. And I had Jordan."

Baz held his breath, his heart pounding. He hated this guy already.

"His pottery was locally famous, and he had mastered this decorative technique—sgraffito. No one could do it like him."

Her voice had gotten small, brittle, and all he wanted to do was gather her in his arms and hold her. But that wasn't what this was. A few nights of whispering through the wall and one kiss—no matter how incendiary—didn't give him the right to treat her like she was his. She wouldn't want that anyway. Right?

"We got married three years ago, right after I sold him half the business." Baz sucked in a breath and instantly hated himself for it when she winced in response. "That was my parents' reaction too. They hated him from the beginning. My dad refused to give him his blessing before we got married." She paused, shaking her head, though whether she was disappointed in her ex or her father, Baz wasn't sure. "I thought we were going to be partners—in everything. I thought he loved me."

"What happened?" He hardly recognized the deadly calm of his voice.

"He was having an affair with the florist next door." She turned her head to look at him then, a tear sliding over the bridge of her nose and into the comforter beneath her cheek. He brushed the pad of his thumb over her cheek to wipe away the trail it left behind. "He said he wanted a family. Children. And I…" She blinked away the ghosts in her eyes, tucking away whatever she'd been about to say, and continued. "He didn't want me anymore. He said he wanted it to be easy. To marry her. They'd already decided which room to turn into a nursery.

In the house *we* lived in together. The house that was only in his name. They'd picked out wallpaper and everything."

Baz couldn't take the sadness in her eyes. He wrapped her up in his arms, bundling her against him. Her arms went around his waist and she let him clasp her to him, nestling her beneath his chin as he loosed a string of muttered curses and oaths to castrate the man if he ever crossed his path.

She buried her face in his chest and exhaled the last of her story. "He wouldn't give up his half of the business. Of the studio *I* built. I didn't want to leave my little house and my coffee shop and the life I'd made for myself there. But the divorce had been dragging on for over a year. And the florist who slept in my bed with my husband was pregnant. He was never going to let me have the business. He said he needed it to support his new family. I let him buy me out so I could be done with it. To be done with him."

He rubbed circles over her back, pressed a kiss into her hair, even as his stomach dropped. "You were still in love with him."

"What? No." She pushed herself up enough to meet his eyes. "No. I realized as soon as he told me about the affair that I didn't love him anymore. Maybe I never had. Maybe I was stupid and mistook infatuation for something more." Her eyes scanned his. "I am not still in love with him." Baz swallowed around the lump forming in his throat and tilted his chin to show he believed her. "I couldn't stay there and watch the bastard run *my* business. He turned the place into a paint-your-own-mug thing, a glorified bar with a side of arts and crafts. I needed to start over. So I left."

Her eyes blazed with anger. She'd never looked more beautiful.

"Why Aster Bay?"

Her eyes dropped to his lips before returning to meet his gaze, and his hands suddenly felt heavy, clumsy as he settled one on her hip.

"Aunt Lucy is there. And it seemed like a good place to open a pottery studio. Quirky small town stuff, you know? And…"

"And?"

"And you were there."

He sucked in a breath, some wild, impulsive thing crashing around inside his ribs, like a bird let loose in too small of a cage. "You thought I hated you." His hand slid across her lower back, shifting her closer, settling her hips against his own.

Her tongue darted out to wet her lips as she nodded, the painted nails on one of her hands digging into his bicep. "I wanted to be close to you. Even if you hated me."

"Why?"

A pretty pink spread over her cheeks and he imagined where else she was pretty and pink. He ached for her, a fact she must have known with their bodies pressed so tightly together.

"Because you were the last person to look at me like maybe I was something special."

"No maybe about it, wildflower."

Her eyes darted all over his face, tracing his brows and the line of his jaw, his lips and the slope of his nose. He felt each sweep of her gaze like a fingertip on his skin, a touch too soft to be satisfying, too heavy to be ignored. He wanted her eyes on him all the time, on every part of him. Wanted to watch as she mapped the muscles of his torso, as she discovered the carved lines at his hips. Wanted to see the realization dawn in her eyes that the thick ridge of his cock pressing into her belly was hard for her. To peel back the layers of her fancy clothes and be the one to uncover the real Sabrina beneath.

She rocked her hips against him and he sucked in a breath, his hands digging into her soft curves to keep her still. With that one small movement, he knew how it would be between them. The way they'd burn so brightly it would hurt, how she'd burrow under his skin and stay there long after they'd gone their separate ways.

And maybe that was okay. Maybe he couldn't be the man she wanted forever, but he could be the man she wanted right now. He wasn't made for forevers. Maybe this, right now, the two of them together, maybe that would be enough.

"Sebastian?"

"Yeah?"

"Kiss me."

# Chapter Eighteen

This kiss was nothing like any of the ones that came before it. Sebastian ran his nose along the line of Sabrina's jaw, breathing in her scent, before he pressed his forehead to hers, their lips close enough that she could feel each exhale as a puff of air against her skin. When she was about to scream from the anticipation, he set his mouth against hers.

Soft.

So light she would have sworn she'd dreamt it if she weren't plastered along the length of him, if she couldn't feel the tension in his muscles and the pulsing heat of his growing erection caught between their bodies.

Then his lips were back, firmer this time, exploring, but still not nearly enough. She wanted more, wanted to lose herself in the feel of him, in the fantasy that this man—her husband— was really hers. That they weren't on borrowed time.

She caught his bottom lip between her teeth and a low growl sounded in his throat before he dug a hand into her hair, cradling her head as he flipped them over until he was on top of her. His weight pressed her into the mattress, her hips pinned beneath his.

He kissed her in earnest then, using his grip on her hair to angle her head the way he wanted it, and licked into her mouth. It was filthy and delicious and still she wanted more. He cupped her breast through her dress and she silently cursed every layer of fabric between them, every inch of her skin that wasn't touching his. He trailed his lips over her jaw, licking at the sensitive spot beneath her ear. She sighed happily and rocked her hips up against him to feel his hardness between her legs.

He chuckled darkly, the kind of laugh that conjured images of being tied to his bed, of being completely at his mercy, of every filthy fantasy she'd ever had about him. He pulled back to look at her, gave her breast one more firm squeeze before trailing his hand back down to her hip. "We should stop."

"No." She fisted her hands in his shirt and tugged him towards her. "I don't want to stop."

His eyes were wary as they assessed her. "You've had an emotional day. I don't want to take advantage of you."

She huffed out a frustrated breath that instigated a quirk from the corner of his lip. "It's not taking advantage if I'm asking you to do it. And I *am* asking you, Sebastian."

"Asking me to do what exactly? To kiss you?" He dropped a kiss to the hollow of her throat. "To touch you?" His fingers trailed up her thigh, stopping just beneath the hem of her dress. "To fuck you?"

"Yes. All of the above."

"We agreed to a marriage in name only. Some health insurance. Playacting around our parents. Sex wasn't part of our deal," he said, but those fingers kept climbing higher, pushing her skirt up as they went.

"Then I want a new deal," she huffed, something hot and needy twisting between her legs.

"Why?"

"What do you mean, *why*?" She ground her hips against him, and he cursed under his breath, tightening his hold on her hip.

"Tell me why, Sabrina."

His tone was as icy as his eyes, and she didn't understand it. He obviously wanted her—he could probably do some serious damage with the steel bar he was walking around with between his legs—but there was something else there too. Something she couldn't quite make sense of, like he didn't *want* to want her. Like he had kissed her more out of instinct than desire. Like he half hated himself for the mindless way he rocked against her.

"Because we're obviously attracted to each other."

"I'm attracted to plenty of people I don't fuck."

"Because we're married."

"For now."

*Okay, ouch.*

"Then we might as well enjoy it while it lasts."

His eyes scanned hers, narrowing slightly, as though he were searching for the lie, for the part of her that knew if she slept with Sebastian, she'd never get over him. Who was she kidding? She'd probably never get over him anyway. If ten years, a failed marriage, and Sebastian's misdirected hatred hadn't gotten him out of her system, it was unlikely anything would.

Maybe that was the real reason why she wanted him. Because this—wanting him—was going to destroy her either way. She might as well wring every last drop of pleasure out of this arrangement while she could.

He sat back on his heels and she let out an impatient huff as she scooted back on the bed until her back was against the headboard.

"I'm not fucking you here," he said. She opened her mouth to protest, but he continued on before she could, his voice a low resonance that sent goosebumps prickling over her skin. "When I fuck my wife for the first time, it won't be with her parents down the hall. It'll be somewhere I can make you scream." She shivered, her breathing coming faster, and a slow half smile tilted up the corner of his lips. "You like that idea?"

"Yes."

"Good. Hike up your dress."

Her eyes darted to his. "I thought you said we weren't—"

"We're not going to fuck, but that doesn't mean you can't come. Now pull up that dress and show me what's mine, wife."

*Holy shit.* She should have known Sebastian would be the dirtiest of dirty talkers.

She scrambled to comply, hiking her dress up over her hips and letting her knees fall open, revealing the gusset of her thong. His eyes fixed to the spot, to where she knew the cotton was already damp. Who needed a physical touch when he could look at her like that, when he could make her clit pulse with the power of his gaze alone?

"Show me," he demanded.

She trailed her fingers down to her panties, hooking her finger over the edge of the fabric, and stopped. With a lick of her lips, she met his eyes again. "You first."

His eyes blazed as his hand dropped to his belt, undoing the buckle singlehandedly. He held her gaze as he lowered his zipper and reached into his pants, watched her like a dare until she broke the connection to steal a look at the hard cock in his hand.

*Good lord.*

Sabrina wasn't generally inclined to describe a cock as beautiful—she made and smashed replicas of the organ for a living, after all—but there was no other word to describe Sebastian in that moment, his hand wrapped tightly around the base of the thickest, most perfectly shaped dick she'd ever seen. He ran his hand up the length of it, a slow pump that highlighted the raised vein along the side, the angry red flare of its tip. And there, at the crown, a shiny silver barbell piercing vertically straight through the tip.

She sucked in a breath and felt more than saw his answering smirk. "You're pierced."

He nodded once, another slow pump. This time his thumb

skated over the ball on the underside of the piercing. "It's called an apadravya."

Like she could remember some long, fancy word for penis jewelry at a time like this. Sebastian Graham had a *pierced cock* and—maybe not tonight, but someday—he was going to fuck her with it. A fresh rush of wetness pooled between her thighs and she ached to know what it would feel like to have him inside her.

Another slow pump. She was mesmerized by his movements. "Your turn, wildflower."

*Right. My turn. Stop staring at his dick. Even if it is staring at me too.*

She slid her panties to the side, the cool air on her exposed skin somehow making this whole thing even more erotic.

"Open yourself up for me, baby. Let me see where you want me."

Using her thumbs, she parted her lips, revealing every inch of herself to his hungry gaze. His cock kicked in his hand, a bead of precum sliding down the tip as he continued his slow strokes.

"Such a pretty little pussy," he purred. "I can see how wet you are from here." She whimpered, her hips rocking up against air as he examined her. "Are you ready to come, baby?"

"Yes, please, Sebastian," she groaned, dropping her knees farther apart.

"Show me how you get yourself off." Her breath caught in her chest and she tore her eyes away from the world's most perfect cock to meet his challenging stare. He chuckled again, the sound like a spark racing down her spine. "I want to watch my wife play with her pussy. Now be a good girl and show me how you make yourself come."

Tentatively, she let her index finger ghost over her clit, barely enough to test how stiff and swollen she already was. What she wouldn't give for it to be his finger, his tongue. Another slow swipe and then she dipped her finger into her wetness, drawing it back up to her clit as she began to stroke in earnest. Small, tight circles that had her wishing she'd thought to pack a bullet vibe, but no, like a fool she'd left her toys at home.

"How does it feel?" he asked, his own hand moving faster over his erection.

"It's not enough." She dropped her head back and cursed. She wasn't going to be able to come like this.

"What do you need?"

"You," she said on a desperate laugh. But he seemed unamused by this answer. "I usually use a vibrator," she admitted softly.

He hummed, a dark sound low in his throat that had her nipples furling so tightly they stung. "I'd like to see that."

She lifted her head to see his face again. "You would?"

Another hum. Christ, this man could get her worked up just with his *noises*.

"I can't wait to use your toys on you. Get you one that sucks on your clit while I fuck your tight little pussy." He grunted as his hand moved faster, as though the image were making him as desperate as it was making her. "Get that clit all nice and plump for me, so stiff and sensitive that you'll hardly be able to take it when I lick you. But you will take it. Won't you, baby?"

"Yes—oh, God, Sebastian."

Her orgasm shimmered out of reach, a tantalizing mirage she could almost touch.

"Fuck, I won't be able to stop playing with that pussy. Need to keep you wet for me all the time. Ready for me to slide in and give us what we both need." His hand was flying now, almost as fast as her own. She couldn't have looked away if she tried, hypnotized by Sebastian Graham and his filthy words and his beautiful, pierced cock. "Tell me how it feels."

"It's—Keep talking."

"You like when I say dirty things to you?"

"Fuck, yes," she whimpered.

"Will you let me do all the dirty things I talk about, wildflower? What if I tell you I want to fuck your pretty mouth, smear that lipstick all over my cock? What if I want to make you come over and over until you beg me to stop, until you can't remember what it felt like not to have my cock inside you?" She nodded, a whimpered sound that might have been agreement. "Put two fingers inside yourself. Show me how you like to be filled up."

She drove two fingers from her free hand inside, pumping them between her legs and pressing on her front wall. A shiver jolted through her, and Sebastian growled a command for her to do it again. Her thighs began to quiver. She was so close. *So close.*

"You're going to let me play with your pussy any time I want, aren't you, baby? In the middle of the goddamn grocery store, if I want to pinch that little clit, you'll spread your legs and say please. Isn't that right, wife?"

"Yes," she gasped, her abdominal muscles shaking. *Oh God, was she actually going to come just from her fingers and his filthy words?*

"I'll make it so fucking good for you, wildflower. Let you bounce on my cock while I take my fucking conference calls. Finger your pretty pussy while you're teaching your pottery classes. That's what you want, isn't it? You want me to make you come."

"Sebastian please!"

"Fucking come, Sabrina," he commanded.

And she did. Fireworks shooting down her spine, a searing heat behind her clit radiating outward as she curled in on herself. Her clit pulsed beneath her fingers as her hips drove up into her hand, her mouth open on a silent scream. Sebastian grunted as he furiously stroked his fist over his length, and then his cock somehow grew longer, thicker, and white ropes of cum spurted over his hand. He fell forward, bracing himself on one hand as his other continued to pump himself until every last drop had been expended.

When at last it was over, he took hold of the back of her neck and pulled her to him, crashing their mouths together in a kiss that was more teeth than lips. Dropping back onto his heels, he dragged a hand over his jaw and met her eyes, the icy blue a mere ring around his blown pupils. He took her hand, the one that had been inside her, and sucked her fingers into his mouth, scraping them clean with his tongue and teeth. But it was the open-mouthed kiss he pressed to her palm that eviscerated her, made her want to gather him into her arms and whisper all her secrets.

"You still want that new deal?" he asked.

"Yes! Of course."

How could he possibly think she wouldn't after he'd painted all those obscene images with his words? She wanted all of it, things she'd never considered before, things she couldn't imagine doing with anyone else.

He nodded once, tucking himself back into his pants as he climbed off the bed and made for the en suite. "Here's to enjoying it while it lasts then."

*While it lasts.*

*Oh, God. What did I do?*

# Chapter Nineteen

Labor Day in Aster Bay meant two things: the carnival set up shop on the Town Common, and Jamie and Ethan threw a huge barbeque at Nuthatch Vineyard for their families and friends. This was the first year since they were in college that Baz wasn't standing next to the grill giving Jamie shit while he cooked corn and burgers. What Baz wouldn't give to be having a beer with the guys instead of listening to one of Richard's work associates drone on about the failure of the local Historic District Commission to enforce the restrictions on acceptable signage colors.

Except if he had stayed in Aster Bay this weekend, he and Sabrina might never have given in to the sexual tension between them. He might never have seen her come apart on her own fingers while he said filthy, depraved things to her, things that made her face flush and her eyes go liquid. He certainly wouldn't have woken with her tucked against his chest. He wouldn't have agreed to be fuck buddies with his wife.

Despite his cock's adamant declarations to the contrary, he knew this was a terrible idea. As he tried to feign interest in the conversation about which shade of blue was most acceptable for restaurant signage, his eyes kept seeking Sabrina out. A flash of red hair across the lawn, a whiff of her wildflower scent on the breeze. But who could blame him? She was by far the most beautiful woman at this party—and not merely because he'd had the pleasure of seeing her naked the night before.

Well, not *completely* naked. Christ, they'd never even undressed. They were doing this all out of order.

*What does that matter? It's not a real marriage. It's just sex. And health insurance. And pretending to be in love.*

Which was really for the better, if Baz was honest with himself. After all, what did he know about being in love? He'd already made the mistake of thinking one Page woman was in love with him, and he saw no reason to revisit that particular brand of humiliation a second time around with her sister. It was just fucking and a convenient arrangement, making lemonade from lemons or whatever that saying was.

But then Sabrina caught his eye from across the lawn where she stood, alone for the first time all day, and her lips curved up in the smallest of smiles. He excused himself from the dullest conversation known to man and strode across the manicured grounds of her parents' home.

"Hi," he said, his eyes drinking her in. She wore a white dress in some kind of slippery, smooth material that hugged her curves and fell slightly above her knees. Bright red wedges the same shade she'd painted her lips and her ever-present gold chains disappearing into the neckline of her dress completed the look. Her hair fell around her shoulders in perfect waves that he knew she'd spent nearly an hour perfecting in the mirror of the guest room en suite.

"Hi," she said back, amusement tugging at the corner of her mouth. "Having fun?" He must have made a face, because she giggled, dipping her head as though she'd hide her smile from him. "I hear Marty has very strong opinions about signage colors. Maybe we should invite him to give a talk to the Merchants' Association."

"Don't you dare."

She laughed again, this time tilting her head back, her hair swaying around her shoulders. Christ, he liked making her laugh.

But the laughter died on her lips, her eyes shuttering themselves as they locked on something across the lawn. He looked over his shoulder, following her line of sight, to see Maryann making her way towards them with two older women, clearly intending to make introductions. He moved next to Sabrina and rested his hand on her lower back, a silent reminder that they were in this mess together.

"Sabrina, there you are!" Maryann said, exasperation coloring every flutter of her hands. "I've been looking all over for you. You remember Mrs. Prindiville and Mrs. Connolly."

"Of course," Sabrina said, her body swaying ever so slightly closer to Baz. "It's nice to see you both again."

"And this must be your husband. Baz, was it?" the one on the left—Mrs. Prindiville?—asked. "Maryann, he's even more handsome than I remembered."

"Sebastian Graham, ma'am. Nice to meet you," he said, holding out his free hand to shake hers and ignoring the implication that this woman had been at his almost wedding.

"Have we met before?" Mrs. Connolly asked, squinting her eyes as though that would help her place him. "You're not one of the Wellesley Grahams, are you?"

What was he supposed to say? *Yeah, we probably met back when I was engaged to my current wife's sister.*

"No, the Aster Bay Grahams."

As if sensing the potential for a social faux pas, Maryann grabbed Sabrina's left hand, holding it out to the other women, who were immediately distracted by the sparkling rings on her finger. Baz raised an eyebrow in Sabrina's direction, as if to say, *See, new rings were a good idea.* He might as well have said it out loud for the way Sabrina pursed her lips in response.

"Good job, young man," Mrs. Connolly said. "Maryann was

just telling us about your wedding."

"She was?" Sabrina asked, glancing at her mother.

"It sounds lovely. A small, intimate wedding out of town," Mrs. Connolly sighed dreamily. "So much more personal than these flashy weddings young people are having now-a-days."

"I know exactly what wedding you're thinking of, Karen," Mrs. Prindiville replied. "No daughter of Maryann's would be so gauche as to throw the kind of wedding the Hanley girl threw last spring." She dropped her voice conspiratorially and leaned towards Baz and Sabrina. "I hear her father had the flowers flown in on a private jet to make sure his daughter got the right color lilies."

"Oh," Sabrina said, glancing at Baz.

"Sounds…expensive," he said.

"I'm sure that was the point," Maryann replied with a smirk towards her friends.

"Your mother was telling us you're opening a new gallery in your husband's hometown. How enterprising of you," Mrs. Connolly gushed.

"I'm not sure I'd call it a gallery," Sabrina said, glancing at her mother.

"Of course, it's a *gallery*," Maryann laughed stiffly, her eyes bulging as she tried to communicate something to her daughter. "Sabrina specializes in ceramic sculptures."

Baz bit back a smirk. "She makes many of the sculptures herself."

Sabrina shot a panicked look his way as her mother's face paled.

"My Rebecca wanted to be an artist, you know. Loved to throw paint around like Jackson Pollock. Thank heavens her father talked her into going to law school with Holly instead!" Mrs. Connolly burst into laughter.

"Speaking of Holly," Mrs. Prindiville said, tilting her head towards the back of the house.

There, at the edge of the perfectly manicured lawn, was Baz's ex-fiancée. He braced for the anger he expected to come, the disgust, the hurt that had hollowed him out and left him devastated a decade before. Instead he found himself studying her, this woman he'd almost married, a woman he hardly knew—even then.

Her hair was dyed an almost-white blonde and cut into a short style that hung around her chin. She was as beautiful as she'd always been, in a severe sort of way, her tailored, apple-green jumpsuit emphasizing all the angularity of her form, as though she were the physical embodiment of some geometric ideal, all elbows and straight lines. Nothing like the woman at Baz's side, whose softness invited his touch and whose curves fit against him as though their edges could blur until the line between them disappeared completely.

"Holly!" Mrs. Connolly called, waving a hand above her head. "Over here! Come say hello!"

Holly's narrowed eyes searched the lawn for the summons, finally landing on Mrs. Connolly. Her expression pinched even further as her eyes moved over Baz and Sabrina. Baz's hand flexed on Sabrina's back, pulling her tighter against his side.

With a word to the nondescript man at her side—her husband, presumably—Holly made her way across the lawn to their little group. If she noticed the frantic way her mother glanced between her two daughters  or the smug expectant expression on Mrs. Prindiville's face as the distance narrowed between them, she made no indication. By the time Holly reached their group, she wore the same practiced smile that Baz had seen a thousand times. Had he ever noticed how disingenuous it was before? How it didn't reach her eyes?

"Mrs. Connolly, Mrs. Prindiville, so good of you to come," Holly said as she came to a stop at the edge of their little group. She leaned across the circle to her mother, pressing her cheek against Maryann's and making a kissing noise even though her lips had come nowhere near her mother's skin. "Mom, was that Marty I saw talking Dad's ear off?"

Maryann's answering laugh bordered on shrill. "Yes, yes, it was."

"I owe him a return call, but he cannot harass my assistant every time he wants to sue someone over their signage," Holly sighed. "I've already told him he doesn't have a case, and even if he did, I don't practice property law."

"I'll make sure your father reminds him," Maryann promised.

Holly finally turned her attention to Baz and Sabrina. Her eyes flitted over him and moved quickly to her sister, as if he hardly merited that fraction of a second of consideration. "Sabrina," she said, her voice sharp. "I wasn't sure you were going to make it."

"Where else would I be?" Sabrina asked.

Again, Holly's eyes flicked towards Baz, her nostrils flaring slightly. "On your honeymoon, perhaps."

"We were just getting to know your sister's new husband," Mrs. Connolly said, oblivious to the tension between the two sisters. "Have you two met before?" She pointed a finger between Holly and Baz.

"Yes. Baz and I know each other quite well," Holly said, sparing him a final withering glance before she turned her back to him and Sabrina. "Mom, I have to go rescue Sheldon before Marty corners him."

With each step she took away from them, Sabrina seemed to relax. He swept his thumb back and forth over her spine. They'd come face to face with her sister and lived to tell the tale. Now all they had to do was survive the rest of the evening.

"You must be so proud," Mrs. Connolly said to Maryann. "Both girls married and settled, and now Holly's made partner."

"She always was our overachiever. Set her a task and she'll exceed expectations every time," Maryann replied. "We never had to worry about her. Did you know she only clerked at her first firm for two months before she was promoted to junior associate? She worked countless late nights that year, so many holidays. It nearly destroyed—" Maryann cut herself off, shooting Baz a wide-eyed look, before moving on, "—well, she hardly had a personal life that year. But nothing can stop her once she's made up her mind to go after something."

*Ahh, there's the anger.* Because now he knew exactly *how* Holly had become junior associate in record time. At the time, he'd been proud of her, the woman he was going to marry, climbing the ranks of one of Boston's top rated law firms. Little did he know she was screwing a partner.

Sabrina leaned into him, her arm sliding around his waist, and the tension in his back and shoulders began to melt away. She looked up at him, furrowed brow and earnest eyes, because she *knew*. She'd known all along. And if it hadn't been for her, he would have married Holly, would have legally bound himself to a woman who had been lying to him the whole time.

In that moment, he'd never been more grateful for Sabrina, for the loyalty she'd shown him long before he had any right to expect that of her. Warmth spread in his chest, making him just reckless enough to press a kiss to her temple and breathe in her wildflower scent.

Slowly the conversation around them came back into focus as Maryann loosed a wild laugh. "I should have known right then," she guffawed, dabbing at tears in the corners of her eyes. "Holly sat at the counter, hands clean as could be, eating her peanut butter and jelly in prim little bites, an extra sandwich beside her—for me, she said—and there was Sabrina!" She laughed again, as though the story were too hilarious to recount.

"Mom, I was three. No one wants to hear about—"

"Covered!" Maryann cackled, as though her daughter hadn't spoken. "It was like those mud baths at the spa on Boylston Street. Peanut butter everywhere! She was up to her elbows in the jar and it was streaked all over her face, in her hair!"

"Mom, please." Sabrina stiffened in his arms, her jaw quivering despite the way she clenched it shut.

But still Maryann continued. "We had to get rid of the carpet, of course. No amount of cleaning could get the smell of peanut butter out of the wool. And I knew right then and there, I was destined to have two very different daughters: one who did what was expected of her, who could accomplish the task at hand with flying colors, and one who would cover herself in peanut butter!"

"Enough," Baz barked.

Maryann and her laughing companions froze, casting startled glances his way. "I beg your pardon?" Maryann asked.

"Enough." He slid his hand across Sabrina's back, curling it over her hip and moving her slightly behind him.

"Sebastian," Sabrina said softly, shaking her head, as though her embarrassment wasn't a good enough reason to stop playing by this stupid society script.

But Sabrina was blinking back tears, and Baz had never been very good at fitting in with people like the Pages and their friends. He could not stand there and let these women talk about Sabrina as if what should have been a charming childhood story was somehow an omen of future failures.

He turned his attention to Maryann and, for the first time, he really saw her—the way she clamored for any scrap of approval from these people she called friends, how she was willing to sacrifice her own daughter for the sin of imperfection on the altar of her own social standing. And she'd never see it, never understand how much pain she caused. His heart ached for Sabrina, for the times he'd been cocooned in his own mother's love as Sabrina had never been in hers.

"You've done nothing but insult Sabrina since we got here," he said, eyes locked on Maryann, despite the anxious way she avoided his gaze. "My wife may be too polite to tell you off, but unfortunately for you, I wasn't raised with her sense of decorum."

"Honestly, this is all a bit much," Maryann tittered anxiously.

"You're right. The way you talk about your own daughter is *a bit much*. And it ends now." He slid his hand into Sabrina's and squeezed. When she squeezed back, he felt like a king. "No one speaks poorly of my wife. Not even you. Not anymore." He pressed his lips to Sabrina's templed and murmured, "It's time to go."

Without another glance at his mother-in-law, Baz led Sabrina across the lawn, away from these people who had never deserved her in the first place. They didn't stop to acknowledge Richard, despite him pushing through a group of guests in an attempt to intercept them as they passed, and they definitely didn't stop to say goodbye to her sister, standing off to the side with a look of annoyance pinching her features. Instead, Baz led her up the stairs to the guest room, realization dawning that he hadn't thought past getting her away from her awful mother to figure out what happened next. Would Sabrina want to go back to the party? Would she be angry with him for making a scene?

*Did I fuck up again?*

The door closed behind them and Baz found himself unsure of what to say. Their still-clasped hands hung between them and he knew he could let her go now, but he didn't want to.

He scraped his free hand over his jaw. "I'm sorry."

Her eyes flew to his. "You're—what?"

"I'm sorry," he repeated, his stomach churning.

"What exactly are you sorry for, Sebastian?" Her eyes narrowed. "For defending me? For caring about my feelings?" She took a step closer and his breath stung in his lungs at her nearness, at the wild, reckless feeling flinging itself against the inside of his ribs. "That was... Thank you."

She rose up on her toes and pressed a kiss to his lips, her free hand gripping the lapel of his jacket and pulling him close. Relief mingled with that reckless thing in his chest, as though he'd been waiting his whole life for the movement of her lips on his and now, finally, she'd put him out of his misery. He wrapped an arm around her waist, dug his other hand into her hair, and kissed her back.

Baz spun her around, pressing her back against the closed door even as he pulled her hips tight against his own. He poured everything he didn't understand about the way she made him feel into that kiss. Every unrestrained flutter in his gut turned into the slide of his tongue against hers, every rush of hunger that pulsed through his veins transformed into the way he nipped at her bottom lip.

She pulled back, panting, and he pressed his forehead to hers, his lips still chasing hers. She tugged on his lapels. "Let's go home."

# Chapter Twenty

**Jamie:** Baz, why does Tessa want me to ask you to ask your wife about a ceramic dick?

**Ethan:** Can you not talk about my daughter and dicks in the same sentence?

**Jamie:** Don't blame me. Blame Sabrina.

**Gavin:** Kyla wants to talk to Sabrina too. Something about planning a dick smashing party for her friend Jo...?

**Ethan:** What the hell is going on?

**Baz:** Sabrina will call them tomorrow. We just got back from her parents' house and she's exhausted.

**Gavin:** You're back early!

**Jamie:** I thought you were staying the whole weekend.

**Ethan:** Everything alright?

**Gavin:** If you're home, that means you can come with us to the carnival tomorrow.

**Baz:** Maybe.

**Gavin:** It's tradition!

**Jamie:** We let you off the hook for the cookout today but you are coming to the carnival. They brought back the big slide this year.

**Gavin:** I got a friction burn on my elbow the last time we went down that thing.

**Baz:** That's because we're too fucking old for carnival rides.

**Ethan:** You're never too old for the Ferris wheel.

**Gavin:** Even if you don't go on any of the rides, come hang out.

**Jamie:** And then Tessa can ask Sabrina her ceramic dick questions directly instead of going through me.

**Baz:** I'll ask her if she wants to go.
**Baz:** But I'm not promising anything.

"Would you believe those men are all in their forties?"

Sabrina followed Kyla's amused head tilt to where Sebastian, Gavin, Jamie, and Ethan stood sizing up one of those games where you threw the ball to knock over a tower of milk bottles. This was their third lap around the carnival games, pausing to discuss the likelihood that each game was rigged—highly likely—and which one of them was the most viable option for winning a stuffed animal—the consensus seemed to be Sebastian or Jamie. Halfway through their second circuit, Tessa had pulled Kyla and Sabrina off to the cluster of food stalls. Snacks procured, the women had retreated to a nearby bench to watch the men's continued posturing as dusk settled and the streetlights came on.

It shouldn't have been cute. Four grown men standing around a child's carnival game and arguing over which one of them could win the most stuffed animals should have been the antithesis of cute. And yet, every time Sebastian scowled at one of his friends, each time they playfully jostled one another or burst into boisterous laughter she could feel in her bones, Sabrina's heart cracked open a little wider, making room for Sebastian and his friends, for this town, for the two women seated beside her.

Tessa popped the final bite of her malasada into her mouth, licking the sugar off her fingers and moaning with pleasure as she ate the last of her fried treat. "God, that's good. I swear, you'd never know this kid is only a quarter Portuguese with how much they like malasadas."

"You don't need to be Portuguese to appreciate fried dough," Kyla said, tearing off another bite of her own fluffy, fried confection.

"Last week, all I wanted was chicken Mozambique. And chouriço. My God, did you know the Pizza Stone has a chouriço and French fry sandwich? Heaven." Tessa ran a hand over her baby bump, frowning. "Shit. Now I want French fries."

"On it," Sabrina said, pushing to her feet.

"Sit down," Tessa said. Then, raising her voice, "Jamie?" Her husband instantly turned his full attention to his pregnant wife. "Could you get me some fries? With extra honey mustard to dip them in?" He was moving towards the food stalls before she'd even finished speaking.

"He takes such good care of us."

Kyla rolled her eyes, though she was still smiling. "We know, we know. Best sex of your life. You've told us already."

"Just wait until you get pregnant. I'm telling you, the sex is on a whole other level." Tessa sighed happily and rested back against the bench, her hand continuing to move over her belly with an absent-minded affection that made Sabrina's throat feel too tight. She turned away, focusing her attention on the last dregs of frozen lemonade in the paper cup in her hand.

"Tessa and I have been talking," Kyla's lips curled into a smile as she glanced between Sabrina and Tessa. "We'd like to be the first to book a penis party in your new studio."

Sabrina coughed as a chunk of frozen lemonade went down the wrong way at the phrase 'penis party.' "You heard the part about *smashing* the clay penises, right? Normally the women who book my parties have recently broken up with someone."

Kyla's grin widened. "We know. My friend Jo broke up with someone a few days ago and she couldn't stop laughing when I told her about what you do. It's the first time she's laughed all week."

"If you need help getting the studio set up, count us in," Tessa said. "Well, Jamie will help on my behalf. I want to smash some pottery dicks before I go into labor."

"We'll all help," Kyla agreed.

"It's pretty much all set up," Sabrina said. "I had workmen in the space the second I got to town."

"Before you had your permits to open?" Tessa said with a mock gasp. "I knew I liked you. You're a rebel."

Sabrina laughed. "Hardly. I'd already purchased the kiln, and I figured I might as well get the studio set up."

*More like I blew every last penny I got from the divorce*

*settlement on new equipment and the security deposit on the storefront. More like I suddenly realized boxes of equipment and a shiny new kiln couldn't be stored in Aunt Lucy's guest room. I hadn't considered that it might take a while to get the proper permits to open the damn place before I spent everything I had on start-up costs.*

"Either way, sounds like you're basically ready to open! When can we do the party?" Kyla asked, her eyes sparkling with excitement. "Not that we want to rush you! But maybe in three or four weeks you'll be ready? That should let us squeeze it in before the baby comes."

When was the last time she had friends like this, real friends who immediately accepted her as one of their own? Maybe never... "Three weeks sounds great."

"Perfect! I'll text Jo. I know she's got some modeling jobs lined up for the next few weeks, but maybe we can do it after those." Kyla dug out her phone and began typing away as Jamie arrived with Tessa's French fries.

"Have I told you lately how much I love you?" Tessa asked as she settled the cardboard tray of fries on top of her stomach.

"Are you talking to me or the fries?" Jamie asked. Tessa rolled her eyes but tilted her chin up to accept his kiss. "Now watch while I win our baby their first teddy bear," he said before striding back over to his friends.

"He's going to be such a good dad," Kyla said, nudging her shoulder into Tessa's.

"He is." Tessa popped a fry in her mouth, then turned a quizzical look Sabrina's way. "Do you and Baz want kids? I bet he'd be adorable with a baby."

"Oh, I—we haven't really talked about it." Sabrina stumbled through the answer as she got to her feet, that tightness in her throat back with a vengeance and a restless energy settling into her limbs. "I'm gonna go grab a drink. Water. Or something. Do you guys need anything?" Tessa and Kyla shook their heads, their eyes wide as they watched her freak the fuck out. "Okay! I'll be back!" she said too brightly as she turned and walked away from the bench, away from the group of men jostling for position at the carnival game counter.

She ducked around the corner of the hall of mirrors, leaning against the wall of the vividly painted trailer and tilting her head back as she willed her heart rate to slow. Did she and Baz want kids? If only *that* were the question.

Ever since she was a teenager, when she'd spend every other week doubled over in pain as her ovaries did everything they could to twist and force her into submission, Sabrina had been cautioned that kids might not be in the cards for her. Sure, the worst of the pain had gone once she'd hit her mid-twenties—except, of course, for those times when her ovaries created cysts the size of citrus fruits, as if they wanted to be sure she hadn't forgotten about her diagnosis.

Incurable—except with surgery.

Controllable with medication—sometimes.

And the reason she'd never let herself seriously consider wanting children, at least not intentionally. At thirteen when the doctors had first diagnosed her PCOS, becoming a mother was the farthest thing from her mind. But at thirty-one…

*No. You will not feel sorry for yourself. You will not mourn things you've never even wanted before.*

But what if Sebastian wanted them?

*All the more reason to remember that this is nothing more than sex. And health insurance. And convenient co-habitation.*

*All the more reason to remember that it's temporary.*

Because Sabrina knew how this story ended, no matter how good it was right now. This was the honeymoon phase, and she knew from experience that didn't last. She knew at some point, whether it was next week or three years from now, at some point she'd look at Sebastian and she wouldn't even recognize him anymore. At some point he'd remember that she wasn't what he wanted. She wasn't enough.

And yet. After the way he'd stood up for her with her parents, after the way he'd looked at her as he demanded she touch herself, she'd let herself start to believe.

*Don't be stupid, Sabrina.*

One way or another, this was going to end. She had already given away too much of herself in her last marriage. She couldn't risk that happening again, no matter how different Sebastian seemed. Once she could purchase her own health insurance, they would file for divorce, like they'd agreed. And the sooner, the better. No need to wait until Christmas. Maybe then she'd at least have a hope of preserving the friendships she was beginning to form. Maybe this time, when the papers were signed and the dust settled, she could keep her place in this town, even if she couldn't keep her husband.

Still, she couldn't help but hope that maybe they could always be…whatever they were, even once they were no longer married.

"Sabrina?" She opened her eyes to Sebastian's scowl, and her chest ached. It was his worried scowl, so different from his angry scowl or his embarrassed scowl or the thousand over scowls she'd begun silently cataloging over the last few weeks. "Are you alright?"

"Fine!" she chirped, and the word sounded false even to her own ears. "Did you win?"

He eyed her carefully, as though debating whether or not to allow her to change the subject. "Not yet. But we can go if you're not feeling—"

"I'm fine," she repeated, this time making more of an effort to mean it. "Besides, we can't go yet. We haven't ridden the Ferris wheel."

"I thought you were afraid of heights."

"Why would you think that?"

"On the plane—"

"Oh! No! It's not the heights, it's more the giant metal deathtrap hurling through space at a thousand miles an hour." She chuckled and some of the worry seemed to slip from his face, his shoulders relaxing.

"But a giant metal wheel of doom is fine?" His lip turned up as he teased her.

God, how she loved that little quirk of his mouth.

"Bring it on," she said.

He held out his hand to her and her heart fluttered in her chest as she took it, interlacing her fingers with his. There was something unexpected about holding his hand like this, alone, with no one scrutinizing their every move, something unbearably intimate about feeling the roughness of his palm against hers just because they wanted to. Just because they could.

Something that didn't feel temporary at all. Something that made it all too easy to imagine how it would be if this thing between them was real. If she could keep him.

# Chapter Twenty-one

The five-story-high Ferris wheel at the edge of the Town Common was the centerpiece of Aster Bay's annual Labor Day weekend carnival, the entire block of greenspace covered with brightly colored rides and stalls. From the top, you could see over the roofline all the way down to the bay in one direction and view the stained-glass Garden of Eden in the steeple at St. Anthony's head on in the other direction. As night settled over the town, the lights on the Ferris wheel blinked to life, beckoning Baz and Sabrina closer.

There was no line when they approached—the youngest carnival-goers had all been shuffled away by parents and indulgent grandparents when the streetlights came on a half hour ago, and most of the teenagers wouldn't make their appearance until dark had well and truly fallen. Baz handed over a strip of day-glow orange tickets to the bored-looking attendant and followed Sabrina into a waiting car.

She'd gone quiet on him again, shooting glances his way when she thought he wouldn't notice, her lips pinched tightly the way she did when she was holding something back. He hated that look—not as much as he hated the various stages of embarrassment and hurt he'd seen flicker across her face the day before at her parents' house, but still, he hated it all the same. Ever since they'd gotten home from Brookline, she'd seemed…distant.

It shouldn't have bothered him that much, but that pinched look on her face now, here, made him itchy all over, like he could *feel* the things she wasn't saying.

They hadn't talked about what happened in her parents' guest room, the things he'd said to her, the boundaries they'd blown right past. Yesterday as they'd driven home, each mile that brought them closer to Aster Bay also pushed them further apart. By the time they'd arrived back at his condo, the awkward weight of all the things they weren't saying was a physical presence between them.

So even though he'd wanted to protest when she'd said goodnight and slipped into the guest room with a shy smile, he hadn't. Because she didn't owe him anything. The only modification to their previous arrangement had been an agreement to indulge in their physical attraction to each other, to act like fucking idiotic teenagers and pretend he could be fuck buddies with his wife.

*No, you agreed to enjoy it while it lasts. Stop being such a whiney fucking asshole and enjoy it.*

The ride attendant secured the door on the Ferris wheel car and the ride slowly began to spin, bringing them higher and higher. But Baz didn't care about the view. He cared about what had put that look on Sabrina's face. What wasn't she telling him?

"Seemed like you were having a good time with Kyla and Tessa," he said.

"They're great," she confirmed. "All your friends are."

"They're your friends too. If you want them to be."

"Maybe they won't want to be my friend when they find out we've been lying to them." She flashed him a small, apologetic smile. It was almost worse than the pinched lips.

"The lie is a technicality," he said, but even he didn't believe it.

"I'm not sure they'll agree."

He blew out a frustrated breath. "We're married. That's not a lie."

"No, but—"

"Anything else is between us. We decide what's true."

It was Sabrina's turn to make a frustrated sound. "That's not how truth works."

"Then tell me what's true, Sabrina. You're living in my apartment. That's true. You're wearing my ring. Your name is next to mine on the goddamn insurance forms. That's true, isn't it?"

She ran her eyes over him appraisingly, like she could see what had crawled under his skin and made him irrationally adamant. But it was *her*—her wildflower scent and her auburn hair and her fucking freckles and the little huff sound she made when there wasn't enough cereal left in the box for a whole bowl and all her goddamn flirty little skirts and just *her*.

Something in her eyes shifted, as though she'd heard his thoughts, and maybe she had. Maybe the way she was seeping into all the cracks in his life and filling them up was written all over his face, how badly he wanted more from her, and how much he hated himself for that. Maybe she already knew.

Maybe she felt the same way.

"Yeah, Sebastian," she said, her tongue flicking out to wet her lips. "That's all true."

"Why do you do that?" he asked, digging a hand into his hair.

"Do what?"

"Say my name like that? *Sebastian*. No one calls me Sebastian."

"Do you want me to call you Baz?" she asked carefully.

"No, I don't fucking want you to call me—"

"Then I don't understand what the problem is."

"I didn't say it was a problem."

"If you want me to call you Baz—"

"Just tell me why, Sabrina!"

They stared at each for a long time as the Ferris wheel continued to turn, before she finally gave him an answer that leveled him. "Because *Baz* was engaged to my sister. And *Sebastian*…is mine."

He pulled her against him, one hand curled around the nape of her neck and the other gripping her waist as he pressed his lips to hers. The kiss was urgent and a little angry, like every kiss they'd shared, and he wondered if it would always be like this—bruising and needy and so damn good.

But even as she melted against him, even as she flicked her tongue against his and arched her body closer to his, somewhere in the back of his mind a dim little voice tsked and reminded him that words like 'always' didn't apply to them. They didn't have 'always.' They had now, until Christmas, until she didn't need him anymore. And there was something seriously fucked about how hard that made him, how desperate he was to take everything she'd give him for every minute that he could, to suck every last drop of good out of their time together before she decided she'd had enough. Maybe if he did, he could save up enough of this feeling to last after she was gone.

He kissed across her cheekbone, trailed his tongue down the line of her throat and sucked on the tender skin on the underside of her jaw. "That's right, baby," he crooned against her skin when she whimpered. "So tell me where the fucking lie is."

He was burning up with the sudden, unmistakable need to show her how right she was, that she *was* his, and that he'd be hers if only she'd let him. To touch her and taste her and claim her for himself. The need mixed with anger, a tight, hot swirl in his gut clawing up his throat, reminding him how fucking stupid he was to let himself feel anything for this woman, how much better off he'd be if he could let it be about nothing more than sex.

He hooked her knee with one hand and lifted her leg over his own, the frilly skirt of her sundress draping over the empty space between her legs. His fingers dug into the soft flesh of her thigh, and her knees fell apart, an invitation that felt like a trap.

"Are you wet for me, wildflower?" he asked against her ear before taking the lobe between his teeth and tugging gently. She gasped at the sting of his bite and rocked her hips against the air, his hand sliding an inch higher, disappearing completely beneath her skirt now. "Have you been a good wife and kept this pussy ready for me?"

Her head fell back with a groan, but he held her in place with that hand on her nape, his lips whispering all manner of filth against her throat. "Touch me," she whispered, her hips moving mindlessly as he traced circles ever higher on the inside of her thigh.

"Dirty girl." He wasn't sure if it was praise or admonishment, but whatever it was, she liked it, her green eyes sinking into darkness. Some foolish thing that felt an awful lot like pride bloomed in his chest.

He slid his hand higher, his fingers finally brushing against the damp gusset of her panties. He traced the edge of the fabric with a single finger, then slid them to the side. She shivered in his arms as the night air met her exposed skin. It took all his self restraint not to flip up that frilly little skirt and let himself see her, wet and swollen and goddamn perfect. But it was one thing to play with her in public, to move his hand between her legs where no one could see, even if they might suspect, and quite another to risk someone else glimpsing the heaven beneath her skirt. No, that view was just for him.

"I'm still waiting for an answer, Sabrina," he said in a low warning tone as he slid one finger over her slit. He settled the pad of his finger against her clit, stroking in slow, small circles the way she'd shown him the other night. She released a shuddering breath and captured his mouth again, but he pulled away with a nip on her lower lip. "What exactly is the lie? You're my wife."

He increased the pressure of his circles, wanting to make her come hard and fast, to force her to the edge of her own pleasure before she could really get her arms around it, to steal her orgasm from her the way she was stealing his heart—unexpected and sharp and a little bit wrong and somehow still so good he couldn't stop.

"This is your husband's hand fucking you." He plunged two fingers into her opening and curled them against her front wall as his thumb continued to work her clit. "I'm the one who's going to make you come, here, with all these people around."

Her inner muscles fluttered around his fingers and he nearly came in his pants like an inexperienced teenager. He swore under his breath and fucked her harder, faster, the obscene sounds of her pleasure as he pumped his fingers in and out mixing with the distant laughter and carnival music floating up to them from the ground.

"You like when I touch you like this?" he asked in an awe-tinged growl.

"Yes. Oh, God, Sebastian." She gripped his forearm where it disappeared beneath her dress, her short, manicured nails digging into his skin as she urged him on, rocking her hips into his touch with increasing urgency.

"So what's the lie?" he asked again. "It can't be the way you're riding my hand right now. Fuck, I wish I could see it. But I can feel it, baby. Feel how much you need to come. There's no lying about that, is there, wife? Give it to me. Want to know how it feels when this pretty pussy comes. Show me now, here, on my fingers, with all those people down there wishing they knew how good you feel. And then I'm taking you home, wildflower, and you're going to show me again. You're going to come on my tongue and on my cock, over and over, until you can't remember anything about a fucking *lie*."

She arched away from the back of the seat, folding over herself as her thighs shook uncontrollably and she came apart on his hand. He worked her mercilessly until she began squirming away from his touch, pressing her thighs together, trapping his hand between her legs, buried deep in her cunt but stilling their motion. He lifted her chin up to him and kissed her softer than he would have thought possible when her pussy was still pulsing around his fingers. As the Ferris wheel slowed, their car making its final loop, and he reluctantly removed his hand from between her legs, and he knew: the only lies were the ones they were telling themselves.

# Chapter Twenty-two

Sebastian's friends were waiting for them when they climbed out of the Ferris wheel. Heat rushed to Sabrina's cheeks and she wondered if anyone could tell that only moments before she'd had the best orgasm of her life riding Sebastian's hand while the ride turned to give her the most breathtaking views of Aster Bay. If they suspected, they didn't say anything, but she thought she saw a knowing smile cross Tessa's face before she took another bite of her cotton candy.

"Where to next?" Gavin asked. "The Rookery?"

"We could go back to the vineyard and play cards," Ethan offered.

"I'm in more of a Scattergories mood than a Go Fish mood," Kyla said. Gavin slung an arm over her shoulder, pulling her against him and pressing a kiss to the top of her head.

"I think we're headed home," Jamie said. "Tessa's been on her feet enough today."

"I'm fine." Tessa popped another wisp of pink spun sugar into her mouth.

"You're six weeks from your due date," her husband reminded her. "Let's go home, princess. I'll rub your—"

"Watch it," Ethan grunted.

"—feet," Jamie finished. He shot a look at Ethan. "Weirdo."

"What about you two?" Gavin asked, turning his attention to Sabrina and Sebastian. "Scattergories?"

"We're going to call it a night too," Sebastian said. He wrapped his arms around Sabrina from behind, and pulled her back against him so she could feel his hard on.

*You will not grind against your husband in front of his friends. You will keep yourself together until you get behind closed doors. You will not do anything inappropriate in public—well, anything else.*

"You married people are no fun," Gavin said, but his smile made it clear he was teasing.

"Better watch it. You're next," Jamie reminded him.

Kyla held up her left hand, her engagement ring sparkling even in the low light. "Yeah, but we'll still be fun after we're married."

Sabrina couldn't help but smile as the friends teased each other. Somehow these people had become her friends too, and she longed to be a part of their easy laughter. It had been too long since she'd had friends that were *easy*, not since she was younger, before she'd become the black sheep at the fancy private school her parents had sent her to, more interested in spending time in the art studio than shopping or hanging out in the mall food court in hopes some boy would notice her. But this was something different. She wanted to know these people, and have them really know her in return, to be a part of their lives and welcome them into hers.

This, here, with the people Sebastian spent most of his time with, Sabrina finally understood what it meant when someone talked about the family you choose. These people were Sebastian's family as much as his mother. The kind of family that saw you fully, flaws and all, and still loved you, still chose you. The kind of family you *wanted* to spend time with. The kind that made you stronger.

For a moment as they all said their goodbyes and she was

pulled into one hug after another, she let herself imagine what it would be like if they were her family too. What would it be like to have a family she chose—and that chose her back?

*So choose it.*

She released Kyla with a promise to meet her for lunch the next day, feeling lighter than she had in years. She could choose this family, this life that had opened up before her. She could choose to keep these friendships, to belong to this town, and maybe even to let herself trust her feelings for her husband.

As if Sebastian could tell her thoughts were wandering to dangerous places, he swatted her butt, a smug grin spreading across his face. "Let's get out of here."

They didn't get far before reality came crashing back in. Sabrina saw her first, though she supposed that made sense. She'd had years more practice spotting, and avoiding, her sister. But she knew the second Sebastian caught sight of Holly leaning against his car in the public parking lot on the edge of the Town Common. His hand went stiff in hers, his back rigid, as every last trace of playfulness disappeared from his face.

Sabrina squeezed his hand, a silent reminder that they were in this together.

"It's about time," Holly said with an impatient sigh, crossing her arms over her chest. "How much is there for two grown adults to do at a *carnival*?"

"What are you doing here, Hol?" Sabrina asked.

"Aunt Lucy said I'd find you here. I almost thought she was joking." Holly's upper lip curled in disgust as she glanced around the Common. "Really, Sabrina? You'd rather be *here* than at Mom and Dad's?"

"I would." It wasn't even a question. She'd choose Aster Bay, this carnival, anywhere over another second of her mother's Labor Day party.

"You embarrassed yourself when you left like that," Holly said.

"Embarrassed *you*, you mean," Sebastian said.

Holly blinked at him, as though she'd only just noticed he was there. "What would *I* have to be embarrassed about? You're the one who ran off to Vegas to marry my little sister." She turned her sharp glare towards Sabrina. "*You're* the one who couldn't wait to get your hands on my sloppy seconds. Is that why you divorced Jordan, to go after Baz?"

"We're not doing that," Sebastian said, stepping slightly forward, as though he could put his body between Sabrina and her sister's hateful words. "You don't get to come to my town and—"

Holly waved a dismissive hand. "Yes, yes, we all know, you love your precious town."

"What do you want?" Sabrina asked.

"I want to know what game you're playing." Holly's eyes darted between them.

"No game," Sebastian said.

"Please. Of course it's a game. Why else would she have married *you*?"

"What's that supposed to mean?" Sabrina asked.

Something dangerous sparked in Holly's eyes. She turned her attention back to Sabrina, and Sabrina braced for the impact of whatever venom her sister was about to release.

"Ever since we were kids, it's been the same tired story. If I had something, you wanted it. And if you couldn't have it, you did everything you could to ruin it for me. It wasn't enough that you broke up my wedding to Baz. You had to go and marry him yourself?"

"Listen to me," Sebastian said as he took a step closer to Holly, his hand slipping from Sabrina's as he did. His voice was low, as icy as the blue of his eyes, and Sabrina told herself that was why she shivered, not because she missed the feel of his hand in hers. "My marriage has nothing to do with you."

"Doesn't it?" Holly asked with a mock quizzical tilt of her

head. "Come on, Baz, you're not that stupid. Can't you see she's using you? She wanted to take you away from me then and she wanted to prove some silly little point now." Holly turned her poisonous stare to Sabrina. "If you'd run into one of my high school boyfriends rather than Baz, would you have married them instead?"

A muscle jumped in Sebastian's clenched jaw and Sabrina hated that her sister was right. Not about her other boyfriends, but this had all started as a way to prove a point, to get under Holly's skin. But somewhere along the way it had become more than that, at least to her. She hazarded a glance at Sebastian. His face was unreadable.

What if it hadn't become more for him?

"Did you really drive all the way here to be a jerk?" Sabrina asked.

Holly rolled her eyes and dug into her Louis Vuitton handbag. Her hand reappeared clutching a familiar envelope, one Sabrina had very purposely left on the drink cart in her mother's parlor. Holly held it out to Sabrina. "You left this at Mom's."

Sabrina snatched the envelope from her sister. "You could have mailed it."

"Nice to see you, too, little sister. Let's not make a habit of it." With that, Holly walked away from them, sliding into the driver's seat of a sleek, black car. At the last moment, Holly turned and shot a pointed look at the envelope in Sabrina's hand. "For once in your life, do as you're told."

Sabrina and Sebastian watched until her tail lights disappeared from view. Only then did Sabrina feel like she could actually take a deep breath as she shoved the envelope into her purse. She'd shred it later.

Still, something in the air had shifted.

"Sebastian?" she asked, taking his hand in hers again.

He stared at their joined hands for a long minute, that

muscle in his jaw continuing to tick. "Is she right?"

"About what?"

"That you would have done this with anyone if it meant pissing off your sister. If you'd found someone else in Vegas from Holly's past, would you have married them instead?" His eyes flicked to hers, guarded and icy in a way that made her feel cold all over.

"I didn't mean to marry anyone," she said softly.

"But you did. You married *me*."

"I don't know what you want me to say here. We both got drunk that night. We both decided to get married. I didn't do that on my own." His eyes were back on their interlocked hands again, as though he were seeing them for the first time. "What exactly are you accusing me of?" she asked, doing her best to hide the tremble in her voice.

Finally, he met her gaze, his brow furrowed. He blinked and ran his free hand over his jaw. "Nothing. Forget it."

"Sebastian—"

"It's late. Let's go home." He released her hand and rounded the car to the driver's side.

Sabrina felt the absence of his touch like a vibration in her bloodstream, like the warning shot over the bow of a ship.

"Are we okay?" she asked.

He flashed her one of his charming smiles that didn't reach his eyes and she thought she might be sick. "Yeah. We're fine."

Oh, what she would have given to believe him.

# Chapter Twenty-three

Baz tossed his keys into the bowl on the kitchen counter and sifted through the overcrowded kitchen cabinet until he found his best bottle of Scotch. Since when did he have four different kinds of breakfast cereal and at least as many packages of cookies in his cabinets? *Since Sabrina.* The thought only stoked his frustration as he pulled the mostly empty bottle from the back of the cabinets and poured himself a drink. Behind him, he heard the soft snick of the front door as Sabrina entered the apartment, and there was that irrational anger he'd first felt in the carnival parking lot.

Anger that she was in his space—in his life—for who knew how long, but certainly not forever. Not for keeps.

That he was another temporary safe harbor for her, good ol' punching bag Baz who'd always be there to take one more punch, no matter how bloodied and bruised it left him. Dependable, disposable Baz. That's who he was to her, just like he'd been for her sister once upon a time.

That he even gave a fuck about any of it.

This was supposed to be about sex, and only until Christmas. So why did that thought make him angrier than any that had come before it?

Despite having his back to her as he nursed his Scotch, his

free hand braced on the kitchen counter, he was all too aware of her moving through the apartment. Kicking off her shoes by the front door, sliding into a seat at the kitchen island. Watching him. Waiting.

"Sebastian—"

"Not now."

If he talked to her now, when every part of him was itching for a fight, when he wanted to push and push and push until there was nothing left but him and his Scotch and the quiet—if he talked to her now, he'd say things he couldn't take back. And even though he was angry, he'd been angry often enough before to know that the feeling always abated eventually, that lashing out at her wouldn't actually make it go away.

"Yes, now." He froze at her words, low and assured, like she was holding a lit match above a keg of gunpowder and daring him to open the lid.

"Go to bed, Sabrina." He threw back the last of the Scotch and set the glass down on the counter a little too hard, the sound of the glass hitting the marble making him wince.

"You know this is what she wanted, right? We didn't follow their script, so Holly wanted to come and throw a grenade into our lives. She *wants* us to be fighting right now. You can't—" She broke off with a growl and he couldn't help but turn to look at her over his shoulder. "You can't seriously think I would have married one of her other exes."

He shrugged one shoulder. "Why not?"

"Why not?" she shouted. She was up out of her seat now, pacing the length of the room with the kitchen island between them. "First of all, you're an even bigger idiot than I thought if you believe that."

"Why shouldn't I believe it? I just happened to be the one who was there."

"Do you know how happy I was to see you? That wasn't about Holly, you big idiot. That was about—"

"Will you stop calling me an idiot?"

"—*you*. I wanted to talk to *you*. To make things right with you."

"Why?"

"Because I missed you!"

"Why, Sabrina?" He pushed off from the counter and braced his hands on his side of the kitchen island as she continued to pace.

"Because—" She broke off, planted her hands on her hips and turned to face off with him across the slab of marble. She opened her mouth as though she had more to say, her eyes darting between his, but whatever she saw there had her closing her lips without saying a word. With another one of those frustrated noises, she turned away from him, retreating to the far wall of the open plan space, staring out at the bay in the moonlight.

"You had ten years to make things right between us. Why now?" He rounded the island to move towards her even as he kept a careful distance between them. Blood rushed in his ears and his whole being practically vibrated with this restless energy he didn't trust.

"This whole thing was *your* idea," she muttered in reply.

"My idea?"

"Yes! You're the one who had the brilliant plan to make her think we were together." She turned to face him, her back to the wall of glass, as he slowly advanced on her.

"I didn't mean for us to get married."

"Neither did I! I never wanted to get married again *ever!*"

Her words hung in the air between them. He couldn't explain why it should matter, but it still slashed to ribbons his secret, fragile hopes of keeping her.

Her voice was softer when she spoke again. "My first marriage took everything from me. Not just my partner, because now I know Jordan never was that, but my home, my town, my work. I signed away half of everything and was left with barely enough to scrape by. Marriage is a trap."

He rocked back on his heels. "You think I trapped you?"

"*I* trapped *you!*" She spun away from him, pressing her hands and forehead into the glass in a posture he'd adopted himself on far too many occasions. His hands clenched at his sides as he fought the desire to go to her. "You offered to help me for one night and I've saddled you with months of dealing with my problems."

"I did that willingly," he said, stabbing a finger at his chest. "I'd do it all again."

"Why?"

"Why did you miss me?" He threw the question back at her and watched as she once again dodged it.

"I don't know." Her refusal to answer felt like a challenge, that lit match dangled over the powder keg, held so loosely it could fall at any moment.

He scoffed, some sick part of him lighting up with satisfaction at the incredulity in her eyes at the sound.

"Why did you offer to help me? First, to make Holly mad and now, with the health insurance?" She advanced on him, but he held his ground, refusing to back away from the fiery redhead threatening to send his whole life up in flames. "Why come to my parents' house? Why stand up for me? Why—"

"Because you're my *wife*," he roared, the words ripped from his chest. "Maybe you did trap me. That's how I feel. Trapped, Sabrina. I can't let you go, but I can't keep you. What am I supposed to do?"

"I—I'll go," she said, her wide eyes turning glassy. "If that's what you want—"

He gripped her arm and pulled her towards him. "That's not what I said."

"Yes, it is!" She pulled her arm out of his grasp. "I don't understand. What do you want?"

He took her face in his hands and kissed her before he could think better of it, before she could misunderstand that too. There was nothing gentle about the kiss. It was tongue and teeth and her nails digging into his biceps as they crashed together. He pressed her against the wall, trapping her between the glass and his body, as he trailed biting kisses down the column of her throat. She moaned his name, one hand buried in his hair and holding him against her.

"Tell me what you need, wildflower, and I'll give it to you," he promised.

And he meant it. She could ask for anything—*anything*—and he'd tear himself apart to give it to her, as if that wasn't the worst trap of them all. But a trap he welcomed, one he'd cling to willingly, even if he didn't understand it. Even if it would break him to watch her leave when it was over.

Her hand in his hair tightened as he lifted his face to meet her eyes. With the slightest pressure, she pushed him down, holding his gaze the entire time, and it was as though she'd finally dropped that match, as though his entire being was consumed by flames as he willingly went to his knees at her feet. Because this he could do. He couldn't fix her awful ex or her horrible parents or even whatever secrets she was keeping, but right here, now, he could make her feel good.

He slid his hands up the back of her legs, over the strong calf muscles and sensitive skin at the back of her knees, over the thighs hidden beneath her sundress and the perfect curve of her ass, until he hooked his fingers in the waist of her panties and pulled them down.

She watched him, her chest rising and falling with rapid breaths and one hand still lost in his hair. Her touch gentled, the insistent tugging on his hair turning to soft strokes, and suddenly it wasn't enough to be on his knees for her. He wanted to see her, every inch of her skin, every freckle that marked her, every secret, soft place she'd kept hidden away.

Baz tugged on the hem of her dress. "Off."

She only hesitated for a moment before she gathered the hem in her hands and pulled it over her head in one fluid motion. She unhooked the strapless bra that caged her torso and that, too, fell away. Baz sat back on his heels and took in the sight of her, completely bare for him.

He sat up on his knees and skated his hands over her hips, the dip of her waist, the angry red marks wrapping her ribs where the bra had been, until his thumbs came to rest on a small tattoo on her side.

He ran his fingers over the small, colorful bouquet of wildflowers, usually concealed beneath her clothing, and the buzzing in his blood grew louder, faster, tangling in knots in his chest and wrapping tendrils of flame over his skin. When had she gotten his nickname for her permanently inked onto her skin? The idea of it, of her sitting in some tattoo parlor getting this particular tattoo while he was thinking the worst of her, was enough to make him dizzy with wanting.

He leaned forward and pressed his lips to the tattoo, murmuring, "My wildflower," into her skin. "My wife."

Her hand returned to his hair, moving the loose strands away from his face, so he knew she saw when he lifted his eyes to hers and began kissing a path across her skin, down the soft curve of her belly. He pressed his face to her mound, breathing in the scent of her arousal as his hands curled around her body and cupped her backside, kneading the flesh there.

"Is this where you need me, wife?" He nipped at the tender place on her inner thigh and smiled against her skin when she sucked in a breath in reply. "Can I taste you now? Please?"

She exhaled her permission and used that hand in his hair to guide him to the apex of her thighs. He dragged his tongue through her slit, forcing himself to take his time, to memorize the taste of her.

She whimpered. "Stop teasing me."

"You like when I tease you."

He grabbed great handfuls of her ass, spreading her cheeks as he licked into her pussy, burying his nose in her soft curls. She spread her legs wider to accommodate his shoulders and he rewarded her with the scrape of his teeth over the pert little bud at her center. She gasped and melted against the glass behind her as he tipped her hips towards his waiting mouth.

"You can't pretend with me, Sabrina. This pretty pussy tells me the truth." He licked her again, deep and slow, humming in satisfaction at her taste on his tongue. "You get so wet when I tease you like this. Maybe I should tease you all night, keep you needy and wanting." She groaned, her hips rocking into his touch. "You like that idea, baby?" Another burst of wetness against his tongue and he chuckled darkly. "Yeah, I thought so."

"Sebastian, please," she groaned.

He slid one hand between her legs, probing at her entrance with a single finger as he resumed his slow exploration of her with his tongue and teeth. She squirmed against him, as though she could get closer to his touch. When her thighs began to quiver with need and her soft exhales were tinged with desperation, only then did he slide a second finger inside her and suck her clit between his lips, drawing her pleasure from her in long pulls and the quick flutter of his fingers. She came apart around him, one hand in his hair and another on her breast, and her eyes locked on his as he drew every last drop of her orgasm from her.

He was tempted to stay there at her feet forever, but there was so much he wanted with Sabrina, and he was suddenly struck by the certainty that he was running out of time. He got to his feet and gathered her into his arms, all her bare skin scraping against his clothing as she kissed herself from his lips. With a single hand, he undid his belt and zipper, shoving his pants to the floor while she fumbled with the buttons of his shirt. At last he was naked, her soft smooth places against the coarse hair of his legs, his chest, sparking fire along his nerve endings every place that they touched.

Her hand wrapped around the base of his cock and he slammed a hand against the glass beside her head, gritting his teeth to keep from coming at that first demanding touch. He took her chin between his thumb and forefinger, tilting her face up to his as she explored the length of him, her clever fingers lingering over the piercing at his tip.

"Tell me what you want, Sabrina," he demanded.

"I want you inside me."

"You want me to fuck you," he clarified, rocking into her fist. She nodded.

He dropped his hand from her chin and stepped out of her grip, reaching for the wallet in his pants pocket and retrieving a condom. He held her gaze as he slid the latex over his shaft, her wide-eyed anticipation tangling with that fiery knot in his chest and growing into something bigger, something more urgent, something he'd never felt before.

He hooked one of her legs over his hip and captured her nipple between her teeth, tugging gently until she melted back against the glass behind her. Lifting his mouth back to hers, he lined himself up with her entrance, pressing against her.

"You want me to fuck you here, baby? Like this? Where anyone out on the bay tonight could look up at this window and see what a good wife you are?" She sucked in a shocked breath, but her hips rocketed forward and he slid inside her— not all the way, but enough for them both to groan in relief. "Fuck, you're tight like this."

He dropped one hand between them, stroking her clit in those rough little circles she liked until she relaxed around him and he could push another inch inside.

"Sebastian," she whined, watching the place where he disappeared inside her in disbelief.

"You can take it." As if to prove his point, he pushed forward again, her gasp setting off a riot of warmth blossoming in his chest. "I'm going to make it so good for you," he promised, pressing his forehead to hers as he slid the rest of the way into the hot clutch of her.

"I know you will," she said.

And fuck if that trust didn't lash against his skin, stinging and sharp, and yet he wanted more despite the burn. He pulled almost all the way out and thrust back in, her surprised inhale urging him on to do it again and again, tilting his hips until he was sure his piercing teased at the right spot. Her hands were everywhere—in his hair and scraping over his back, digging into his ass and pulling him into her over and over, and still he wanted to be closer, to slow down and feel each slide of his skin over hers, each spark along his nerves, to speed up and lose himself in the inexorable rhythm of their coupling.

"Why?" he whispered against her lips. He wasn't sure what exactly he meant—*why are you letting me be with you like this? Why did you come back? Why didn't I know it could be like this, why didn't you find me sooner, why do you have to go? Why does it feel like I'm being unmade and remade all at once?*

She laced her fingers with his and guided his hand from where it had been toying with her nipple to press against the tattoo on her side, their fingertips brushing the bottom curve of her breast. As she held his palm to the ink on her skin, she stared into his eyes, as though inviting him to read the answers there if only he would look hard enough. But all he saw were more questions—his own mingling with hers and tangling into this knot of doubt that urged him to fuck her harder, faster, to race against that distant ticking clock taunting them.

She cried out his name as she came, her inner walls clutching at him with each frantic thrust until he joined her with a roar, the pleasure racing down his spine and tearing him open. It was too good, too bright. His cock jolted within her, and he tried to get closer, deeper, to fuse himself with her in ways he didn't understand. He wanted to keep her like this—face frozen in pleasure, his name on her lips, her body pulling him in—until they both forgot all about anything other than this, this perfect moment, this pure bliss where there was no time and she was his.

As the pleasure receded, she dropped her forehead to his chest, the aftershocks of her orgasm fluttering around his softening cock. He dropped a kiss to the sweaty mess of her hair, then reluctantly pulled away to dispose of the condom. He returned to the living room to find her exactly as he'd left her, slumped against the glass with a hazy look on her face that mimicked the tentative satisfaction in his own chest.

He took her hand and led her to his bedroom, leaving their clothing scattered about the living room. He tucked her into his bed and pulled her into his arms as if he could calm the panic clawing up his throat if he held her tight enough. And if, half-awake in the night, he slid into her from behind and held her against his chest so he could feel her shake in his arms when she came, if he slept tangled between her legs with his lips pressed to her tattoo, it was only to calm that restlessness he still didn't understand.

# Chapter Twenty-four

Sabrina pressed the foot pedal and the pottery wheel whirred to life. She hadn't intended to throw on the wheel today, but after the night before, after waking up alone with a hastily scribbled note that Sebastian had gone into work early, she had to do *something*. She could not spend the entire day in the condo she'd begun to think of as theirs with nothing to do but replay the hottest night of her life with a man who couldn't have gotten away from her faster this morning if he'd tried. She'd arrived at the studio intending to hang the vinyl letters on the window that would announce to Aster Bay that Get Clayed was open and ready for business, but she knew there was only one thing that steadied her when she was feeling shaken up like this.

She worked the clay, drawing it up and flattening it out in an endless cycle. It had been too long since she'd had her hands in the clay, the greyish brown coating her skin in familiar ways, the hum of the wheel, the rhythm of the clay taking shape and dissolving back into shapelessness. The movements became meditative, but even this, even the place she felt most herself, wasn't enough to calm the voices in her head.

*You will not read into anything that happened last night. Or this morning. You will not confuse oxytocin and dopamine and whatever other feel-good sex chemicals for actual feelings.*

Her hands moved of their own accord as she tried to convince herself that nothing had changed. It was a trick of biology, an evolutionary impulse that had long outlived its usefulness. She was confusing friendship and lust for other things she didn't dare name, emotions that left her vulnerable and ripe for heartbreak. She'd had quite enough of that already, thank you very much.

And there was that other pesky piece of the puzzle to consider. If there were actual feelings involved, if the way he'd looked at her when he'd pulled her close in the middle of the night for rounds two and three was about something other than hormones and proximity, then she'd have to face all the ways she'd fucked up yet again. All the ways she wasn't going to be enough for him. *Like you weren't enough for Jordan.*

She froze at the thought and in that moment of hesitation, her clay became uncentered, the fragile walls she'd been building crumbling in dramatic fashion into a heap of mutilated clay on the wheel. The wheel slowed to a stop and she cursed under her breath, using the heel of her hand to move a loose wisp of hair off her forehead.

Of course, Sebastian chose that moment to appear, as if summoned by her incessant thoughts about the ways he used his fingers and tongue and cock—

"What's that look about?" Sebastian asked with a knowing twitch of his lip as he rounded the worktable at the front of the studio and made his way to Sabrina where she sat at the wheel.

She blinked, shaking her head and starting up the wheel again. "Nothing. I'm trying to get back in the habit. For Kyla's friend's party."

"The penis party," he said casually as he leaned against the worktable.

"The break-up party."

She gathered the clay back together in the center of her wheel and started working it again. If she focused on the clay then she couldn't notice how out of place he looked in his three-piece suit in her studio, nor could she notice how that thought stung, how much she wanted him to fit here with her. But Sebastian fit with the Sabrina that wore silk blouses and pencil skirts, not the Sabrina who wore leggings and an oversized t-shirt knotted up at her waist, hands coated in clay.

"I thought you'd done these a hundred times before."

"I have. But Kyla wants…something different." The messages she'd woken to from Kyla that morning had been enthusiastic, bursting with excitement for the two-evening party she was hosting for her friend. And they'd contained a very specific request, courtesy of Tessa.

"She doesn't want to smash a clay dick?" he asked.

"She does. But she also wants to make a second piece. One she can keep." Heat rushed to her cheeks, which was stupid considering she'd had Sebastian's *piece* inside her repeatedly the night before.

"Will you show me?"

Sabrina glanced up from the clay, meeting Sebastian's eyes long enough to clock the challenge lingering there.

"Aren't you supposed to be at work?" she asked.

"Being self-employed has its perks."

He braced his hands on the worktable behind him, affecting a casual pose that belied the tension in his jaw, and Sabrina had the distinct impression that he was a predator toying with his prey, coiled anticipatory strength waiting for the most opportune moment to pounce. And there was that fizzy, shaken up feeling again, coursing through her limbs and gathering in a deep ache between her legs.

Sabrina began shaping the clay, keeping her eyes on her work. "Did you know Tessa painted a mural in the baby's room?" she asked, eager for a distraction from the fact that he was watching her with those ice blue eyes.

"No."

*Some distraction.*

"She told me all about it at the carnival. One whole wall is some kind of fairytale forest theme. Kyla helped. And her friends Jo and Molly too. Jo's the one we're having the party for. Tessa found a picture in a children's book and they painted it on the wall. Life size trees and fairies and a unicorn. Well, I guess who knows if the fairies and unicorn are life size, right? Since they're not real. I mean, the painting's real. You know what I mean."

"Oh, yeah. I vaguely remember Jamie talking about that."

"She showed me a picture. It looks incredible. That baby is going to be so lucky. To have a mom who's that artistic."

Baz's eyes narrowed as he studied her. When he spoke, she got the sense that he was picking his words carefully, almost as though he wasn't sure they were what he actually wanted to say. "Is that something you would want someday?"

"I can't paint. Not like that. Not trees and fairies and a whole freakin' unicorn. Glazing pottery is as far as my painting skills go. And what if you painted a forest and later you wished it was a castle or a beach or a jungle? I guess a jungle is a kind of forest. But you wouldn't put unicorns in a jungle. Or fairies. Not that fairies couldn't be in a jungle if they wanted to be. But it doesn't seem like a fairy place. Jungles, I mean." She hazarded a glance and found herself unable to look away from him as she cataloged the deep crease between his brows, the intensity of his focus on her. Her mouth was suddenly dry when she asked. "Is that something you want?"

"A mural?" he asked with an arch of his eyebrow. She shrugged. He scraped his hand over his face and did that word-picking thing again. "Maybe someday. With the right person."

She forced a chuckle that felt wrong even to her own ears. Of course he wanted murals someday—dark-haired, blue-eyed murals. Why shouldn't he?

"Right, you wouldn't want to do something as permanent as paint a mural with the wrong person. You could end up with purple trees or—or—or a unicorn without a horn. Which I guess is basically a horse."

"Why are you doing your nervous babbling thing?" he asked.

"My what? I'm not babbling."

"You are." He pushed off from the worktable and moved towards her. "What's making you nervous? Me or the conversation?"

"I'm not nervous talking about murals," she scoffed. *As if that's what we were actually talking about.*

"So, it's me, then."

She could feel him moving behind her, the heat of his eyes on her back. "I'm not nervous. I'm just not used to someone watching me when I'm…sculpting."

"You teach classes. I'd think you'd be quite used to being watched."

"That's different."

"How?"

"Because my clients are sculpting too. Not watching me work."

She heard the scrape of metal across the tile floor as Sebastian pulled a chair up behind her stool.

*Please drop it. Please pretend with me for a little longer.*

When he sat, his knees bracketed her hips. He pressed his lips to the nape of her neck and she nearly destroyed the clay she'd been carefully shaping as electricity sparked across her skin.

"I like watching you," he said in that low, resonant way she could feel in her bones. Another kiss, more electricity. "But if you want me to go, I will."

"No. Stay."

He hummed in approval and moved closer to her, pressing himself flush against her back as she continued to work. For a while he watched in silence as she shaped the clay, the way she changed the pressure of her thumb to create the flared tip, the way she smoothed the ridge.

"Is this one for keeping or smashing?" he asked.

"Keeping." She'd need to test the firing and glazing to be sure she could deliver what Kyla and her friends were looking for, after all. Making a tester only made sense.

That hum again, another kiss below her ear.

"What will you use it for?" he asked as he snaked an arm around her waist.

"I'm…not sure." Sabrina stopped the wheel, the perfectly shaped clay dick staring back at her. She carefully marked the depression in the center of the tip, smoothing the clay as she went and gathering her courage. "Maybe I'll use it. Could be fun."

His fingers teased along the waistband of her leggings, and for a moment she was lost in their movement, in the heat of his body at her back. She turned her head to look at him over her shoulder, that fizzy, shaken up feeling pressing at the back of her lips.

"You left so early this morning," she said quietly.

His eyes found hers, holding her captive, but his words were unusually hesitant. "I wanted to let you sleep."

"Did you? Or did you want to sneak out before I woke up?"

He swallowed, wetting his lips with a flash of his tongue, and her heart fell to her stomach.

"I didn't want it to be awkward." She narrowed her eyes in confusion, and he blew out a breath as he searched for his explanation. "I'm not used to waking up with someone. I panicked. It won't happen again."

Warmth washed over her at his matter-of-fact promise. Maybe it didn't matter if she didn't want to paint murals—maybe he was indifferent to murals and nurseries and all the soft, fragile beings that belonged there. And maybe she was getting way ahead of herself. They'd only been married a few weeks. It was far too soon to even be thinking about murals. Right?

She pressed her lips tentatively to his. He tasted like his morning coffee. It didn't take long for him to deepen the kiss, to slide his tongue along hers as his fingers slipped beneath the waistband of her leggings. He pulled back to meet her gaze as his fingers continued to stroke the skin below her bellybutton, a question posed in his eyes.

She wasn't sure how she knew, but she *knew* deep in the marrow of her bones that if he asked that question, if he spoke whatever words were dancing behind his eyes, it would change everything. And she wasn't ready for things to change again. They'd only just gotten *here*—to nights full of the most delicious sex, to heated glances, to promises that made her feel warm all over. Couldn't they enjoy *this* for a while before they were confronted with whatever question haunted his ice blue eyes?

She let her knees fall to the side, resting against his powerful thighs behind her, and guided his hand lower as she kissed him again, bringing them back to something safer. At the first brush of his finger over her clit, she melted back against him, relief washing over her to have his touch exactly where she wanted it. He played with her in slow glides of his finger as he kissed her like he had all the time in the world. She made to turn towards him, to pull him closer, but remembered her clay coated hands and stopped herself with a groan.

Baz pulled back, chuckling, his eyes affectionate. He nuzzled into her hair, his lips at her ear. "Keep working on your sculpture, wildflower."

With shaky hands, she reached for the clay phallus, smoothing out the flare at the crown, adjusting her pressure to add the more lifelike ridges and veining, and all the while, he stroked her clit in too-gentle strokes that never quite got her where she wanted to be.

"Sebastian," she grumbled, squirming on her stool.

He chuckled and slid his other hand up the front of her

t-shirt, pinning her against him fully. He pulled down the cup of her bra and pinched her nipple, but still the hand in her pants remained gentle. Her eyes flitted to the door on the other side of the shop. True, they were mostly hidden behind the shelving unit at the front of the studio, and the brown butcher paper still covered the windows of the storefront, but the door was unlocked. Anyone could come in and find them like this, find *her* like this, being slowly tortured for want of an orgasm.

"Will you fuck that cock when it's done, baby? Will you use it to get yourself off and pretend it's me?" he asked. Her breathing hitched, and, as if in reward for being turned on by the idea, Baz slid two fingers inside her, slowly pumping against the spot on her front wall that drove her wild. "It won't be enough for you. You'll need more, isn't that right? But it could be a good warm up. Get you ready for the real thing."

He rocked his hips against her, the unmistakable weight of his erection pressing against her backside as he continued to work her beneath her clothes. She whimpered at the idea of it, and her hands stilled on the clay.

"I didn't say you were done, Sabrina," he tsked in her ear. "You stop, I stop." With a frustrated sound low in her throat, she went back to work on the clay. "There's my good wife." He rewarded her with increased pressure on her clit, winding her up as little shock waves of pleasure radiated out from her center, curling her spine in on itself, shooting down to her toes. "Tell me what you need."

"I need to come," she moaned, rocking her hips against his hand.

"I know you do, baby." He nipped at her neck, left sucking kisses along her throat. "You finish making your toy and I'll make you come, just like you'll come all over that clay cock when it's ready."

"I *am* finished," she protested.

"Not yet," he growled.

She turned to meet his eyes, searched the intensity she found there as her thighs quivered under his renewed ministrations. She was so close and he knew it, the bastard. He was keeping her on that knife's edge until she figured out whatever he thought was missing—

Reaching into the tray of tools at her side, she withdrew a long, thin metal rod. "We'll have to wait until it's fired to add the barbell," she said. Then she stuck the rod through the head of the clay penis, piercing it the way he was pierced, making the toy a replica for the man behind her. He hummed his approval and kissed her deeply. Finally he brought her to climax, holding her against him as she rode out her orgasm, her vision going white around the edges as she shuddered against his hand.

She'd hardly stopped shaking when he pulled his hands from her clothing and stood. As she watched, he sucked her wetness from his fingers, then bent down and kissed her again.

"See you at home, wife."

# Chapter Twenty-five

"I'm sorry we're late!" Tessa burst into the ballroom at The Barclay, the boutique waterfront hotel at the center of Aster Bay's tourism industry, a Styrofoam to-go cup clutched in one hand. Jamie trailed behind her. He set a tray of mini pastries in the center of the round table at the edge of the room that the Food and Wine Festival Committee was using for its meeting.

"We had to stop for a milkshake at Dockside," Jamie explained with a good-natured roll of his eyes. "That's the big craving for month eight. Milkshakes."

Natalia, the lingerie shop owner, stacked a few of the mini pastries on a napkin as she asked, "Why didn't you make the milkshake yourself?"

"Apparently mine don't taste as good," Jamie said.

"It's not that they don't taste as good. But they're different." Tessa lowered herself into an empty chair with a sigh. "It's the ice cream. You use a different kind."

"I use local—"

"It's very good ice cream," Tessa said in a way that made it clear they'd had this argument many times before. "But it's different. Don't argue with me. Argue with the baby." She pointed at her swollen belly. "I don't make the rules."

Gavin stifled a laugh, wincing when Kyla elbowed him in

the ribs. "We were just talking about what packages we should offer this year, and how to gamify them."

"The easiest thing to do is create a passport program," Sabrina explained, handing Jamie and Tessa copies of the notes she'd distributed earlier. She'd been up until well after midnight putting all her thoughts together, perfecting the language, the visuals, and she would have kept going if Sebastian hadn't insisted she come to bed—not that she needed all that much persuading. She pushed away the thoughts of all the ways her husband had found to use his tongue the night before and forged ahead. "Between all the tastings, the opening dinner, and the bonfire on the beach, there are plenty of events and we want to encourage people to attend them all. If they attend at least four events over the course of the weekend, they'd earn an entry in a raffle for some kind of fantastic prize."

"Tell him about the themed tracks," Kyla said, nodding encouragingly.

"You all already did a great job curating themed packages of experiences last year. This would take it to the next level. We create themed tracks of activities—a girls' weekend, for example. A mini photo shoot at the boudoir studio, a visit to the lingerie shop, a manicure or facial at the spa—"

"A breakup party at Get Clayed," Kyla chimed in, grinning.

"Exactly. And if you do all the items in the track you get extra entries in the raffle. That way we can encourage people to visit all the businesses in town, not just the ones participating in the festival," Sabrina said.

"I like it," Jamie said.

"You better watch out, Sabrina, or they'll make you the next chair of this thing," Tessa cautioned with a smile.

"It worked out alright for you," Jamie said.

Tessa shrugged, dissolving into laughter when Jamie tickled her side.

The rest of the meeting flew by as the group brainstormed

tracks that would send tourists all over town and introduce locals to places they might not have otherwise had occasion to visit: a session of goat yoga at the goat farm; a walking tour of the filming locations from *Once Upon A Town*, the reality dating show where Gavin and Kyla had gotten together; an escape room-style game at Aster Place, the historic mansion in town; a mulled cider workshop at Longfield Farm; a pub crawl through the bars, breweries, and distilleries in town—the list went on and on.

By the end of the meeting, Sabrina had her own list of places she wanted to visit in town. When the meeting was over, Tessa slid into a seat beside Sabrina. "Did you get an appointment with Dr. Rosenbaum?" she asked.

"I did! Thank you for the recommendation. I go next week. I can't believe he got me in this fast."

"Good gynecologists are hard to come by. I'm happy to help. Those of us who are newer to town have to stick together," Tessa said. "Trust me, though, by the end of the year, it'll be hard to remember why you ever wanted to live anywhere else."

Sabrina turned Tessa's words over in her mind as she said her goodbyes and drove back to Sebastian's condo. It was already hard to remember why she'd ever wanted to live anywhere else. She'd always loved Aster Bay—the people and the waterfront, the shops and restaurants—and her summers visiting Aunt Lucy were some of her happiest memories, especially that summer ten years ago when she'd spent most of her time stocking food pantry shelves with the man who was now her husband. If things hadn't gone south all those years ago, if she hadn't believed that Sebastian would run her out of town with an angry pitchfork-wielding mob, she probably would have stayed in Aster Bay instead of skulking off to Maine to lick her wounds and rebuild.

And now, all these years later, she could truly call Aster Bay home.

She paused, a strange sense of dread creeping up her spine. Homes could be lost. Homes could be *taken*. If she wasn't careful, she'd once again have to give up her favorite coffee shop and local ice cream and the friends that had come built-in with her marriage. Even her position on the festival committee, where for the first time in years other people were looking to her for answers, could be taken from her—after all, these people had been Sebastian's people long before they became hers.

And where would she go then, when Aster Bay was no longer welcoming to her? How many lives was she going to fall in love with and have to give up? How many times would she be forced to start over?

It was exactly what she'd been afraid of, why she'd promised herself never to get married again.

*Fat lot of good that promise did you. All it took was forty-eight hours in Vegas with Sebastian Graham to get you to abandon that plan.*

Sabrina put her car in park in the spot designated for Sebastian's guests and dug through her purse for her phone. She refused to lose another home. It was too late to go back in time and stop herself from marrying Sebastian, but it wasn't too late to protect herself against the inevitable day when he decided he'd had enough of playing house.

Her fingers hesitated over the name on her phone screen.

What if she was overreacting? What if she and Sebastian could actually make it work? What if the man who growled filthy things in her ear and brought her to ecstasy over and over again didn't pull the rug out from under her?

*And what if he does?*

She couldn't risk it.

She jabbed the name on the screen and fired off a quick text to her father.


**Sabrina:** I'm ready to talk about that post-nup.

"Jesus Christ!" Jamie slammed a hand over his heart and glared at Baz, who had been too deep in Lemon and Thyme's bookkeeping software to even notice his friend had come into the back office at the restaurant. "When did you get here?"

"About an hour ago."

Jamie glanced pointedly at the clock on the wall across from his desk. The restaurant didn't open for the dinner rush for another two hours.

"Is something wrong with the books?" Jamie asked, coming into the office and dropping into the seat on the other side of the desk.

"Just wanted to get a head start."

Jamie eyed Baz warily. "Did you and Sabrina have a fight or something?"

"Everything's fine."

"Right. That's why you're hiding out in *my* office in *my* restaurant."

Baz held up the shiny silver Monopoly dog without missing a beat in his endless scroll of the last month of the restaurant's expenses. "You had something of mine."

Jamie laughed, a deep, full laugh that set Baz's teeth on edge for some reason he didn't want to examine too closely.

"Did you really spend twice as much as usual on cleaning last month?" Baz asked.

"Baz, come on. You're not here to look at my finances."

Baz closed his fist around the Monopoly dog and continued clicking through the accounts on the computer screen.

Jamie sighed. "You leave me no choice. I'm going to have to call in the other guys." Baz glared at him over the top of the computer monitor. "Or you could tell me why you're really here."

"Fuck you." Baz pushed away from the desk and stared

down his friend, turning that little metal dog over and over in his hand.

The truth was, he wasn't sure why he'd come here. He'd woken up in bed with Sabrina, their legs entwined and her perfect ass pressed to his groin, her auburn hair and her wildflower scent all around him, as he had every day for the last few weeks—and he'd panicked. He hardly recognized himself anymore. Baz didn't do sleep overs. He did meaningless sex, no emotions involved, and certainly no cuddling. But after the last month, it had gotten harder to remember that he wasn't the guy who woke up after an incredible night with a woman feeling raw, like his insides had been scraped out—he wasn't the guy who had sex and woke up *feeling* at all.

He'd thought a shower would take care of it, washing her scent from his skin, but the entire time, he'd heard her voice in his head. *I never wanted to get married again ever,* and *Marriage is a trap.* Words he'd been trying like hell to forget but that kept pushing their way to the forefront of his mind, growing louder every day. Each time he remembered her words, that restless feeling grew until he had to get out of there, away from the bedroom where their clothes still lay scattered across the floor, away from the wall of windows overlooking the bay where anyone could have seen them that first night, away from the condo that smelled like her and the sound of her soft breathing in his bed.

But he hadn't been able to stay away for long. Guilt gnawed at his bones for leaving her without saying goodbye, for acting like she was another hook-up when she was his wife.

*Even if she didn't want to be.*

Or did she? She'd sculpted a clay version of his cock. She slept in his t-shirts. And then there was that thinly veiled conversation about having children. Great, now he was picturing it—little redheaded kids with her freckles and his eyes and he wasn't even sure if he wanted that, but he also wasn't sure he didn't want it, so what the fuck was he supposed to do with that?

His own office had been too quiet for too long, and it was hours yet until Sabrina would be home from the studio. He needed to get it together before he saw her again. He'd intended to go to the vineyard, to camp out in Ethan's office, but somehow he'd found himself at Lemon and Thyme instead, using his key to enter the restaurant through the kitchen and helping himself to the dark office at the end of the hall.

Now, looking at Jamie, at the pictures of his and Tessa's wedding that littered his desk, at the framed sonogram picture of their baby, he knew why he'd come here.

Baz pushed out of the chair and paced the length of the small office, scraping his hand over his face. He was grateful for Jamie's silent patience, almost like he knew Baz needed a minute to collect his thoughts. And maybe he did know. Maybe that's exactly why Baz had come here.

"I need to say some shit and I need you to listen and let me get it out, okay?"

Jamie nodded, leaning back in the chair and waiting for Baz to continue.

"Sabrina and I didn't mean to get married. It wasn't planned. We had too much to drink and things got out of hand and the next morning…" Baz held up his left hand and Jamie nodded in understanding. "Did you know there's no such thing as an annulment in Rhode Island?"

"No shit?"

"So fine, whatever, we'll get a divorce. Only something's wrong with Sabrina. She's sick—I mean, not sick exactly, but she gets this pain." He gestured vaguely to his stomach. "Not all the time. But too damn often. And—get this—she didn't have health insurance. Couldn't afford to get any until the studio's up and running. Fine, I think, we're already married, she'll go on my policy. No big deal. And once she's on her feet, then we'll get divorced."

"Makes sense," Jamie said. "You always take care of the people in your life."

Baz made a face and pushed away the compliment. "Only now our families think we're married for real. And you remember how the Pages are." Jamie nods. "I couldn't let her go to that party Labor Day weekend alone. They would have torn her apart. And I think, fine, I'll get to rub it in Holly's face. I'll get to show her she didn't break me when she left."

"And did you?"

"I don't give a shit about Holly," Baz scoffed. *Then why did her words the other night send you into a tailspin?* He shrugged off the thought and barreled ahead. "Except there's this *thing* with me and Sabrina. This sexual chemistry or whatever. And I can't remember ever feeling that way with Holly. Like I had to kiss her or I was going to explode. You know?"

"Yeah, I do know," Jamie said with a chuckle.

"I don't remember it being like that with Sabrina either. Before. She was a kid, and I liked her well enough. Wanted her to be happy. Liked making her laugh. But she was a kid. She wasn't this… It doesn't matter. Point is, it was supposed to be paperwork. Roommates. Married in name only."

"How's that working out for you?" Jamie said with one of his goddamn eyebrow arches.

"*Let's enjoy the time we have*, she said. Like it'd be that easy. And I'm the fucking idiot who agreed. Because of the exploding thing." Jamie nodded, but Baz was pretty sure he was making less and less sense as he went on. Baz dropped onto the couch at the edge of the office and braced his elbows on his knees, hands clasped like he could keep himself together if he could hold on long enough. "How did you know? With Tessa. How did you know it wasn't just sex?"

Jamie blew out a long breath as he considered his answer. "There were a hundred little ways, but I think it was when being with her started to feel inevitable. Like she was the shore and I was the wave. There was never a world in which we didn't end up crashing into each other. I think it was when not being with her started to feel harder than being with her."

Baz hung his head and scraped his hands through his hair. "When we knew each other before, I used to call her 'wildflower.' Her shampoo or something had some kind of floral smell and she seemed…chaotic, but in a good way. I was the only one who called her that." He turned helpless eyes towards his friend and pressed his hand to the side of his ribs. "She has a tattoo. Right here. Wildflowers." He struggled to string together his next thoughts. "She's my wife. I don't think I ever want her to be anything less than that."

For once, Jamie didn't smile and Baz had never been so grateful. This didn't feel like a smiling matter. It felt big and messy and out of control. It felt like careening down a highway in a rainstorm and that second when the water got under your tires and for a moment you were weightless and wild and terrified, but you also felt a little bit like a god, like you could do this impossible thing and survive. Only this time Baz wasn't sure how long it would be until his tires touched the pavement again.

"Does she know how you feel?"

"She doesn't want to be married. Not to me. Not to anyone. Her last marriage… She doesn't want to do it again. If I tell her… Fuck, I don't even have the words to tell her."

"Don't you?" Jamie leaned forward, bracing his elbows on his knees and looking directly into Baz's eyes. "You tell her you love her."

The words stole Baz's breath and simultaneously settled something inside him, like for the first time since that bar in Vegas, the buzzy restlessness in his chest calmed to a dull hum. He loved her. *He loved her.* He silently repeated it to himself a few times, as though he were trying it on for size, and was awe-struck by how well it fit. He loved her. As the words were settling into his bones, becoming a part of him he hadn't even known was missing, something new wrapped itself around his heart, an echo of a long-ago pain.

"And what if I tell her that, and she doesn't want it? What if she's not all that different from her sister after all?"

"Then at least you know."

# Chapter Twenty-six

Baz was working on his laptop at the kitchen island when Sabrina got home. For the last two weeks, he'd taken to working the end of the day from home, timing his arrival to coincide with her typical return from the pottery studio. It would be another few days before she held her first break-up party there for Kyla's friend Jo, but since opening last week she'd welcomed a group from the senior center, led by Mrs. White and Aunt Lucy, to make bowls for the food pantry's latest fundraiser, and a local mommy-and-me class. It was a slow start to be sure, but Baz was certain that once word got out about the break-up parties, business would be booming.

Even if she never booked another event, he was so damn proud of her. She'd built a whole new studio, started from scratch and had it up and running in record time, and she'd done it all on her own. And he was the lucky bastard who got to stand by her side while she did.

He couldn't imagine not standing there for the rest of his life. He certainly couldn't fathom giving her up simply because they'd met an arbitrary deadline on the calendar. But he wasn't sure if she felt the same way.

Most days he came home early to hear about what was happening in the studio. So far, he'd learned all about the difference between slab building and throwing on the wheel—well, not *all* about it, but enough to understand what she was talking about when she enthusiastically recounted her day.

But today was different.

Today, she'd had her first appointment with a new doctor—someone Tessa had recommended in Providence—and Baz had been on edge all day waiting to hear how it had gone, if she'd gotten whatever she needed to keep her from being in pain again. Sabrina had tried to explain that it wasn't that simple, that even with medication there still might be bad days, but it had to be better than what he'd seen on that first day back from Vegas, right? And if that was a mild flare up…

He hoped this doctor was good.

He glanced up from his laptop when the door closed behind her. "How was your appointment?"

"Fine." She stepped between his legs, into his waiting arms, and tilted her face up to receive his kiss. It was all so…domestic. Simple. Easy.

"You got what you needed?"

"Mmhmm. One shiny new prescription for birth control pills."

"And that will help?"

"It should." She rested her hands on his biceps, her fingers skating over the muscles beneath his shirt. How did that simple touch feel that good? "What do you want to do for dinner tonight?" she asked.

If someone had asked him a year ago—hell, two months ago—if he'd ever be the kind of man who waited for his wife to come home from work, who felt lighter with each passing week of these everyday conversations and joint decisions, he would have laughed in their face. Well, to be fair, Baz didn't laugh all that often even two months ago. Yet another thing Sabrina had changed about his life.

Baz curled his hands around the back of her thighs and

pulled her closer, nuzzling into her neck. "I have a few ideas." He nipped at her skin and she laughed, the throaty, fluttery kind that meant she was already turned on. "Let me take you out tonight."

"Like a date?" Her voice was breathy, unsure.

"Yeah, wildflower. Like a date."

*Simple.*

Could it be simple?

Sometimes he could almost forget that none of this was meant to happen. Not taking her out on a date, not sleeping every night in her arms, or waking up and reaching for her. Not the way she looked at him like she was always on the brink of saying something he hadn't let himself want in years—not since her sister.

It all seemed close enough to touch, as real as the feel of her silken hair wrapped around his fist or her breath on his neck.

They hadn't done anything in the right order, and yet maybe that was the key. With Holly, Baz had followed the rulebook: he'd waited until after their third date to ask her up to his apartment, he'd gotten down on one knee, he'd smiled for the overpriced engagement photos—and where had it gotten him?

Maybe he wasn't cut out for traditional. Maybe he and Sabrina were meant to forge their own path. Maybe *simple* was a feeling, not a plan.

Like eating ice cream at two a.m. as the moonlight danced on his wife's skin.

Like watching the town he loved open its arms to her, and watching her embrace it right back.

Like the feel of her freckles beneath his lips as he traced their path across her clavicle.

*Simple.*

Baz watched from the bathroom doorway as Sabrina put small diamond studs in her ears, the finishing touch on her date night outfit. She was always beautiful but she was beyond gorgeous in the form-fitting dress in a green color that made her eyes seem even more vibrant, her long legs on display and the neckline low enough to tease at the shadow between her breasts. He was half tempted to call off this plan and take her to bed straightaway.

*Stop thinking with your dick.*

This was important. They needed to keep their hands to themselves long enough to have a real conversation—about their future, about whatever was going on with her health, about the feeling in his chest that he was afraid to name. And the longer he went without naming it, the more he felt like maybe it was all in his head. It had only been a few weeks, after all.  Maybe he was confusing lust with…something more. Maybe he was letting their circumstances muddle his thoughts. Baz had never thought he'd be the kind of guy to find commitment sexy, at least not after Holly, but knowing Sabrina was his wife, that she wore his ring—Christ, it made him half hard just thinking about it.

And yet they'd skipped all the things that were supposed to come before "I do"—the courtship and the slow discovery of one another. Sabrina deserved that. She deserved to be swept off her feet, to feel chosen. Tonight, he would give her that.

"If you keep looking at me like that, we're not going to make it to dinner," Sabrina said with a laugh.

"Just admiring the view." He pushed off of the doorframe and stepped behind her, settling his hands on her hips and his lips on the curve where her neck met her shoulder.

She sighed happily and leaned back against him. "We could stay home. Order in."

He nipped her shoulder, and she yelped in surprise, the sound dissolving into a giggle that made him smile in spite of himself. "Temptress."

She laughed in earnest, then pushed away from him and reached for her lipstick, a bright red he fully intended to see smeared all over his cock later. "Two minutes," she said when he got distracted by the color painting her lips.

He shook his head to clear it. "I'll give you five."

"You know me so well."

"That I do."

When she emerged from the bathroom—four and a half minutes later—Baz had to remind himself to breathe. Then she took his hand, and smiled up at him, and for a moment, it felt like everything was slotting into place. Like this was the way it was meant to be all along.

Their first stop was at Lemon and Thyme. Baz had called ahead and placed a to-go order, despite Jamie doing his best to convince him that the food would taste better if they ate in at the restaurant. But Baz had other plans, a whole evening, and it didn't involve sitting in Lemon and Thyme while half of Aster Bay tried to eavesdrop on their conversation.

The hostess greeted Baz warmly and within minutes Jamie pushed through the double doors of the kitchen in his pristine chef's jacket, a large brown paper bag filled with some of the best food in the state in his hands.

"You're lucky you're practically family," Jamie said, handing over the bag. "I usually don't make my calamari for to-go orders."

"We appreciate you compromising on your impossibly high standards," Baz said.

"You better."

Sabrina beamed at Jamie. "You have a packed house tonight!"

"Every night," Baz said. It was funny, the way pride blossomed in his chest, to brag about his friend's success, to watch Sabrina drink it in, to know that, as Jamie's accountant, he had some small part in that.

"Hopefully it'll slow down a little soon or I'll need to hire even more help for while I'm out on paternity leave," Jamie said.

"How's Tessa holding up?" Baz asked.

"She's great. Sore and she thinks I don't hear her talking to the baby. She's due in two weeks but she keeps telling the baby to stay in a little longer. I told her not to schedule the baby shower so close to her due date, but she's determined to make it until after the shower." Jamie shook his head, smiling.

"And the breakup party this weekend. Don't let her forget," Sabrina said.

Jamie chuckled. "No chance of that. She's been talking about smashing a clay penis for weeks."

Sabrina smiled wider.

"I've been cooking something special in the back for her. I added a dish of it for you. My treat," Jamie said.

"What does Tessa have you making this week?" Baz asked.

"All South American flavors. I think I've finally perfected my fried plantains."

"I thought you hated plantains," Baz said.

"Chef." A young kid, likely a busboy, approached the hostess stand where they stood talking. "Sorry to interrupt. Your wife's on the phone. Something about empanadas."

"Alright, Ben, thanks. I'll be right in." Jamie turned back to Baz, grinning. "You'll see, when Sabrina's pregnant with your first kid, it won't matter what you hate anymore. Anything she wants, she gets."

"Fucking right," Baz said, grinning.

Alone again, the air suddenly felt heavier between them. Baz took Sabrina's hand in his and squeezed. "Ready to go?"

She blinked away whatever shadows had crept into her eyes. "Yeah. Let's go."

# Chapter Twenty-seven

Sebastian drove them to the edge of town as the sun began to set over the bay, eventually turning his car onto the Williston University campus. The leaves had begun to change color, and by the end of the month Sebastian promised they'd be a stunning mix of reds and oranges. Sabrina rolled down her window to let the crisp night air in, hoping it could calm the low hum of panic that had simmered through her veins since their conversation with Jamie.

"Aren't we a little old to be going back to college?" Sabrina asked.

One corner of Baz's lips quirked up. "Taking a short cut."

Sabrina chuckled at the irony. It seemed all they did was take shortcuts.

"What, you don't like shortcuts?"

"I guess some shortcuts are good. Like using store-bought puff pastry instead of making your own—though Tessa would probably disagree."

"Tessa would definitely disagree."

"She's going to be the kind of mom who makes Pinterest-perfect school lunches with sandwiches shaped like dinosaurs and vegetables cut to look like little trees, entire dioramas in every lunchbox. I bet she won't even need the fancy cookie cutters to do it. She'll just freehand a brontosaurus on a Tuesday morning. Like it's easy."

*Tessa probably didn't have any trouble talking to Jamie about their future, didn't look for any shortcuts to get out of those hard conversations.*

"You alright?" he asked, glancing over at her as drove down the winding roads of the college campus. "You've been tense since we left the restaurant."

"Just hungry."

He frowned and shot her a look that made it clear he didn't believe her lie, but he let it go.

The road curved to the right and turned into a dirt path that disappeared into the trees. Baz pulled over to the side of the road and stopped the car, climbing out before she had a chance to register where they were. Sabrina drew in an awed breath as she took in the view over the roof of the car.

They'd parked on the edge of the road, where the pavement and gravel gave way to dirt and then sand, sloping down to form a shallow beach, mere steps from the first set of pilings that held up the suspension bridge spanning the bay. At this angle, the bridge shot out above them, a steel slash across the sky, the lampposts that lined the edges blinking to life as the last of the sun disappeared beneath the horizon. It was breathtaking.

Sebastian slid his hand into hers. "C'mon."

He led her down to the beach, where he lay out a soft, red flannel blanket in a little protected cove at the edge of the clearing. The early October air was still warm in this little section of the beach, even if the sand beneath the blanket was a good ten degrees cooler. As he unpacked the bag from Lemon and Thyme, opening Styrofoam containers and arranging food on actual China, he spoke in a low voice, a continuous stream of words blending with the gentle lapping of the water against the shore.

"When I was a kid, my mom used to bring me here any

time she had anything important to tell me." He gestured with an open container of wild mushroom ravioli to a spot further down along the shore. "That's where she told me about my dad. I never knew him. He left before I was born. Mrs. White used to say there was an epidemic of absent fathers in Aster Bay. I hated being a part of that statistic."

Sabrina's heart clenched as she lowered herself to sit on the blanket, watching as Sebastian worked. He never paused in his movements, never made eye contact. She got the sense that this—the unpacking, the arranging of food—was the distraction he needed to keep talking, to bare himself to her with such vulnerability, like an animal showing her his belly.

"This is where she told me when Gavin's dad died. Where she told me I couldn't go on the high school trip to Europe because we couldn't afford it. I used to think that made this a bad luck spot, but I know better now. She came here because it was peaceful. She could hear herself think. She could hear the things I didn't say." He paused, glancing up at her with a self-deprecating smirk. "I didn't talk much."

"You don't say," she replied with a smile.

He chuckled and turned back to his work, spooning sauce over the ravioli, separating pieces of garlic bread. "I started coming out here on my own any time I needed to think. Something about the quiet here… It's easier to hear my own thoughts. And I'm pretty sure it's the only place in town where there isn't some busybody eavesdropping on everything you say."

Sabrina leaned back on her hands, stretching her legs out in front of her. Sebastian's gaze snagged on the bare skin, and he grazed the curve of her calf with his thumb, almost as though he couldn't resist touching her.

"It's your secret spot."

He hummed an agreement.

"I bet it was very popular with the ladies," she said, and immediately regretted it. *Popular with the ladies?* Ug.

He wrapped his hand around her ankle, squeezed slightly. "You're the first woman I've brought here."

"Oh." The word gusted out on a surprised breath, the admission wheedling its way deeper into her heart.

He cleared his throat, breaking their eye contact, and handed her a plate, each item arranged with care. A lump worked its way into her throat and she blinked back an unexpected wetness in her eyes.

*Don't be ridiculous. It's dinner. Who cries over dinner?*

But it wasn't just dinner. It was every precise movement he'd taken to create this exact plate of food for her, to provide this experience for her, to open himself up, and she suddenly knew the lump was made of things she needed to open up about, too, pushing their way up and out and—

"Sebastian."

"Eat, Sabrina." He held her gaze as he extended a fork her way—an actual metal fork from his silverware drawer at home. "We can talk after."

She wasn't sure if she was grateful for the reprieve or not, but she accepted it, digging into the eclectic arrangement of foods— mushroom ravioli, calamari with little roasted tomatoes and balsamic drizzle, fried plantains, a soft loaf of garlic bread with crusty edges, green beans with little slivers of almond. None of it made sense together, but all of it was delicious.

"Good?" he asked with a knowing grin when she moaned around a bit of calamari.

"So good."

"It's all my favorites from the restaurant. Well, and Tessa's latest pregnancy craving," he said, gesturing with a plantain on the end of his fork.

They ate without speaking, and she was surprised to find the quiet wasn't awkward. Instead they slowly drifted closer together, until she was half leaning against his chest as she took her last bites of ravioli. The sun had fully set by then, leaving them cloaked in the deep blue black of night, the only light from the handful of stars and the lampposts on the bridge. Sebastian set their plates aside and wrapped his arm around her, tugging her against his chest. She sank back against him, watching the bay ripple in the starlight, the reflection of the bridge a flicker on the waves.

"I'm glad you moved back." Sebastian's voice was deep and smooth, a stone polished by the bay. He nuzzled against her temple.

"I am too."

"I know we didn't plan on any of this, but—"

"I don't think I want kids." The words burst from her before she could stop them, and then hung there between them, almost like she could see them twisting in the air, taunting her. She turned so she could see his face in the half-light from the lampposts. "I might not even be able to have children. PCOS can make it harder, and I was always told… I never let myself think about if I wanted them. And the other day when you said you wanted a mural, I should have told you then. Because the thing is, it wasn't about a mural."

His lip twitched. "I'm aware."

"And I don't want you thinking that I'm going to paint a mural with you when I might not be able to, or I might not want to. It wouldn't be fair to you. Since you do know that you want, you know, a mural." Her voice faded away as she realized how absolutely batshit she sounded rambling on and on about *murals* for the second time in as many weeks.

"Can we stop calling our potential children murals now?" There was that lip twitch again.

She shoved him with a little burst of indignation. "Don't laugh. It's not funny."

"It's a little funny."

She tried to shove him again, but he caught her wrist, stroking his thumb over the sensitive skin there. "First of all,

I said maybe. I don't know if I want kids either, Sabrina. After your sister—" He stopped himself, rolling his lips between his teeth. They didn't talk about Holly, not anymore, not now that there was so much more between them. "I didn't let myself think about it either."

"What if you decide you want them and I can't give them to you?"

He pressed his lips to her palm. "There are lots of ways to become parents. If someday we both decide that's something we want."

*Someday.*

There was so much tied up in that little word.

When Sebastian was close like this, trailing his lips along the inside of her forearm, looking unfairly handsome in the moonlight, talking about *someday*, it was so much harder to remember that she wasn't supposed to want any of it. Not the someday promises, not the sweet dating, not the marriage.

But she did.

She wanted it. She wanted right now and she wanted someday and, God help her, she wanted the marriage, even knowing how much he could take from her—not just her business and her sense of home, but this feeling that someone finally saw her, that for once she wasn't a disappointment, that for once she was enough, nervous babbling and questionable career choices and all. Her father's paperwork could safeguard her business, but what about the rest of it?

"Wildflower," he rumbled against her hair, the tip of his nose tracing the shell of her ear, "you're thinking too much."

She met his eyes, like those ice blue irises could anchor her. "This was only supposed to be temporary," she breathed, some strange mix of wonder and worry wrinkling her brow.

"Health insurance and sex," he said with another one of those lip quirks.

She wanted to bite it, to taste the amusement on his lips.

Maybe then she could also be amused instead of so damn scared.

He smoothed the crease between her brows with the pad of his thumb, traced her cheekbone, dragged his thumb over her bottom lip, and she felt it everywhere. Her skin sparked to life under his too gentle caresses and careful touches.

"I don't think we're cut out for temporary," he said.

"I'm scared," she whispered.

His face softened and he cupped her cheek. "I know. Me too. Let's be scared together."

# Chapter Twenty-eight

There was a terrifying moment where Baz thought she might say no.

He could see Sabrina weighing his heart against her fears, like some fucked up version of Osiris' scales. In that moment, he understood how men had gone mad for love. It didn't matter that he hadn't said the words to her—he was no less in love with her for his inability to articulate the emotion. Despite Jamie's advice, it wasn't the time. If he said it now, she'd run, so he'd have to find other ways to tell her until she was ready.

Baz skated his lips over hers, a whisper of a kiss, and he was gratified when she tipped her face towards him, chasing his lips with her own. He kissed her again, longer this time, slanting his mouth over hers. And then again. Over and over until she grew soft and pliant in his arms, melting against him.

This time when he pulled away, she made a little noise of protest at the back of her throat and pulled him back to her, her fingers twisting in his hair as she took control of the kiss, rubbing herself against him like a kitten as she demanded more.

He'd give her more.

He'd give her every-fucking-thing if only she'd take it.

With a growl, he wrapped an arm around her waist and dragged her into his lap, settling her knees on either side of his hips. Her dress rode up with the movement, her creamy skin almost glowing in the moonlight, and he skated his hands up her thighs, reveling in the softness of her skin. He wished he could see her properly, skirt rucked up and hair fluttering in the wind as she ground her core against the place where he was hard and ready for her. Even through clothing she felt incredible, and he promised himself that the next time they did this, they'd be home, in their bed, with the lights on so he could watch every moment.

"Sebastian," she groaned as she rocked against him.

He dragged his tongue along her collarbone, pressing his lips to the hollow of her throat when he spoke in that low rumble she liked. "Can I fuck you, baby?"

"Here?"

He smirked. She might play at being scandalized, but he could see the way her eyes hooded, could feel how she pressed herself against him harder.

"Here." He slid his hands all the way up her thighs and around to cup her ass, her dress fully bunched around her waist now. "I'll slide right in, fill you up, right here on the beach where anyone could see us."

She smiled as she continued to work herself against the bulge in his pants. "It's pretty dark," she teased, pressing her lips together to try to hide her grin. "Not sure anyone could really see anything."

He reached up with one hand and pulled down the front of her dress, exposing her bra. She released an excited little puff of air, her hand in his hair tightening. She loved this game as much as he did, and fuck if that didn't make him even harder. He pulled down each bra cup, her tits spilling over the flimsy fabric that had concealed them. Christ, she was beautiful, a wanton vision of perfection, her skin like a beacon in the dark.

"They could see you now," he said, running a thumb over one puckered nipple. Of course, there was no one around, no one to see how her breathing hitched when his nail scraped the tight little furl, but the fun was in the fantasy of it, the possibility of danger.

He traced a finger between her breasts and down her torso, sliding his hand into her panties. "Off."

She scrambled to comply, jumping to her feet and nearly falling over as she dragged the fabric down her legs and off, tossing it to the side. He gripped her leg and pulled her back towards him, burying his face between her thighs and inhaling her scent. He'd never get tired of this smell that meant she wanted him as much as he wanted her. He slid his tongue between her lower lips and drew a line up the length of her slit, not enough to bring her any pleasure, but enough to gather the taste of her on his tongue. Enough to make them both out of their minds with need.

"Christ, look at you." He looked up at her with his lips still pressed to her mound. He understood now why poets wrote sonnets to the women they loved, how they could rhapsodize on the exact shape of their breasts, the dip of their waist. Sabrina Page disheveled and needy was a sight to behold.

*Mine.*

The word thundered through his veins and he groaned, burying his tongue inside her, as desperate for her release as his own. He licked her hard and fast, winding her up mercilessly, sucking her clit hard and long, until her thighs began to shake.

And when she seemed ready to break, he stopped, pulling away to watch the haze clear from her eyes.

"What the hell?" she panted.

He pulled her down onto his lap and nipped at her bottom lip, harder than he should have, but she didn't seem to mind. "You come when I decide, wife. And I'm not done playing with you yet." She sucked in a startled breath, but her body melted against him further. He pinched one of her nipples, hard enough to make her gasp, and grinned at the sound. "Take me out, baby."

She licked her lips as she considered his request, but they both knew there wasn't a scenario where she said no to him, not like this. Everything else might be complicated, but this one thing had always been easy for them.

Sabrina unbuckled his belt and drew down his zipper. When she reached inside the undone placket of his dress pants and wrapped her hand around his cock, he grunted, fighting the urge to buck up into her grip. She drew him out, stroking him from root to tip. She slid down his legs and bent towards his lap, but he tightened his grip in her hair, holding her back.

He tsked softly, tilting her face up to his and nipping at her lip again. "Not yet." She pouted and he bit the inside of his cheeks to keep from smiling at how goddamn adorable she was.

He slid the hand in her hair down her back and gripped her ass, pulling her back up until their pelvises were flush, then he lay back, tucking one hand behind his head as a makeshift pillow. Using his grip on her to pull her forward, he lined her up so his erection was trapped against his belly, dragged through her slit without ever breaching her entrance. She shivered as the underside of his piercing grazed her clit, then rocked back to glide over him again.

"That's it, baby. Make a mess of me. Then you can suck me clean."

She groaned, reaching up and roughly cupping one of her breasts as she continued to slide over his length. His fingers dug into the plush softness of her ass as he helped her find her rhythm.

"You like that idea, don't you? Can't wait to taste yourself on my cock." She mumbled an assent through her shaky breathing and moans. Christ, what had he done to deserve this woman? "Gonna have to wait a little longer, baby. I'm enjoying the view too much to let you have what you want yet."

She shivered and adjusted her movements to a short, fast slide over his tip, his piercing dragging back and forth over her clit. He let her go on for a minute, cataloging every shiver and shake, the way her breasts moved with each shuddery breath, and, once again, when she seemed ready to burst, he stopped her, holding her still with his cock trapped against her clit. Pressure but no friction. She whimpered and tried, uselessly, to rock against him again.

Fuck, he loved her like this—needy and wild, not thinking, asking for what she wanted. Undone, all the layers of her proper façade messy and stripped away. Because of him.

"You ready for a taste?" he asked, his voice rough with emotion at the idea of being the one who got to see her like this, to feel her.

"Then can I come?"

He slid his hand over the curve of her hip and pushed her back down the length of his erection. "We're just getting started." She let out a little cry of indignation and his cock kicked against his clothed stomach. "Suck my cock, wildflower. Taste the mess you've made."

It should have been humiliating, keening against Sebastian like an animal in heat, practically begging him for an orgasm. But it wasn't. It was the hottest thing she'd ever done, except maybe when she did as her husband asked and bent down to lick up the length of his erection, tasting her own pleasure coating his skin. He swore under his breath and dropped his head back as she took his tip into her mouth, playing with his piercing with her tongue.

Sabrina used her fists to squeeze the part of him she couldn't take in her mouth, working him in slow teasing glides of her tongue and hands. His hand tangled in her hair, gripping the strands until her scalp tingled, but never guiding her movements. She flattened her tongue along the underside and paid extra attention to the ridge of his crown, to the barbell through his tip, to the slit at the top leaking salty precum.

"Fuck, baby," he cursed. She met his eyes as she hollowed her cheeks and continued to suck, the sensitive tips of her breasts brushing against the rough fabric of his dress pants as she moved over him. "Will you swallow me down, Sabrina? Can I come in this pretty mouth?"

She tried to squeeze her thighs together at the fresh onslaught of need buzzing between her legs, and she hummed her consent, unwilling to lose the taste of him. He cursed again and bucked up into her mouth slightly, and her eyes fell closed.

"Eyes on me." She locked her gaze with his. "There she is," he whispered, his hand moving from her hair to skate down her cheek, gently cupping her face even as her lips stretched around his cock.

And then he was coming, shooting jet after jet of his hot release down her throat. She swallowed it all and licked him clean when he was done, only letting his still-half-hard cock fall from between her lips when he pulled her up to kiss him. It was messy and urgent, the way he licked into her mouth and bit at her lips, his hands everywhere except where she needed him.

When at last he pulled away, he tucked himself back into his pants and did up his zipper and belt, an evil glint in his eye that she had come to love. "Let's go."

He couldn't be serious. She hadn't come yet.

He ignored her incredulity as he packed up their things, throwing them haphazardly into the bag they'd arrived with. All except her underwear. That he folded neatly and tucked away in an inside pocket of his jacket. She got to her feet with a huff and moved to right her clothing.

"Stop." She froze and he moved her hand away from her exposed chest. "You cover up when I say you can."

She sputtered in disbelief. "You expect me to drive home with my tits hanging out?"

"I do. I want any car that drives by us to see what a needy thing you are, and I think you want that too."

She didn't. She absolutely did not.

Except now that he'd said it, she sort of did, and the stinging in her nipples as they tightened seemed to agree with him. His eyes flicked to the puckered peaks, and he lifted one to his mouth, worrying it between his teeth. The bastard.

"Is this alright?" he asked softly, breaking the spell for a moment. He was so earnest, the care in his eyes clear, she knew he'd end this little game if she wanted him to. But she didn't want him to.

"More than alright," she said with a reassuring smile of her own.

His grin turned wolfish and he nipped at her breast once more before straightening up, adjusting his suit jacket.

"Get in the car, Sabrina."

On shaking legs, she did as she was told. When he climbed into the car beside her and turned it on, her skin broke out in goosebumps. Anyone who drove by would see. It was fully dark out now, but if their headlights hit the car just right… She squirmed in her seat. Fuck, why was that so hot?

Maybe because she knew Baz would never let that happen. He'd never actually let anyone see her that exposed. He drove slowly down back roads on the way to his condo, and they never passed a single car. As he turned onto his street, she realized she'd trusted him to keep her safe, to protect her, even as he asked her to drive home completely exposed.

She trusted him implicitly with her body. To direct her, to make her feel good, to know how far to push her. Would it be so hard to trust him with her heart too?

She watched his face flicker in and out of view as they drove beneath the street lights, caught the quirk of his lip, the crinkle at the corner of his eyes. He reached across the console and set his hand on her thigh, squeezing reassuringly, and she realized she already did trust him with her heart, more than she'd ever trusted anyone.

She loved him.

She was *in love* with Sebastian Graham.

And she was pretty sure he loved her too.

Baz put the car in park and, without a word, walked around to her side of the car. He opened her door and slid off his suit jacket, then bent over so he could drape the jacket over her shoulders, laying the lapels to conceal her nakedness. He held out his hand to her, waiting for her to accept it, to follow him. It was the easiest decision of her life.

Inside the condo, he threw the deadbolt on the front door and backed her up towards the large windows overlooking the bay where they'd had sex that first time. He gestured up and down at her dress. "Off," he said as he began rolling up his sleeves. Which was really not fair of him. How was she meant to preserve any pretense of control when he was flashing his forearms at her?

She shed his jacket, shimmied out of her dress and bra, and stood in the darkened condo in front of him completely naked. Somehow she felt more exposed than she'd been on the beach.

He circled her like a hunter circling its prey, his eyes assessing every inch of her. In front of her again, he asked, "Did you like driving home with your tits out for anyone to see?"

"No," she shot back. She wasn't entirely sure why she was fighting him, why she felt the need to push back. She *had* liked it. She'd liked it so much she wasn't quite sure what that said about her.

He smirked and cupped her hard between the legs, dragging his middle finger through her slit. He tsked. "Your pussy says otherwise." He continued to stroke her in shallow passes of his finger, a tease, just enough to remind her of all the ways he *wasn't* touching her. He leaned forward and growled at her ear, "I think you loved it." He pressed the pad of his finger against her clit, grinding down against the swollen spot, and a bolt of electricity shot down her thighs, buckling her knees. "I think you're this wet right now because you wanted someone to see."

Then his hand was gone and she practically cried from the disappointment. "Please, Sebastian," she moaned.

"What do you need, wife?" He stepped back, unbuttoning his shirt as though he had all the time in the world, as though she weren't a shivering, shaking mass of nerves desperate for relief. "Tell me, Sabrina. Tell me what you want from me and it's yours."

She glanced at him, dizzy with need, and yet still somehow certain that they weren't only talking about sex. He shucked off his shirt and moved on to his belt, his pants, stepping out of his shoes, losing one piece of clothing at time until he stood in front of her equally naked, his hand slowly pumping over his cock. It was obscene how hard he was again already, though not as obscene as how badly she wanted to drop to her knees and beg him to fuck her.

"I'll give you anything, wildflower," he said, his voice raw as he stared her down. "Everything. It's yours. But you have to trust me. And tell me what you want."

She tore her eyes away from his. "I want you to fuck me. Make me come."

He sighed, as though he were disappointed in her answer, then he advanced on her, throwing her over his shoulder. She released a startled yelp, but he was already moving towards his bedroom. He threw her down on his bed and climbed over her. She hardly registered the sound of the condom packet opening before he notched his tip at her entrance and filled her in one smooth glide that drove all the breath from her lungs.

"Is that all you want?"

He hooked her legs and lifted them over his shoulders, his hands wrapped around her calves as he drove into her in slow, even thrusts. The new angle was better than anything they'd done before and the edges of her vision went blurry. He blew out a harsh breath through his nose as though he'd realized she was too far gone to answer him, too lost to the sensations zinging along her nerve endings.

"I'll make you come," he promised, the words a low, gravely sound that scraped over her skin. "I'll make you come until you think you can't come anymore. And then I'll make you come again. Do you know why, Sabrina?"

"Why?" she panted as the orgasm began clawing its way up her over-sensitized nerves.

"Because you are my wife." He pressed his thumb to her clit and began working her hard and fast in time to his thrusts. As the first orgasm crashed over her, he fucked her harder, never faltering in his rhythm. "Because I'm not done with you yet, Sabrina. I'll never be done with you."

He slowed the movement of his thumb, but kept it pressed tightly against her, as she shook around him. She cried out his name, her toes curling. Everything in her centered on the place where they were connected, where he was carving his name so deeply inside her she knew she'd never be able to forget how it felt to be his. As her heart rate slowed, he began moving within her again, stroking her twice as fast, twice as hard.

"That was one."

# Chapter Twenty-nine

"I'm telling you, my penis was crooked." Kyla cocked her head to the side and lifted a finger, bending it to the left, as though that were an adequate representation of the clay phallus she'd created during the breakup party earlier.

Her friend Jo, a willowy honest-to-God model with a platinum blonde pixie cut, leaned across the small table at the back of the dive bar they'd gone to after the breakup party and bent Kyla's finger even further. "It's not crooked, but it kind of hooks to the left. Plenty of people like that kind of thing."

"The point wasn't to make the perfect penis," Sabrina reminded them. "There is no such thing as perfection in art."

"But there is such a thing as the perfect dick," Jo said. She gestured to Kyla's still bent finger. "And that was not it."

Kyla dropped her hand and reached for her drink, her cheeks turning pink. "I have no need for perfection in clay when I have the perfect real thing at home."

"Kyla Philomena Mitchell-soon-to-be-West!" Jo exclaimed with a delighted cackle.

"Not my middle name." Kyla shook her head and took another sip of her drink.

"It's too bad Ben's dad isn't hot," Jo mused as she dunked another mozzarella stick in marinara sauce. "I could have taken a page out of your book and banged my ex's dad. But Mr. Lewis is short and balding and I'm pretty sure he has a chronic case of pink eye." She wrinkled her nose and took a bite of the mozzarella stick before aiming it accusingly at Tessa. "And my dad doesn't have any hot friends, either. What good are you two? How's a girl supposed to follow in your sickeningly-in-love footsteps?"

"Tessa's dad is still single," Kyla offered.

Tessa groaned. "Can we not?"

"Hypocrite," Kyla teased, nudging her friend's shoulder lightly.

"It's not that! I'm not opposed to Dad finding love with someone I know, per se, but…" She shivered. "Never mind. Very much opposed."

They all laughed as the bartender set another round of drinks in front of them. Sabrina listened happily as the other women bantered, their affection for each other clear with each teasing volley across the table, and marveled at being included. She liked these women.

She liked everything about her life in Aster Bay.

"Sabrina, did you ever figure out how to make one of the pottery penises…functional?" Tessa asked.

Sabrina cheeks heated. "Mmhmm. It wasn't as hard as I thought it would be."

"That's what she said," Jo mumbled.

"Does Jamie know you're trying to replace him with a piece of pottery?" Molly, the dark-haired friend who'd arrived with Jo, asked.

"Not *replace*. Assist," Tessa clarified. She turned to Jo. "Find yourself a man who welcomes the occasional assist. It keeps things interesting."

"Noted," Jo said with a saucy smile.

"Ooo, that should go on the checklist!" Kyla dug in her purse for a notepad, flipping pages until she found the right one. "Right after 'good tipper.'"

"What is this checklist?" Sabrina asked.

"Things my next boyfriend has to have," Jo said.

"Like a job?" Molly teased.

"Yes! Like a job!" Jo laughed, dunking another mozzarella stick. "Like the ability to dirty talk without referring to my *petals*." She shuddered.

"He didn't," Sabrina laughed.

"Oh, he did. And that wasn't even the worst one."

"Flaps," Molly said with a sympathetic nod.

"Sounds like he got his hands on some old school romance novels," Tessa said. "At least the boy wanted to learn."

"But I don't want a *boy*," Jo whined. "I want a *man*. A whole, grown-ass man who's not afraid of toys," she gestured at Tessa, "preferably has some hot-ass kink he's willing to teach me about," she gestured at Kyla, "and can brood so well he can set your panties on fire from across the room." She directed the last at Sabrina.

"Excuse me?" Sabrina laughed.

"Baz is the master of the brood," Molly said.

"And he has a job," Jo said. "And I bet he can dirty talk with the best of them."

All eyes turned expectantly to Sabrina, waiting for her to confirm that her husband did, in fact, have the filthiest mouth she'd ever heard. She squirmed in her seat at the memory of some of the things he'd said to her the night before, the answering soreness between her legs a reminder of how much she'd liked each and every one of those growled commands.

"He's not bad," she said.

"Please," Jo scoffed. "That man looks like he could make you come without ever touching you."

*If only she knew how right she was.*

"He's a good tipper too," Jo continued. "And I bet *he's* not afraid of the assist."

Sabrina thought of her own functional clay cock, newly completed with a shiny barbell all its own and tucked into the bedside table in Sebastian's room. No, he definitely wasn't afraid of the assist.

"Okay, okay, I think we're embarrassing her," Kyla said.

"It's fine," Sabrina said, but she knew her cheeks must be bright red.

Jo sighed. "You got one of the last good ones."

"Bullshit. There are plenty of good ones left," Molly said. "We just haven't found them yet."

"You will," Sabrina said. "Sebastian and I knew each other for ten years before we got married. And for most of that time, he hated me."

She knew it was the wrong thing to say the second it left her mouth. Four sets of interested eyes locked on her, and she could feel the barrage of follow up questions before they began.

"What do you mean *hated*?" Kyla asked.

"Hated is probably the wrong word," Sabrina hedged.

"How *did* you two end up together? Jamie was short on details," Tessa said, doing her best to look as though Sabrina hadn't let slip something she definitely shouldn't have said in front of Sebastian's friends.

"Oh, you know, just one of those things," Sabrina said. *You will not word vomit the details of your marriage to these women. You will not betray Sebastian's trust that way.* "Let's talk about something else. Like penises! Kyla, does Gavin have a good one? Penis that is."

*THAT was the best topic change you could come up with?!*

Kyla let out a startled laugh. "Yeah. He's got a good penis."

"Good. That's good. Good penis is important," Sabrina said. *Oh, shut up.*

"Alright, you guys, I think that's my cue to get Jo home before we're all too drunk to remember this conversation tomorrow," Molly said.

"I want to know more about the good penis," Jo complained. "C'mon. Let a girl live vicariously."

With some more laughter and hugs all around, Molly finally succeeded in guiding Jo out of the bar, leaving Kyla, Tessa, and Sabrina alone.

"Hey, I didn't mean to make you uncomfortable," Tessa said.

"No, no, of course not. You didn't," Sabrina said.

"Kind of seems like I did."

Sabrina sighed and met Tessa's eyes. It would be nice to talk to someone about what was going on. Not the drunken Vegas wedding or the sort-of-fake-but-maybe-now-real marriage thing, but maybe the other parts. The way Sebastain had given her a string of soul-shattering orgasms the other night and then immediately pulled away. Not physically. He'd never left the bed they now shared, had even kept his arm banded around her all night, but…emotionally, maybe? She could feel the difference in the way he spoke to her, the way he looked at her. Like some of those walls from that first night in Vegas were back, keeping her out.

"Things are complicated," Sabrina began.

Kyla smiled. "Then you've come to the right place. The two of us are complicated relationship experts. Engaged to my ex's dad," she said pointing at herself, then, pointing at Tessa, "married her dad's best friend. Remember?"

*Tell me what you want.*

The sincerity in his voice still tugged at her heart. The disappointment in his sigh when she'd demanded an orgasm echoed in her mind the way the memory of his touch echoed through her body.

*I'm not done with you yet, Sabrina. I'll never be done with you.*

She was tempted to believe him. She *wanted* to believe him. But she wasn't sure how. And she didn't know how to ask for what she really wanted from Sebastian.

"I'm fucking it up." The truth of her words twisted in her gut. "I don't know how not to."

"You love him, don't you?" Kyla asked.

"Yeah. Yeah, of course, I love him." Sabrina blinked back the moisture gathering at the corner of her eyes. She loved him, and she was driving him away.

"There are a lot worse places to start than that," Kyla said gently.

Sabrina swallowed a laugh, dashing away the tears from the corner of her eyes. "Gah, sorry, look at me, being *that* girl, crying in a bar."

"Hey, *that girl* is our friend," Tessa said. "And she's allowed to have the full range of human emotions, even when it's messy. And complicated."

"I think I hurt him. I didn't mean to. I'm just so afraid of losing myself again." Sabrina closed her eyes, exhausted by her own hang-ups. For the first time, she really felt the weight of her fears, how they'd held her back.

"Marriage is hard, and trust is scary," Tessa said. "The thing about really loving someone is you do lose yourself, but that's okay, because you find yourself too."

# Chapter Thirty

"Where do you want the cupcakes?" Gavin balanced three pastry boxes against the doorjamb of Ethan's kitchen.

"Over there, thanks." Ethan gestured to the counter, already filled with more food than they were ever going to eat in one afternoon. "Did they make the bananas foster one?"

Jamie scoffed and lifted the lid to show Ethan the baked goods. "My wife's staff know how to follow directions."

Baz climbed down from the stepladder he'd been using to hang the obnoxious stork banner above the kitchen doorway. "What's next?"

Ethan glanced around the kitchen. "I think that's everything for in here."

"Living room's all set too," Jamie said, swiping a mini quiche from the tray on the counter.

Baz glanced at the clock on the wall. "What are we supposed to do for the next hour before everyone else arrives?"

Gavin glanced at a table in the corner of the living room decorated with a yellow baby farm animal tablecloth. "I'll get the cards."

"I'll get the beer." Ethan ducked back into the kitchen.

"Make mine a Scotch," Baz called.

Jamie filled a bowl with tortilla chips and set it on the table as the others returned, each taking their usual seats around the table.

"Give me those. You suck at shuffling." Baz took the cards from Gavin.

"Just because I got multiple draw-fours last time doesn't mean—" Gavin protested.

"That you suck? Yeah, it does," Jamie said.

"And here I was going to suggest you go first, daddy," Gavin teased.

"Hey now. Only Tessa's allowed to call me daddy."

"Jesus Christ—Jamie, how many times do I have to tell you not to talk about my daughter like that when I'm around?" Ethan grumbled.

"Draw two, grandpa." Jamie slapped down his card.

"Holy shit. One of us is about to be a grandfather," Gavin said.

"You're realizing this now?" Baz asked.

"No, but it's weird, right? When did we get old enough for that?" Gavin asked.

"We're not. You two had kids when you were ridiculously young," Baz said, gesturing to Gavin and Ethan.

"And what about you? You and Sabrina going to have any kids?" Gavin asked.

Baz pressed his lips together and focused on his cards. The last day and a half, he and Sabrina had hardly been speaking, never mind planning their future. "We've only been married six weeks."

Gavin played a reverse card, making it Baz's turn again. "I didn't mean right now. You've talked about it though, right?"

Baz played his card. A plain ol' boring two. What he wouldn't give for some kind of nuclear reverse to make Gavin draw ten or twenty cards. He didn't want to think about all the conversations he and Sabrina weren't having. The last week had been so good, so comfortable—she hadn't nervous babbled even once and he was getting used to sleeping next to her. If he was being honest, he wasn't just used to it—he fucking loved it.

But the other night he'd walked right up to the line of what they'd agreed to, come dangerously close to telling her he loved her, and she'd made it perfectly clear all she wanted was sex. A few weeks ago, he would have sworn that was what he wanted too—a gorgeous woman who was his perfect match in bed and wanted nothing more from him. A dream come true.

Except now it felt more like a nightmare.

"Have you and Kyla talked about it?" Baz asked, shifting the attention away from himself.

"Of course. Before I proposed."

"And?" Jamie prompted.

"We didn't definitively say no forever, but it's absolutely no for now. She's still young, though. I know she might want kids later."

"And you'd be okay with that?" Ethan asked.

"Yeah, I think I would be."

Baz felt all three sets of eyes turn towards him. He clenched his jaw tighter and blew out a frustrated breath through his nose. "We're not sure if we want kids."

"But things are going well?" Jamie asked.

Baz caught his eye, saw the hesitance there, and knew Jamie was recalling their conversation from last week. He didn't want to get into all the things that had subtly shifted since then, the ground he'd gained and lost, the things he didn't even know how to quantify that were slipping away with each minute that passed.

Baz nodded once as he played his turn. "Yeah."

"You're definitely going to be the next one to have kids," Gavin said. "You'd have cute kids. Her hair and your eyes."

"Gav," Ethan said, a warning note in his voice as he kept his eyes on Baz.

"What? It's true. Oh! And if you have them soon, your kids could be best friends with Jamie's kids!" Gavin said.

Baz shot a glance at Jamie and Ethan and hoped his message was clear—*shut it down*—as he pushed to his feet and grumbled something about needing to use the bathroom.

"I guess we're done playing?" Gavin called after him.

Baz pushed into the bathroom at the end of the hall and shut the door behind him a little harder than necessary, closing out the sounds of his friends. He braced his hands on the sink and hung his head between his shoulders.

*It'll be fine. Suck it the fuck up and talk to her. It'll be fine.*

The phone in his pocket vibrated and he sighed when he saw his lawyer's name flash across the screen. "Not a great time," he said by way of greeting.

"I'm looking over this agreement and I gotta tell you, Baz, I wouldn't sign this if I were you."

Baz pinched the bridge of his nose. "What the fuck are you talking about?"

"The post-nup."

Baz's eyes flew open as cold dread slithered down his spine. "The what?"

"The post-nuptial agreement your father-in-law's firm had forwarded for your signature." He was going to be sick. "Tell me you know what I'm talking about."

"First I'm hearing of it."

"Shit. Sorry, I assumed…"

Baz forced himself to breathe, to stay calm even though he could feel his hands already starting to shake. "What does she want?"

"You both leave with the assets you brought to the marriage—your business and hers, her inheritance when the times comes. Then it gets dicey. You're responsible for all legal fees in the event of a divorce, both hers and yours. Your condo is to be considered marital property. And this line for spousal support—frankly, I'd be surprised if this thing is even enforceable."

"Shred it."

"I can send it over for you to review—"

"I don't want to fucking review it. Shred it." Baz scrubbed

his hand over his face.

"We can counter," his lawyer continued. "Obviously your father-in-law got overzealous in trying to protect his daughter."

"We're not countering. I'm not signing. Shred the fucking thing."

Baz hung up as his lawyer continued to talk about *negotiations*. As if he was going to negotiate with Sabrina when she was already planning her exit. And not just any exit, but one that would fuck him over spectacularly. As if her family hadn't humiliated him enough for one lifetime.

He'd trusted her. And the hell of it was, if she'd asked him, he would have signed any damn thing she wanted. He'd rip out his own heart and serve it to her on a silver platter if it meant he could keep her, if it meant she'd let him in.

*Idiot. This is why you don't get emotional. This is why you don't let your guard down.*

He stared at himself in the mirror, rolling the tension from his neck and straightening his cuffs. He should have known something like this was coming, that she was another person who wanted to use him up and throw him away.

This time he'd be the first to walk away.

Baz left the bathroom and made his way back into the living room where the party was in full swing. He must have been in there longer than he'd realized. As he made his way through the gathered crowd of familiar faces, he caught bits and pieces of conversation, all blending together into a wall of sound.

"So I said to my Ricky, I said, you have to make a map so the people who get stuck in the corn maze can find their way out again." Cheryl patted her husband's knee beside her, her loud storytelling rising above the din. "And he said, Cheryl, honey, if they get lost in the corn, they can eat their way out." She roared with laughter.

On the other side of the room, Gavin's and Baz's moms ooo-ed and ahh-ed over a hand-knit baby blanket Ethan's mother had sent from Florida. In another corner, Kyla and Gavin chatted happily with Natalia from the lingerie shop, Gavin shooting adoring looks at his fiancée as she grew more animated in her speech. At the center of it all, Jamie and Tessa held court, his hand resting protectively on her belly.

Baz needed to go. Jamie and Tessa would understand. He needed air.

He rounded the corner, determined to slip out the back door in the kitchen, and came face to face with his wife.

Sabrina leaned against the wall, clutching her glass of punch as if it were a lifeline. The sight of her was like a sucker punch to the gut. She wore a silky green blouse that brought out her eyes, the first few buttons undone, tucked into one of her pencil skirts. This one was a cream color, cut above the knee, and for a moment he wanted to drop to his knees at her feet and beg her to love him. To press his lips to the soft skin on the inside of her thigh and plead his case. He could love her enough for the both of them. He could—

He knew the instant she caught sight of him, the way her spine straightened, the smile that spread over her lips. They were painted red again, the color vibrant against her pale skin. Was she paler than usual? Her eyes lit up and she raised a hand in greeting, as though he might not have seen her yet. As though she wasn't always the first person he saw in any room. As though she wasn't the *only* one he saw.

*Enough.*

Her brow furrowed and her head cocked to the side in confusion as she registered his immovable stance. He couldn't go any nearer to her without risking flinging himself at her feet and exacerbating his humiliation. And he couldn't walk away.

How was he supposed to walk away from her?

Christ, how was he supposed to live without her now that he knew what it was like to love her, even if she didn't love him back?

She set her glass down on a nearby table and made her way across the room to him, but she stopped short a few inches further from him than normal. As though she was afraid to touch him.

He should be grateful. If she touched him, he wasn't sure what he would do. Push her away? Pull her closer? Rip off that goddamn skirt and fuck her right there in the middle of the party, as though it would somehow prove that she was his? As though he could fuck her into loving him?

Hadn't he tried that already?

And she was still going to leave. More than that, she was going to burn down the fucking house on her way out the door.

"You alright?" she asked, reaching up to touch his forehead, but then she seemed to think better of it and dropped her hand. "Did something happen?"

Something wasn't right—not only the pain in her lower abdomen, but something with Sebastian. Sabrina had been relieved to see him when he appeared in the kitchen, but then something had shifted. His face had hardened, jaw clenched. And he seemed pale, drawn, like maybe he wasn't feeling well either. Maybe they'd both gotten food poisoning.

She really hoped it was food poisoning.

"You alright? Did something happen?" she asked.

His eyes flitted about the room, clocking the groups of guests talking and laughing, as though he were mapping out his exit. When his gaze fell back on her, she felt the coldness in his stare like the temperature in the room had dropped several degrees.

"I'm not doing this here," he said, pushing past her on his way to the back door of the kitchen.

"Sebastian?"

"No. I'm done being lied to," he barked without bothering to look back at her.

Then he threw open the kitchen door and was gone.

Panic rose in her throat. She was too late. She'd waited too long to tell him how she felt and—*No.* This was not how their story ended. She would not let him march away from her with a head full of assumptions like last time. She would not wait another ten years to tell him how she really felt.

She pushed past the elderly women inspecting the mini quiches on the kitchen counter and followed Sebastian out the door onto a small porch at the back of the house. He stood at the bottom of the three wooden steps with his back to her, his hands in his hair, elbows out to the side, as though he'd just run a marathon. Sabrina knew the instant he registered her presence, the clacking of her heels on the wooden deck causing his shoulders to tense, his back to expand with the slowest, deepest breath.

"Sebastian, there's something I need to tell you."

He whirled around on her, his nostrils flaring, and for a wild, panic-addled moment she thought it must be what a dragon looked like before they breathed fire on their victim. "You had me fooled. I didn't see this coming."

"See what coming?" Another stab of pain and she dug the heel of her hand into the spot.

*Nope. Definitely not food poisoning.*

His eyes shot to the spot and softened for a moment, but he blinked it away, refocusing his anger on her. "Was this your plan all along? Is that why you really moved back here? To get some kind of revenge for—for what?"

"What are you talking about?"

"The post-nup. Your father sent it to my lawyer this morning."

All the breath rushed from Sabrina's lungs and her mouth went dry. "He did what?"

"Don't pretend you didn't know."

"He wasn't supposed to send anything. I didn't—"

"You didn't tell your father you wanted my condo and spousal support?"

"What?" Her head spun, her stomach twisting in on itself. None of this made any sense. "I don't know what you're talking about."

"So you didn't ask your dad to draft a post-nuptial agreement that would screw me over?"

"That's not what—" She winced as another stab tore through her abdomen, this one stronger than the last. Sebastian paced on the lawn, barely looking at her, and she could feel each brick in that wall he was erecting between them. A wall she knew she'd never break through again if she didn't stop this. "I was scared. I told you I never wanted to get married again."

"I didn't force you down the aisle!"

"I know!" They were shouting now. Likely everyone in the house could hear every word of this argument, but she could hardly care about that. She was *losing* him, and he didn't even know she loved him.

"At least when your sister fucked me over, she didn't try to pretend she gave a shit."

His words were a slap across the face, stinging and drawing tears to her eyes faster than she cared to admit. "I didn't— I'm not— I didn't ask him to do that. My parents wanted us to sign a post-nup. I told him I'd consider it, to show me a draft. I knew within minutes that I'd never sign it. I knew—" He released a grunt of disbelief and ceased his pacing, staring her down with eyes that seemed to look right through her. "I was scared," she repeated.

"Of me. You didn't trust me."

"No, that's not—"

"Then why?" he barked.

"Because I have so much more to lose this time! I lov—"

"Don't." He shook his head, swallowing hard, his eyes flashing with fire like he'd been backed into a corner and was prepared to fight his way out. "Don't fucking say that now."

When had she started crying? She dashed away the moisture from her eyes, but it was useless. "I'm sorry I doubted you, even for a minute. I'm sorry."

"I don't know how to trust you." He closed his eyes, shaking his head.

"Sebastian, please."

"I'll find somewhere else to stay tonight." This time when he drew in an overlarge breath, he seemed to shrink under the weight of it, his shoulders slumping.

"Don't do this. Can't we talk about it?"

"No. Not right now we can't."

"Why not?"

"Because I'll say things I can't take back."

She forced herself to breathe through the inescapable feeling that she was being torn apart from the inside out, that her organs had conspired to make manifest the agony of watching Sebastian slip away. "Don't give up on us. Sebastian, please."

"There is no us. None of this was real."

"Don't say that. It was real to me."

He hung his head, then sniffed and looked right through her. "I wish I could believe you."

Sebastian disappeared around the corner of the house as Sabrina stood in shock, unable to move, unable to speak. A moment later, his car kicked up gravel as it turned out of the driveway and down the street, leaving her alone.

She crumbled, dissolving into tears as she sat on the steps of the deck, the ache in her chest warring with the stabbing in her abdomen as she sobbed. She pressed against the familiar spot on her side as the pain seared through her again, hot and sharp and bright enough that the edges of her vision went white, and she gasped for breath.

This wasn't like the last time or the time before that or the time before that when the sharp stab of pain slowly dimmed, when it dulled to the sting of a pulled muscle, flaring with movement but otherwise quiet, until it disappeared altogether—at least until the next time. This pain wasn't diminishing. It was as though someone had her insides in a vise grip and was slowly twisting, twisting. Like she was being torn apart from the inside.

Was this what a broken heart felt like? God, how could she survive it?

"Sabrina." Kyla's voice called to her as though she were underwater, fuzzy and muted, too far away.

And then her hand was on Sabrina's forehead, the other resting on her knee as Kyla crouched in front of her. Kyla was talking to her, but Sabrina couldn't make out what she was saying.

Then everything went black.

# Chapter Thirty-one

Baz threw another stone and watched it skip across the surface of the bay once, twice, then sink. Grunting in frustration, he bent and gathered another handful of the small smooth stones that littered this section of beach beneath the bridge and tried again. Once, twice, gone. He swore under his breath and tried again. And again. Each stone sinking too early.

*Fucking rocks.*

He shed his suit jacket, tossing it onto the beach. As though he were preparing for a fight, he rolled up the sleeves of his shirt, pacing at the water's edge, his shiny dress shoes sinking into the wet sand there. They'd be ruined. He couldn't be bothered to care.

He squared off with the open water, as though meeting an enemy in the boxing ring, exhaled hard through his nose, and sent another stone skipping across the water. When it, too, sank, he threw down the remaining stones, cursing.

This was supposed to be his place, the one place where all the rest of the noise faded away and he could think, but now all he could see were flashes of the other night. Sabrina in his lap, her hair in the wind, those fucking red lips.

He shouldn't have come here. But there wasn't a place in town that didn't hold her memory now. Part of him wanted to go home to her, to shout and fight and fuck until there was nothing left to do but forgive her. He was hurt and angry, all his old wounds pushed to the surface and cut open to bleed, but he loved her. He *loved* her. And yet she'd somehow believed he was capable of leaving her, of taking from her and hurting her the way her ex had.

*Didn't you, though? She wanted to explain herself and you wouldn't listen, just like you wouldn't listen ten years ago. Jesus Christ, she was in pain and you walked away.*

Fucking stupid voices in his head. He wanted to be angry, dammit, not feel guilty.

He'd work off the last of this adrenaline and then he'd go find her. She'd tell him he was an idiot. He'd agree. They'd make up. It would be fine. Couples fought, right? It would be fine.

He threw another stone across the bay, but his heart wasn't in it. She'd hurt him, but he'd hurt her too. His anger dissipated, only to be replaced by guilt, sour and twisting in his stomach.

*Don't give up on us. Sebastian, please.*

*It was real to me.*

He scrubbed his hand over his face. Jesus Christ, he was an asshole. Fuck forgiving *her*, he needed to beg for her forgiveness. And he didn't have any idea how to do that. Baz had never asked anyone for absolution before—aside from a priest during confession—and he wasn't exactly known for being forthcoming with his own forgiveness. Baz was the guy who held a grudge against his friend for ten years because of one sentence in a text message and a handful of things he'd heard out of context. But he didn't want to be that guy anymore. That guy didn't deserve to breathe the same air as Sabrina, let alone to call her his wife.

He would make himself worthy of her. He'd do whatever it took, every day, for as long as they both lived, to prove his love to her.

But first, he had to apologize.

*And get flowers. Flowers probably wouldn't hurt. The biggest bouquet of flowers you can find.*

Baz turned at the sound of a car approaching, only moderately surprised when he recognized Gavin's hatchback pulling up beside his BMW. The car was hardly in park when Gavin threw open the door and stormed across the beach towards Baz.

"Where the hell have you been?" Gavin demanded.

"I know. I'm an asshole. I'll apologize," Baz said, reaching for his jacket.

"What are you talking about?"

"What are *you* talking about?"

"Tessa's water broke. She and Jamie are at the hospital now. And Sabrina—" He paused, scanning Baz's face, his eyes softening in a way that was probably meant to be comforting but sent fear spiking through Baz's heart.

"What about Sabrina?"

"We have to go," Gavin said.

"Gav, tell me."

"She collapsed. In the yard. The paramedics think it might be appendicitis. She's—"

Baz was already pushing past Gavin, back towards his car, his heart pounding in an endless chant that sounded a lot like his wife's name.

*Hold on, wildflower. I'm coming.*

"Baz, you can't drive." Gavin had to run to catch up to him, meeting him at his car door. "Come on. I'll take you."

It had been hours. Or maybe only *an* hour? Time had no meaning in the pale seafoam green hospital waiting room where Baz had been pacing since he and Gavin arrived.

Gavin sat in one of the identical chairs, flipping through

each of the magazines on the little side table until he'd been reduced to doing the hidden picture searches in the *Highlights*. He didn't say a word. He hardly even looked at Baz. And somehow it helped. Knowing Gavin was there, waiting for when Baz needed him, but pretending he was too engrossed in finding the green teacup hidden in the tree leaves to pay attention to Baz's breakdown.

"It's been too long," Baz said, mostly to himself, as he passed Gavin and began another lap around the mostly deserted waiting room.

Gavin glanced up at him, his face a neutral mask. "It takes as long as it takes."

Baz scoffed, scraping his hand along his jaw, and came to a stop in front of his friend. "They have to know something by now."

Gavin set down the magazine. "She's going to be okay. The nurse said she was awake in the ambulance and during her scans, talking to the doctors before they took her in for surgery. Someone will come get you when they know something."

When they'd arrived at the hospital, the astringent scent of ammonia cleaners and the hum of the fluorescent lights had snapped into stark reality. Sabrina—*his* Sabrina—was here, somewhere behind those double doors, in surgery, in pain, scared and alone. He'd left her *alone*.

He dug his hands into his pockets, fingering the rings they'd given him when he'd arrived. Her wedding rings, removed before she went into surgery. He should have been there.

Baz sank into a seat next to Gavin.

*She doesn't even know I love her.*

He scrubbed his hand over his face and slid his hands into his hair, digging his fingertips into his scalp to ground himself in the moment.

*She will not die today. She can't die when she doesn't even know I love her.*

"She knows," Gavin said softly. Baz shot him a look, desperate to believe him. "You should tell her anyway. Women like that. And for some reason, this woman loves you too."

Baz shook his head. "I was an asshole."

"Yeah, you probably were. I didn't say you don't owe her an apology."

"I don't know how to do this."

"You just do it." Gavin leaned forward, bracing his elbows on his knees and leveling Baz with his most parental *cut-the-shit* look. "You wake up each day and you decide she's worth it. You decide to stop letting your baggage get in the way of your happiness." He leaned back, picking up *Highlights* again and flipping through the brightly colored pages. "Let me tell you, when you finally stop pretending she's not the most important thing in your life—" He whistled. "There's nothing better."

Baz pushed to his feet. He couldn't sit there any longer and wait. Sabrina was back there. Alone. He pressed his palms flat against the cool top of the desk at the edge of the waiting room and made sure to keep his voice quiet, even, to project the appearance that he wasn't a few seconds away from completely losing his shit.

"Is there any update? Her name is Sabrina Page and—"

"Sir, I don't have any new information. I promise, as soon as she's in recovery, someone will come talk to you," the woman behind the desk repeated.

"Does it usually take this long? It's been a long time—"

"I promise you she is being well taken care of." The woman looked at him with an expectant eyebrow raise, waiting for him to accept her meager information and go sit in the waiting room for another indeterminate length of time.

*Fuck that.*

"You don't understand. I should be with her," he said, pressing his palms down harder to keep his hands from shaking. "I should be—"

The double doors to the left of the desk burst open, a trio of harried-looking doctors in green scrubs guiding a gurney through the doorway and down the hall towards another set of double doors, already swinging open. And on that bed, a spray of auburn hair against the white pillow, a too-pale face dotted with freckles. Baz peeled away from the desk, turning to follow after the hospital bed as it rolled away.

"Sabrina!"

"Sir, you need to step back."

"Sabrina!" he called again, trying to move around the woman from behind the desk who suddenly seemed a whole lot more formidable now that she was standing. He really didn't want to knock down this poor woman trying to do her job but he needed to get to— "Sabrina!"

"Sir, step back."

"Sebastian?" Sabrina's voice was thin, frail, but it was a balm to his frayed nerves.

"We need you to step back." One of the doctors at Sabrina's bedside turned to Sebastian, blocking his path.

He called after her, moving faster towards her. "I'm here, wildflower. I'm—"

A hand landed on his shoulder, trying to guide him away from her. "Sir—"

"That's my wife!" Baz roared.

Suddenly everything was quiet—no more fluorescent light hum, no more squeaky hospital bed wheel—only Baz's own ragged breathing.

"That's my wife," he repeated, quieter, grasping for some semblance of calm.

The doctor in his path glanced back at his colleagues, seeming to come to some sort of silent consensus, then stepped back. Suddenly he was guiding Baz towards Sabrina instead of blocking his path and Baz didn't think he'd ever wanted to hug a stranger more.

"Your wife has just come from surgery. She'll be groggy for another hour or so, and she'll need to stay overnight for observation, but she did very well," the doctor by Sabrina's feet said as Baz dropped to his knees at her bedside, pulling her hand into his grasp. He held it with both of his hands, pressing her curled fingers to his lips as the doctor continued. Bits of what the doctor was saying floated through the haze of Baz's relief at seeing Sabrina, things like, "ruptured cyst" and "ovarian torsion" and "internal bleeding" and—*fuck*.

"I'm sorry," he said. She looked so small in the hospital bed, surrounded by this small army of doctors. "For everything. I'm so sorry."

"Sebastian, you're here," she said happily, her speech slurred. She used her free hand to stroke his hair, his cheek. A frown stole over her face, her eyes narrowing in confusion. "Why are you here? You're mad at me. Or am *I* mad at you? Someone's mad. Oh! Do you want to know a secret?"

"Always."

She raised her head off the pillow and craned it towards him, whispering in the loudest whisper he'd ever heard. "They gave me pain meds. The good kind! They really work!" Baz bit the inside of his cheek to keep from loosing the relieved laughter bubbling up inside him as she plopped back down on the pillow. "What were you saying?"

Baz turned his face towards her palm, pressing a kiss there. "I'm sorry."

Her eyes fell closed, a smile splitting across her face, and despite the hospital gown and the IV in her arm and how weak she looked, it was the most beautiful smile he'd ever seen. "Don't be sorry. You have the fancy insurance. It's *such* good insurance. Did you know that? They—" She clicked her tongue and spread out her fingers. "—fixed me right up." She looked into his eyes, her face sobering for a minute. "I'm really glad I married you."

"Because of the fancy insurance?" he asked, no longer bothering to hold back his smile. She probably wouldn't remember any of this conversation later.

"No! Because you're cute—" She dragged out the word.

"I'm not cute."

"Yup. You are. You're cute and smart and I like your penis jewelry." One of the doctors cleared his throat and looked away. Not that Sabrina noticed. She was too busy trying to poke Sebastian's nose with the tip of her index finger—something that took multiple attempts before she finally landed on her target with a delighted "boop!" Baz caught her wrist and pressed his lips to her palm. Sabrina sighed happily. "I love you."

Baz's heart stopped, but Sabrina was already flopping back against the pillow.

"We need to get her to her room," one of the doctor's said gently. "Someone will be out to get you as soon as she's settled and ready for visitors."

Sabrina's hand reached out, gripping Sebastian's, her eyes flying open as she searched for him. "You'll still be here, right?"

"Yeah, wildflower. I'm not going anywhere."

# Chapter Thirty-two

"I can't wait to take a shower and sleep without being woken up every hour to check my vital signs." Sabrina sank onto the couch in the condo and dropped her head back against the cushions.

Sebastian kicked the front door closed behind himself, his head and torso hidden behind the obscenely large flower arrangement her parents had sent to the hospital the night before. Sabrina had hardly spoken to them herself, Sebastian filling them in on the details of her surgery and recovery plan, but they'd sounded more concerned than she could remember. Mom had threatened to call the nurse's station and demand to speak to a manager if she wasn't being treated well, which was her mom's equivalent of filling their fridge with lasagna, even if Dad did have an early tee time he wanted to keep and Mom wasn't inclined to reschedule her brunch plans. It stung, but she knew they loved her in their own way.

And besides, Sebastian's mother had already filled the fridge with lasagna, and a chicken pot pie and a frittata, because apparently her mother-in-law showed love with casseroles and her parents did it by threatening the staff. Tomato, tomahto.

Sebastian set the flowers down on the kitchen island and moved behind her at the couch, running his fingers through her hair, lightly massaging her scalp as he went.

"You're spoiling me." She closed her eyes and leaned into his touch.

"I'm taking care of you."

"You're hovering."

"You had major surgery."

"It was laparoscopic."

"You were bleeding internally. They removed an organ."

"A tiny organ."

Sebastian's hands stilled in her hair and she opened her eyes to meet his. He was doing that thing where he tried not to smile but it made his lips twitch. It was ridiculously adorable.

"Let me hover, wildflower. I like hovering."

"I like when you hover."

He leant forward and dropped a kiss on the tip of her nose. "Good."

Sebastian headed to the kitchen, and Sabrina closed her eyes as she listened to the familiar sounds of him moving about. "Did you tell Tessa I want to go see the baby as soon as she's up for it?" she called.

"I told her. She says you're welcome as soon as *you're* up for it. And Gavin and Kyla promised to text us lots of pictures."

"I probably can't hold the baby for a few weeks, huh? Stupid stitches."

"I'll hold the baby and sit next to you, and you can still wrap your arms around him."

"You're going to be the best uncle," she sighed, picturing Sebastian with a baby in his arms.

He chuckled. "I've got some competition."

He came back into view with a glass of water for her, which he set on the coffee table before taking a seat next to her on the couch. He pulled her feet into his lap, peeled off her hospital socks—oops, she hadn't meant to wear those home—and began lazily massaging her feet. "How are you feeling?"

"Tired. Sore. But much better." She sank down further into the couch, giving him more of her calves in his lap. "Can we talk now?"

"Are you still on pain killers?" he asked with an arched eyebrow.

"Tylenol. A shit ton of it, but still."

"Are you sure you're up for this tonight? We can wait until after you've had a good night's sleep, or—"

"Oh my God, will you talk to me already! The longer you make me wait, the more nervous you're making me."

"I'm making you nervous?" He seemed genuinely flabbergasted by the idea, and she couldn't help but chuckle in disbelief.

"Yes! What's with all the build up?" When he didn't answer right away, a wisp of anxiety curled in Sabrina's stomach. "Whatever it is, say it."

His face had gone hard, lips pressed together, jaw clenched, as he seemed to sort through his thoughts. She slid her feet out of his lap as that wisp was fanned to a plume, but he gripped her ankle, hard, and pulled them back towards himself.

At last, he turned that too-serious face towards her, his eyebrows crinkling in concentration. "I'm sorry."

Her stomach sank. "Oh." Was this his way of telling her he was ready to get divorced? Was that why he didn't want to have this conversation while she was still in the hospital, because he was planning on breaking her heart?

"Wait, what's that look?" he asked.

"What look?"

He circled one finger in the air in the direction of her face. "This look. You look like someone killed your cat."

"I don't have a cat."

"Sabrina."

She took a deep breath, in through her nose and out through her mouth. "There. No more look."

He looked skeptical but he took a deep breath of his own and picked up where he'd left off. "I'm sorry for the way I reacted the other day."

"It's okay—"

"It's *not* okay. I was angry and hurt, but instead of saying that, I hurt you too. And that wasn't fair." He tilted his head down to meet her eyes, looking up at her through his eyelashes. "I'm sorry. I can't promise it won't happen again, but I'm going to try to be better."

*Again? Better? Those don't sound like break up words.* "Wait, what?"

"I'm not great at talking about my feelings. In case you haven't noticed. And when someone hurts me, my first instinct is to cut that person off. But I don't want to cut you off, Sabrina. Even when I was mad, even right after I left you at Ethan's, I knew I was being an asshole. I knew I couldn't cut you off. I'm sorry. I'm probably going to fuck it up a bunch of times before I get it right, but I want to do better. I'm going to do better. Can you forgive me?"

His words sank in, and it was like she was coming out of a fog. For a minute she wondered if she had messed up and taken a stronger painkiller by mistake. "So you're not asking me for a divorce?"

"What? No!" His eyes narrowed, nostrils flaring. "Why? Do you want a divorce?"

"No! I thought *you* did!"

"Well, I don't!"

"Good!"

They stared at each other for a moment before they burst into laughter, the relief washing over Sabrina.

"Jesus Christ, wildflower, I'm trying to tell you I love you and you're talking about divorce?"

Her laughter died on her lips, her eyes going wide and she sat upright on the sofa—not as fast as she'd like because, stitches, but fast all the same. "You love me?"

"That's what I've been trying to tell you!" He shook his head, raking his fingers through his hair. "Fuck, I'm bad at this."

"No, you're not. You're doing perfect." She slid closer to him on the couch, her heart pounding in her chest. It was so full she thought it might burst. "Say it again."

He grinned and slid his hands into her hair, tilting her face up to his. He ran the tip of his nose along the line of her jaw and nipped at her bottom lip lightly. "I love you, Sabrina."

"I love you, Sebastian."

He kissed her, his lips moving softly over hers. It felt like new beginnings and possibilities, like gratitude and relief and so much love she didn't know how to contain it. Instead, she let it spill from her lips as she kissed him back, tasting each murmured "I love you" he offered between kisses.

When they pulled away, he reached into his inside jacket pocket and retrieved her wedding and engagement rings.

"I didn't get to ask you properly last time." He took her left hand in his, his smile so wide the corners of his eyes crinkled. "Sabrina Page, my wildflower, will you be my wife?"

An overjoyed burst of laughter fell from her lips and she nodded as he slid the rings onto her finger. "Yes, Sebastian Graham, yes."

He kissed her again, then rested his forehead against hers. "We can get married again. A big wedding in the church."

"Is that what you want?"

"I don't care about the wedding, Sabrina, but I care about you. If it's important to you that we stand up at an altar in front of our friends and—"

"It's not." She peppered his face with kisses, his cheekbones and his temples, the tip of his nose and the underside of his jaw. "I'm already your wife. I don't need another ceremony to prove it."

He hummed contentedly as her lips found his again. "Then

what do you propose we do next, wife?"

"Living happily ever after sounds nice, don't you think?"

When he smiled, she felt it all over. "I do."

# Epilogue

*One year later*

"Are you sure they're coming?" Ethan craned his head towards the front door again. "Does anyone know for sure that their plane landed?"

"Gavin texted a little over an hour ago," Baz said as he took his seat at the table in Ethan's living room beside Sabrina.

"They'll be here," Jamie said. "Calm down, grandpa."

"I hate when you call me that," Ethan grumbled.

"What? You *are* Julie's grandpa." Jamie gestured to his chubby one-year-old daughter who was playing with a set of brightly colored stacking cups with Tessa on the rug in the middle of the living room.

"That's not what you meant," Ethan said.

Tessa scooped up her daughter and carried her over to Jamie, holding her out to her husband. "Julie needs a new diaper. Your turn, daddy."

"Hate that even more," Ethan muttered.

Tessa laughed. "Here, Dad. Have a cupcake." She set an elaborately decorated cupcake in front of Ethan, dropped a kiss on his forehead, and then sank into Jamie's newly vacated seat.

"How'd I end up being the seventh wheel?" Ethan asked.

"Seventh wheel? Is that a thing?" Jamie asked from the changing table in the corner of the living room.

"It is now," Baz said.

"Don't worry, Dad. We'll find you someone. A nice, age-appropriate grandma—" Tessa said, breaking off with a laugh when she caught Ethan's horrified expression.

"Since when does anyone here know anything about *age appropriate*?" Ethan grumbled.

"Age is just a number, isn't that right, daddy?" Tessa asked, turning her face up for a kiss as Jamie came back over with the baby.

"Jesus Christ," Ethan muttered as Jamie kissed Tessa on his way past to set Julie back down amongst her toys.

"Can I be the dog this time?" Tessa asked, reaching into the open box on the table.

"No. The last time your husband got his hands on the dog, it disappeared for months," Baz said.

"Yeah, but that's him. You can trust *me*," Tessa said with a smile.

"No dog. You can be the top hat." Baz handed her the small metal token.

"Oh, man, I wanted to be the top hat."

They all turned at the sound of Gavin's voice in the doorway to the living room. Ethan and Tessa sprang to their feet, rushing to greet Gavin and Kyla with exclamations about how happy they were to have them home. They'd only been gone for a week to visit Gavin's son in Los Angeles, but from the reception, you would have thought it had been months.

Sabrina moved to stand, but Baz took her hand, pulling her back down into her seat. She laughed. "Let's go say hi."

"In a minute." He pressed a kiss to her cheek, then moved his lips to the shell of her ear. "One round, no hotels, then we're out of here."

Her cheeks heated and her hand dropped to his knee,

squeezing. Christ, even that simple touch and his cock was already taking notice.

"I thought you liked game night," she said.

"I love game night. But we only just left your parents' house this morning. I haven't gotten to fuck my wife in two days," he growled.

"No one said you had to keep your hands to yourself while we were visiting them." *Tease.*

He grunted. "Their walls are too thin."

She laughed. "I remember. I still don't think Mom's recovered from last Christmas."

They'd settled into a comfortable rhythm with Sabrina's family—twice yearly visits, never at the same time as Holly. It seemed when faced with the ultimatum they'd leveled at her parents in the months following her surgery—criticism was not helpful or welcome, and if her parents insisted on imposing their standards on Sabrina, then they wouldn't be a part of their lives any longer—her parents had been surprisingly willing to try. To do better for their youngest daughter.

It wasn't perfect. Maryann still sometimes made a comment about Sabrina's clothing and Richard was still quick to offer unsolicited business advice, but they were trying. It was enough for now.

Holly hadn't been as open to their terms. Baz couldn't say he was surprised, or that he missed seeing his sister-in-law, but he knew Sabrina still mourned the loss of the relationship she had hoped to have with her sister. Nights like this with their friends helped, when Kyla and Tessa would wrap Sabrina in their friendship like a cloak, a warm and welcome weight.

He nipped at her bottom lip, then pulled her to her feet, leading her over to greet their friends. "No hotels, Sabrina. I mean it."

Sabrina had put hotels on every one of her properties. He wasn't sure if she was *trying* to torture him or if it just came naturally to her, but either way the effect was the same. By the time they said their goodbyes and climbed into Baz's BMW to head home, he was ready to crawl out of his skin with need.

He was already removing his tie as he followed her into their condo, smacking her ass when she paused to look at the mail on the kitchen counter. "Bed, Sabrina. Now."

She yelped, a delighted sound that filled his chest with a fuzzy, warm feeling, and scampered down the hall towards their bedroom. He took his time following her, dropping his tie on the counter by the mail, unbuttoning his shirt as he rounded the corner into their bedroom. It was a clear, autumn night and the moon sparkled on the bay on the other side of the sliding glass door that led from their bedroom to the balcony. Sabrina stood by the door, slowly sliding the zipper of her dress down. She knew how much he liked the moonlight bouncing off her skin. With a mischievous glance over her shoulder at him, she let the dress fall and pool at her feet.

Baz sucked in a breath at the sight of her, mostly naked and bathed in the moonlight streaming into their bedroom. "You went to game night in your fuck-me panties?" He banded his arm around her waist from behind and pulled her back against his still-clothed body, his fingertips toying with the waistband of the little slip of sheer mesh and lace barely covering her. "Your fuck-me bra," he tsked.

"It's a new set," she said, guiding his other hand up to cup her breast through the barely-there lingerie set. "To replace the one you tore last time."

He hummed and scraped his teeth over the curve where her neck met her shoulder. "I'll have to be more careful."

She reached behind herself, squeezing him through the rough fabric of his pants. He exhaled hard through his nose, the unexpected touch testing his control. As he unhooked her bra, he dropped kisses along the column of her throat. "Next time we go to Brookline, we're getting a hotel room. Two days is too long."

Sabrina laughed. "We've gone longer."

"When?" Her bra joined her dress at her feet.

"There must have been a time."

He slid his hand into the waistband of her panties, his fingers stroking over her. "Not since your surgery." He dragged his knuckle through her slit, pressing hard against all her soft places, then pulled away. "Off."

"I love when you get all demanding," she said with a grin as she shimmied out of her panties.

Christ, she was beautiful. He'd never get used to the fact that he got to see her like this, to touch her and be the one to make her feel good. That he got to keep her. Swallowing down the sudden onslaught of emotion, he tilted his head towards the bedside table. "Get your toy."

"Which one?" she asked.

He swatted her ass on the way past and followed her over to the bed. "You know which one."

While he stepped out of his shoes and shed the rest of his clothes, carefully folding each item to draw out the anticipation, Sabrina retrieved the pierced ceramic dildo she'd made last year. How had a year gone by so fast?

Sabrina scooted up on the bed, leaning back against the ridiculous array of pillows that had been accumulating there since Sabrina had officially moved into his room.

Baz sat on the edge of the bed and turned to face her, drawing his hand up her calf until he could press gently at her knees. Sabrina dropped her knees to the side, opening herself up to his view.

"Show me," he said, his voice hoarse.

It didn't matter how many times they'd done this, it still overwhelmed him each time to see her tease herself with the piercing at the tip of the clay cock, to watch as she slid it inside herself. She always sucked in a breath when the dildo entered her, as though the stretch were still a surprise after all this time. He fucking lived for that sound.

As he watched, she slowly fucked herself, her hips rocking against the hard length within her. "How does it feel?" he asked.

"So good," she moaned.

They'd played this game before, and each time he tried to drag it out a little longer, to let her control the pace for a few more seconds. Each time he tried to memorize the way she looked like this, spread out for him, touching herself as much for his pleasure as her own. "Fuck. You're beautiful." She sighed happily and rocked her hips against the toy. "That's right, baby. Get yourself ready for me."

"I'm ready."

"Not yet."

He ran his hand from her knee up to her thigh, pressing her legs back even farther, making room for himself between her legs. As she continued to work herself on the toy she'd created, he bent forward and fixed his lips to the stiff bud at the apex of her thighs, sucking it into his mouth. She cried out and bucked against him, so he did it again.

Sebastian wrapped his hand around hers where it gripped the base of the clay cock and took over the movement, driving it in faster, twisting on the way out so the barbell scraped against her g-spot, until she was a quivering mess of incoherent moans, pleases and oh Gods, and don't stops. What he wouldn't give to keep her like this forever, mindless with the need to come, begging him for her release.

He lifted his mouth from her and pressed one hand low on her abdomen the way she liked. "Come for me, baby. Come and I'll give you my cock."

She dug her hands in his hair and dragged his face back between her legs. Fuck, there was nothing better than her demanding what she wanted from him, and he was all too happy to give it to her. He worked her clit with his lips and tongue and teeth as he fucked her with the ceramic dildo until she arched off the bed and came with a startled cry.

She'd barely stopped coming when he tossed the dildo aside and drove himself inside her, the lingering flutterings of her pussy gripping his length.

"You did such a good job," he praised as he shifted so they were lying on their sides, her back to his front, and continued to work himself in and out of her tight heat.

He lifted her top leg, bending it back over his hip to give him better access to her clit. She whimpered when he pressed his finger to it, already sensitive from her first orgasm, but he knew she could take another. His wife would take each one he'd give her and still be ready for more.

"Such a good fucking girl letting your husband play with your pussy. Such a good wife, taking my cock like this, letting me fill you up. Look at how pretty you are stretched around me. Look at how well you take my cock. Do you want to come again, baby? Do you think you can?"

She groaned and turned her head to press a hard kiss to his lips over her shoulder. "Yes."

"Good. So do I." He increased the pace of his thrusts, the pressure on her clit, and there were those telltale flutterings again, her inner walls already anticipating her next orgasm. "Gonna fuck you all night, wife. And if you're a very good girl and come for me when I tell you to, I'll let you come on my tongue on the balcony as the sun rises."

She shivered in his arms, bucking her hips back against him, and came again, shouting his name. Her pussy clamped down on his length, milking him hard and fast, pulling his orgasm from him. With a groan, he buried his face in her neck and pumped her full of his release, stroking her clit through it all, only stopping when she pressed her hand to his to still his movements.

"I love you," she said, sleep already pulling at her.

He wrapped his arms around her waist and pulled her snugly back against himself. He pressed a kiss to her temple and let his eyes fall closed. "I love you, wife."

*The End*

# Also by Cara Dion

**Love Song Series**
*Irreplaceable*

*Indiscreet*

*Undeniable*


**Aster Bay Series**
*Whisking It All*

*Just For Show*

*First Comes Marriage*


**Visit my website to learn more and
download free bonus content:**

# Acknowledgments

I was incredibly lucky to grow up with six grandparents—an embarrasement of riches, really. Now, only one of those grandparents is still with us.

The two year anniversary of my maternal grandmother's death passed while I was finishing this book. Grief is a funny thing. It both speeds things up and slows them down—it seems like just yesterday she was here, and also like it's been forever since I last spoke to her.

And when I am missing her most, characters like Aunt Lucy appear on the page. Wise, wonderful matriarchs who love fiercely and unconditionally, whose support is unwavering, who revel in the joy of their loved ones. Nana was all that and more, and I know she'd be tickled pink if she knew she made guest appearances in my books. Somehow, I suspect she knows.

Though there is nothing I would not give for one more day with her, one more afternoon spent making bread, one more time to hear her laugh, I am beyond grateful for the incredible women she has left behind, who love as fiercely as she loved—my great aunts, her sisters; my aunts; her daughters; my mother, who has stepped into that wise, wonderful matriarch role in her stead.

Thank you, Nana.

As happens each time I find myself trying to write these notes, there are so many other people to thank:

Mom and John, I am doing things I hardly dared to dream of because of you. There are no words for how much I love and appreciate you.

My husband and son, for making this wild, wonderful life possible and sharing it with me, for your endless support and the look in my little boy's eyes when he tells someone Mama wrote a book—here's another one, baby boy. (Please don't ever read it!)

Ann and John, Megan and Phil, Devon, Alysa, Sam, thank you for always being in my corner, for laughing with me when things are hard and celebrating with me when they are good.

Ginny, for putting up with my endless texts and mini meltdowns on the path to completing another book, for the hours of Zoom calls and countless thousands of words of encouragement and ideas—there is no one else I'd want to be on this journey with.

Sophie, Marty, Liz, Maria, and all the other romance authors who I've had the privilege to get to know over the last few years. I'm so grateful for each of you and for the ways you have helped me grow as an author.

Brittany, Nicole, and Jess, my bookstagram lifelines, thank you for your belief in me, for your friendship, and for always being game when I slide into your DMs with a "can I run something by you?"

And to you, my readers, for wanting to read these stories, for asking for more, for always being ready for the next book. Thank you for letting me do this crazy thing that I love, and thank you for loving it right back.

# About the Author

Cara Dion writes steamy, contemporary romance, often with a forbidden or age gap relationship.

Cara has always had an overactive imagination and spent much of her teenage years watching 80s and 90s romcoms with her aunt. She read her first romance when a friend snuck one of their mother's Harlequins into their Catholic school and passed it around like contraband, but she didn't return to romancelandia until the pandemic.

She has been an English teacher, professional musician, and nonprofit administrator. When she's not reading or writing romance, Cara loves cooking, Broadway musicals, and all things Disney.

Cara lives in a small town in New England with her husband, son, and two very demanding cats.

Follow Cara on Instagram at caradion.author and contact her at cara@caradion.com. Visit the website and join Cara's newsletter to get insider information on upcoming books and exclusive content.